To Devon
Library

The School
of
Opportunity

by
Eric J Brown

Brown Eric J (Eric John) 1947 -
   School of Opportunity/Eric J Brown

ISBN 978-0-9812980-1-6

1. Title

PS8553.R68497S362009   C813'.54   C2009-904889-2

Printed and Published by
Magnolia Press
Box 499
Entwistle, Alberta
T0E 0S0

Dedication

This work is dedicated to those teachers who braved often adverse conditions to give the gift of literacy to children who lived in remote areas. Having the ability and patience to teach several grades simultaneously in a single classroom is a testament to their great courage and stamina. It is to them that so many of us owe so much for laying the foundation for our own success in life.

Other Books in Print by Eric J Brown

Ginny – A Canadian Story of Love & Friendship 1998
Ingrid – An Immigrant's Tale 2000
Anna – Her Odyssey to Freedom 2002
The Promise 2004
To the Last Tree Standing 2006
Third Time Lucky 2009

First Edition May 2010

Copyright 2009 © Eric J Brown

Acknowledgements

First, I would like to acknowledge my wife Isabella who has always served as first line critic in all of my works. She has shown particular enthusiasm and support in this work as first proof-reader and I would like to thank her for her encouragement in my endeavour.

Secondly, I would like to thank Charlie Goulet; fellow author and retired teacher, for taking time to review this work. His experience as a teacher in the one-room school system has been an invaluable resource.

Thirdly, I would like to thank Eileen Harrigan for her work as principal editor and for her thoughtful comments to make this work run smoothly.

As this work is about a school teacher, I would also like to give special acknowledgment to two teachers who had the most profound impact on my education.
First, George Meyer, who presided over my first three grades at the Matthews Crossing School. Through his efforts I learned the basics of literacy and general knowledge that contributed so much to all that I am.
Secondly, Barbara Storms, my Grade eight teacher. It was in her class that my urge to write began to blossom. In knowing this, she would generously supply me with foolscap paper so that I could write my thoughts down in my first faltering steps towards becoming a novelist.

While I had many very capable and even exceptional teachers during my school years, these two will always stand out above the rest.

A Word From the Author

It seems like yesterday that on a September morning in 1953 I walked beside my brothers up the road, wearing my best new homemade clothes. We walked up the dirt road that cut through the "big muskeg," navigating the deep ruts and bits of corduroy logs that protruded through the track they called the main road. I remember that the air was pungent with the odour of muskeg as I walked to my first day of school.

At the other end of the muskeg on an island that rose out of the surrounding swamp was the school they called Matthew's Crossing. My school; I couldn't imagine any other kind because Matthew's Crossing was where everybody went. It was school.

As we turned into the entrance way, past the cabin that served as the teacher's home, several students were already there playing outdoors awaiting the call to class. I was not frightened at all as I knew everyone there, even the older kids. A cheery lad named Jimmy who was dressed in raggedly clothes came up to me to ask if I wanted to be on his side in the game of prisoner's base that they were playing. Several greeted me as if I was a guest of honour on my first day of school. Perhaps I was in a sense as I was only one of the two Grade One students starting that year.

When placed in our desks, I was second from the front in the row by the large windows that faced the road. Ahead of me sat a boy named Glynne, the other Grade One pupil. Glynne was my friend and would always be until his untimely death in a car accident as a young man.

Looking across the room to the far row by the side blackboard I could see my oldest brother Allen, who was in Grade Eight - the highest grade offered at the school. He had two peers in his grade, Janet and Ethel. The older kids in the row between were, my other brother Howard, some Christensens and MacMurchys among others. In the row beside me were the Grade Two students, because of age closeness they were also friends of sorts; Valerie and Trudy, two Leroys, and Arnold. Behind me sat an older boy named Walter, he was different. He grinned and slobbered and could not talk properly, they said he was simple; today he would be called severely mentally challenged.

We were issued our readers, perhaps not on the first day but soon afterwards. It was a little red book. When opened, it showed a picture of a boy named Dick and the next page had a picture of his sister Jane. "Dick, Jane, oh, oh, look see," were the first words I learned to read.

There was recess where we all went outside to run and play games. There was a diamond for those who wanted to play ball. For those who didn't, there was an open area at the south of the school where the ground was worn bare from so many footsteps. Here, they played prisoner's base or a similar game called stealing sticks. Sometimes we played hide and seek using the whole south wall of the school for home base. Often they would play anti-I-over, a game that involved throwing a ball over the roof and amazingly, at least in my time, no windows were broken. In the shade by the south end was a large sand box. Our toys were tin cans and sticks. Walter would sit in the middle of the sand box and throw sand up in the air, letting it fall down all over himself while he would exclaim "Halifax!" a word he learned somewhere along the way. Other children were not bothered by him, they knew he was different and they were indifferent.

At lunch time we would all go to the sunny south side of the school to have our lunch. Lunch pails were exactly that, usually lard pails or jam cans. We had a large pail in which my brothers and I shared a common lunch. I didn't like it when Mom made us pork and bean sandwiches as they were all soggy and stuck together.

At the end of the day we walked home though in a larger group; walking with us were Carl, Henry, Roy, Marilynn and

Elsie. Our home was the closest, only a mile away. Now I was a student, about to embark on a marvelous journey of learning how to read and write.

The halcyon days at Matthew's Crossing came to an end two years later when I finished Grade Three. The teacher had moved on and a replacement couldn't be found, so the little school at the edge of the muskeg closed down. That September of 1956, I began a wondrous new experience. I got to ride on a school bus all the way to Seba Beach to a big school where the classroom was full of kids of the same grade, and it even had indoor toilets. The world had suddenly got so much bigger. Though Seba Beach would remain my school until I eventually graduated from Grade Twelve, my years at Matthew's Crossing would always seem like a golden time of long, long ago.

Introduction

The School of Opportunity is the ongoing story of Jane Phillips, the ever resourceful and indomitable woman determined to see her dream come true. Jane Phillips, nee Brody, was introduced in the prequel to this work, *Third Time Lucky*. She was portrayed as a frumpish, unattractive woman who came west as a mail-order bride for Ethan Phillips, her husband-to-be, a crusty, unsophisticated bachelor whose life changed dramatically as he and Jane became embroiled in a rather tumultuous courtship. This ultimately included a love triangle involving Sean O'Malley, the loveable Irish moonshiner, before she and Ethan formalized their relationship. Their neighbours, the Higgins and Kepler families and various members of the Grimstad clan, appear again in this work as does Jane's friend Mary. Audi, the notorious womanizing Dutchman, is also back with a surprising new role.

At the request of her neighbours and driven by her own secret wish to become a teacher, Jane finds herself teaching in a tiny one-room school two miles from her home. Since the school is not sanctioned by the school board and Jane lacks proper training and a teaching certificate, she and her school soon run afoul with the authorities, leading to several dramatic confrontations. While there is no doubt that Jane is a gifted teacher, the question of what really makes a teacher is brought to head. The school board wants to shut her and her school down, and the parents of her pupils are adamant that she stays. Behind the scenes, the school has a mysterious benefactor who anonymously donates books and supplies, and is the largest single contributor to the fundraising drives.

The School of Opportunity is a portrayal of the rural school system as it existed in the first half of the 20th century, particularly in remote areas where children had a choice of travelling several miles to school on foot or growing up illiterate. This is a story of a child's right to be educated under reasonable conditions verses dogma and regulations.

Chapter One

"Thank you for the cup of milk." Thomas read from a sentence that Jane printed for him, the last of several sentences printed on the piece of paper.

Jane smiled and said, "Very good Thomas and now I have one for you, Herman." She handed Herman a piece of paper and he read, "Und, I mean and ze uh…the, cookies were very good also."

"Very good Herman, your English is coming along well." Jane smiled. "Well, that will be all for today. When you come back on Thursday, we will do arithmetic."

Both boys rose from their chairs and said in turn, "Thank you Mrs. Phillips," though Herman struggled to say the TH sound properly. His parents were German, and he tended to mimic their strong accents.

Jane sighed as she watched them leave the house. *To bad they didn't have a proper school to go to, they should have been in school years ago.* She stood at the door and watched them walk down the hill to their horses as her year-old son Robbie came over to her and said "Boys go home."

"Yes sweetheart they're going home now. Oh look Robbie, Daddy is coming."

"Daddy coming," little Robbie's eyes lit up at the mention of his name.

Jane saw Ethan drive by the barnyard fence and come up the hill to the house with his team and buggy. She was thinking that it was two years ago nearly to the day when Ethan had brought her to his place in the lumber wagon and she reminisced about the rather eventful summer that followed as they adapted to each others ways. She was happy now as Ethan was a good man and his apparent grumpy moods were more show than substance. Now they had a son.

She looked at her garden that covered most of the hillside just past the barnyard. She remembered how it started as a small patch of upturned clay that she and Ethan developed in their first weeks together as part of the bond that drew them together. She thought that she would have to get busy and finish the planting tomorrow. The two afternoons a week that she tutored Thomas Higgins and Herman Kepler cut somewhat into her busy schedule, but she was satisfied that they would be able to read and do basic arithmetic.

Ethan stopped by the house with the buggy, and Jane held the door for him as he carried in a box of groceries with a sack of flour balanced on one shoulder. "Stay out of Daddy's way," Jane said as she drew their toddler to one side.

Ethan set down the groceries and then turned and swept young Robbie into his arms to fuss over his son.

"Daddy," the boy gurgled as Ethan picked him up.

"How's my little helper today?" Ethan grinned at his son.

"I remember a time when you scoffed at the idea of being a father," Jane laughed.

"I remember you saying the same thing about being a mother," Ethan replied. "Now you have someone to inherit your diary."

"And you someone to show your war medals to," Jane replied.

"So how did your class go today?" Ethan asked. "You always said you wanted to be a teacher and now yer doin' it by the backdoor."

"Those kids need a proper school to go to," Jane sighed. "They should have been in school three years ago and now Helen and Wilhelm are old enough to start." She was referring to the younger siblings of Thomas and Herman.

"That Russian fellow who moved in north of Keplers, Ivan Malov, has a couple of twin daughters he'd like to get into a school," Ethan added.

"Wasn't Dave Higgins going to the school board today

to see about building a school in our area?" Jane asked.

"Yeah, wonder how he made out," Ethan said as he sat down and tussled Robbie on his knee.

"So do you officially own that quarter section out by the main road?" Jane asked as she poured Ethan a cup of coffee.

"Thanks dear," he said in one breath. "I got the paper right here in my pocket that says I own it. Maybe in a couple of years or so if ambition and money allows we can move there. The soil is better and less rocky, and there ain't so much muskeg on that quarter." He handed the document to Jane saying, "Put this in with the other papers."

"Yes, it's also two miles closer to town and our good neighbours the Higgins and Keplers," Jane replied as she took the land deed. Then looking out the window she added, "Well, I suppose it's time to get the cows." After the birth of Robbie, Jane struck a bargain with Ethan; when practicable, he would come to the house in late afternoon and watch Robbie while Jane went to fetch the cows from the back pasture to give her a break from housework and Robbie.

"Wanna bring Robbie and come out to the barnyard with me so I can unharness the horses," Ethan replied.

Jane led Robbie by the hand and followed Ethan as he unhitched the horses and led them to the barnyard.

Down at the barn, Ethan had just finished hanging up the harness and had just taken Robbie into his arms when Thomas Higgins rode into the barnyard at full gallop.

"What did you forget?" Jane asked with a smile. Thomas had left there scarcely a half hour before and she was surprised to see him back.

"Nothing," he said hurriedly. "I met Dad on the main road and he wants all the neighbours to come to our place tonight to discuss the school."

"Robbie won't be old enough to go to school for another five years," Ethan said in his usual grumpy voice.

"I'd like to go," Jane chimed in.

Ethan turned and frowned at her while Thomas said, "I

got to go and tell more neighbours. Try to be there by 7:30."
Thomas turned and rode away.

"Why are you so interested in the meeting, afraid the
school will do you out of a job?" Ethan said with a crooked
grin.

"No, anything to do with a proper education for these
children and ours, when the time comes, is of interest to
me," Jane replied emphatically. "Look at it as planning for
the future."

"I suppose," Ethan grumbled. "Who is gonna look after
Robbie if we go to that meeting?"

"Take him along," Jane replied. "I'm sure Helen and
the other kids will be glad to watch him when we attend the
meeting."

Ethan gave her a doubting glance.

"Look Ethan Phillips," Jane continued in her ever
resolute tone, "I'm going to that meeting even if I have to
walk and you can stay home and put Robbie to bed."

"I wished he'd a come before I unharnessed the horses,"
Ethan said ever grumpily.

"Oh quit complaining," Jane scoffed. "You know in
your heart that the school is important to us." She turned to
head out to the pasture to find the cows. As Ethan watched
Jane walk toward the pasture, he thought of the wonderful
woman who was his wife — with her long, brown hair drawn
back and tied loosely she was beautiful. Her long neck and
prominent nose, features that made her so self-conscious
two years ago were of such insignificance in the greater
scheme of things, particularly in the face of her powerful,
but loving personality.

That evening they arrived at the Higgins' place alongside
Wolf and Hella Kepler, Ivan and Raisa Malov, and the new
Polish family, Stan and Lyudmila Gogowicz. The latter
arrived at the same time as Jane and Ethan. Ethan, who
had previously met Stan, whose full name was Stanislaw,
introduced Jane. Stan in turn introduced them to his wife

Lyudmila.

"Just call me Ludy for short," she smiled. They brought their four children with them, three who appeared to be of school age. Helen Higgins appeared and eagerly took Robbie off their hands and offered to do the same with the younger Gogowicz child, whose name was Maria. Robbie, who was familiar with Helen, followed her eagerly while Maria was at first hesitant. As Ethan and Jane were about to go into the house, Axel Rutland, owner and operator of the local sawmill, arrived. Curious that Axel, who lived in Grimstad, was there Ethan said to him, "Come a long way for this meeting did yuh?"

"Dis last quarter I vas sawing on looks like good land," Axel replied with his Norwegian accent. "I am tinking of setting up a farm around here if dere is a school for my *shildren* to attend."

Jane, who had not previously met Axel, cleared her throat and taking cue Ethan introduced her and with a laugh added, "Axel is the only Norwegian in Grimstad, not related to the Grimstad clan."

The older children were instructed to look after the younger ones and play outside in the warm spring evening. Meanwhile, the adults gathered in the living room where Sari Higgins provided tea and fresh cinnamon buns.

Dave Higgins, in his distinct English accent, called the meeting to order and said, "As you know I paid a visit to the school board today to see about getting a school for our area, but I'm afraid I have a bit of bad news. The school board turned me down."

There was a loud exclamation from the others, and Wolf with his German accent exemplified by his frustration, demanded, "What is ze reason for zis?"

"They say there aren't enough students. They need twelve to justify a school and a teacher; we only have nine counting those of Stan and Ivan."

"What we going to do with our cheeldren?" Ivan asked

in his strong Russian accent. "I come to dees country so Sonya and Tanya can go to school. Dey don't have many schools in Roshya." He was referring to his six-year-old twin daughters. His wife Raisa smiled in agreement, though she could barely understand English.

"They say we should send our children to Grimstad to go to school," Dave continued.

"Zhat is fifteen miles for Herman und Wilhelm," Wolf piped in. "Zhey would spend so much time travelling."

"Ya und zhey vould haff to get up so early in ze morning," Hella added with her shrill voice. "Zhey vould be so tired zhey vould be no good for chores."

"It would be a shame if these children didn't have an opportunity to go to school," Jane added. "I think it's a crime that a child should grow up to be illiterate and with no idea how to do simple arithmetic."

"Is there nothing we can do?" Ludy Gogowicz said. Her English was quite clear though with a slight Polish inflection.

"Surely we can find some solution," Sari added. "We can't expect Jane to give some of our children piecemeal education in her home forever."

"Why not build our own school?" Ethan interjected. He'd been sitting in the background thus far absorbing the discussion. "Ta hell with them. I ain't gonna send Robbie all the way to Grimstad when he's old enough, and I ain't gonna let him grow up uneducated neither."

There was a general murmur among the others and Jane smiled at him.

"Ya zhat's it. Ve vill build our own school," Wolf added.

"Yes, but they still won't supply a teacher," Dave said. "A school is no ruddy good without a teacher."

"Yuh got one sittin' right in this room," Ethan smiled cryptically as he looked at Jane.

"Ya Jane could be our teacher," Hella said picking up on Ethan's implication. "She taught me how to speak English.

If *mein*, I mean my English is not so *gut*, it is not her fault und now she is teaching Herman."

There was a ripple of laughter and Jane blushed at being the centre of attention. "M-me," she stuttered. "I'm not qualified."

"The way you have been teaching Thomas you're as good as any of them," Sari interjected. "He can't wait to go to your house for his next lesson."

"Ya und ze same goes for Herman," Hella piped in.

All eyes turned to Jane. "I don't know what to say, I have a child to raise and so much work around the farm," she flustered.

"Do you zhink zat you could spare Jane to teach at ze school?" Wolf asked Ethan.

"If that's what she really wants and I think it is. It'll be her choice to see her dream come true." Ethan replied.

"I vould look after Robbie during ze day," Hella volunteered.

"And I could take him on days that Hella is not available," Sari added.

"But what will the school board say when they find out I'm not qualified?" Jane replied.

"To blazes with them," Dave replied. "They won't educate our children so we'll do it ourselves." There were cheers among the others.

"We can build the school on my land and it'll be on private property," Ethan added.

"Away back there?" Sari asked in an anxious tone.

"As some of you may know, I bought the quarter just in on the trail to my place with the idea I might relocate there. I can spare a corner for the school and it can stay there even after I set up and start farmin' the quarter."

There was a general murmur as only Dave was aware that Ethan was even considering acquiring that quarter section. He restored order and said, "I think that's a splendid idea. The school would be central and not too far away for anyone."

"It's done then," Ethan said. "Maybe Dave and Wolf can come with me and pick a spot, then we need to build it."

"We should form an organisation, both to plan for the school and to raise money, and then to manage it once it is in operation," Dave suggested.

"In that case I nominate you as president." Ethan added. Everyone cried in agreement and Sari volunteered to be secretary.

"I nominate Wolf as treasurer as he seems to have a head for figures." Dave added.

"I will try my best," Wolf replied.

"I think yuh ought to be the one to organise the construction for the school, as you seem to be skilled at that sort of thing," Ethan said to Wolf. "We can use logs from my quarter. It'll help me clear the land."

"I vill donate planks for da floor and boards for da roof," Axel declared. "You can have all da slabs you need for firevood and odder buildings."

"Thank you Axel," Dave said. "It is more than generous of you. For your efforts I have a stand of trees on my place you may take for free."

"Und me too," Wolf added. "I haff some timber you can have."

"I suppose we ought to get together and work out a work schedule," Ethan added.

With that, the men huddled together under Wolf's direction to work out a schedule, while the women clustered around Jane to offer whatever help they could.

On the way home that night as they rode in the buggy through the gathering dusk, Jane said, "Did you really mean it, that you won't mind if I volunteer to teach?"

"That's what you really wanna do, you said it many times," he replied. "I wouldn't volunteer yuh if I didn't want you to do it."

"Thanks dear," Jane replied as she leaned her head against his broad shoulder while still holding the soundly sleeping Robbie in her arms. "Robbie will be the biggest thing to deal with."

"We'll figure somethun out, besides Hella said she would look after him."

"I'll really have my work cut out with trying to grow my garden, do housework, and trying to cook your supper as well as teach."

"You can handle it," Ethan grinned confidently. "If there's one thing I learned about you Jane, there's nothun you can't do if you put yer mind to it. I can tell yer real excited about this teaching thing."

"Oh Ethan, this is like a dream come true," Jane said in an elated tone and then more downcast added, "I hope the school board won't try to stop me."

"If they do, they'll have a hell of a fight on their hands," Ethan rumbled. "The neighbours want you and I know you can do it, so you don't worry none."

"Thanks dear," Jane grinned.

They rode along in silence with the horses moving in a trot, listening to the croaking of hundreds of frogs. The croaking receded before them and started up behind them like the parting waves of a boat moving across a lake. Jane thought of her first night travelling with Ethan two years ago. She looked at the profile of this powerfully built, rugged-looking man with his crusty manner. Some might say he was ugly or cantankerous, but to Jane he was warm and loving and his craggy features were a mark of great distinction. He glanced at her and smiled momentarily at her adoring gaze.

That night Jane wrote in her diary:

I am ecstatic about becoming a teacher at the little school they are building. It is like a dream come true. I am pleased that Ethan is fully supportive of me. I thought he might complain, but that man surprises me every day — God how I love him.

Eric J. Brown

I am overwhelmed at the vote of confidence that my good neighbours have given me as the teacher of their children. I truly hope I won't disappoint them.

Chapter Two

A corner of Ethan's property near the main road was selected for the school site. It was cut off from the main part of the quarter section by a small muskeg and an adjoining slough since it was only a three acre patch. It was too small for farming, but ideal for the school. Ethan, Dave, Wolf and Ivan devoted two full days for felling logs from the main part of the quarter and the crown land across the road and skid them to the school site. Stan was only able to devote one full day. The school was set off the road behind a dense thicket of spruce and poplar that offered maximum shelter from the prevailing winds and made it invisible from the main road. This was Dave's idea as he said, "That way if they come snooping around looking for this school, they will have a devil of a time trying to find it."

They were able to find a few large tamaracks from the muskeg to serve as the base logs as tamaracks were known for their great durability and resistance to rot. The older children, like Thomas and Herman, were employed to peel the logs with draw knives. Later, Ivan who was skilled at log construction, showed them how to square the logs for closer fitting. Sari supplied lunch one day and Hella the other. On the second day, Sean O'Malley showed up driving his Model-T and offered to lend a hand.

"What brings you here?" Ethan asked Sean as Sean drew up beside him. Ethan had Bessie and Clyde, his two horses, hitched to a pair of large long logs and was dragging them to their place at the school site.

"Someone said they were buildin' a school for Jane and

since me praties are all planted, I thought I would give a hand."

"We can always use a hand. If yuh got an axe come back to help cut and yuh can either fall or limb."

"I brought me axe, but I will ask ye not to put me workin' with the Englishman."

"I thought you and Dave were on speakin' terms," Ethan rumbled.

"Well, at a distance, but there's no use in pushin' it yet," Sean said gravely.

"We're all workin' together here for a common good. Come join us today and you can talk to Wolf," Ethan said. "He has a schedule and you can work on days that Dave isn't here. But personally I think you ought a get over this foolishness."

Sean offered no comment as he grabbed his axe and followed Ethan back to the cutting area where the sounds of axes could be heard. Then someone cried, "Timber!" A great spruce tree crashed to the ground. Its feller was Ivan and Dave, who was standing by during the felling, started to limb it. Wolf came by Ethan and Sean with his team dragging three logs. Stopping abreast to them he said, "*Hallo* Sean, are you coming to fall trees?"

"Yes, I thought I'd lend me hand to things," Sean replied.

"I think he's plannin' for the future," Ethan laughed.

"Ya zat's right you courting mit your own school teacher."

"He's bin seein' her for about two years now and ain't hitched yet," Ethan remarked.

"Maybe I'm waitin' for the school to be built first." Sean laughed making light of things.

"Zhat's vhat I call planning ahead," Wolf chuckled.

"Ethan tells me you're the boss," Sean said.

"Well, zhey put me in charge und if you are looking for somezing to do, you can start limbing." Wolf suggested nodding at the tree that Dave was limbing.

Sean gave Wolf a look as if he had been just handed a dangerous job.

Wolf added, sensing Sean's discomfort, "We are all working togezer here und if we want zis school built, we haff to put personal feelings aside."

Sean sighed and reluctantly started toward the tree that Dave was limbing. Just then Stan felled another tree a few dozen yards away. "I'll go help him limb," Sean said as he started toward the tree Stan had felled. Ivan was already attacking another tree with his double bladed axe.

"He's a good man but awful hard-headed," Ethan commented to Wolf as Sean walked away.

"Well, if he is going to help us he will have to get along mit Dave. I don't like Poles eazer but have no problem mit Stan helping."

"I agree," Ethan said as Wolf nudged his horses to carry on.

Meanwhile, Jane spent every available moment trying to devise a learning program for her students. She thought lots about it when attending her garden or flower beds, doing housework, or tending to little Robbie. She bought some children's scribblers from the store and made lists and notes of things to teach her proposed pupils. Jane felt she'd have little problem teaching them how to read and write or how to do arithmetic, but in science, history and geography she was a little fuzzy. History was not her strong suit in school, but she felt she might at least teach them about the explorers. Since her pupils were beginners, she would not have to worry about too much detail in these subjects though she sensed she had aroused a strong appetite for knowledge in both Thomas and Herman. She believed that soon they would be taxing her knowledge in such areas.

Finally, one evening after going through her extensive notes, Jane said to Ethan, who was busy sewing up tears in some of his grain bags, "Will Sean be working on the school tomorrow?"

13

"Let's see," Ethan said as he thought for a moment. "Probably, as Dave won't be there. Why?"

"I would like him to bring Mary over here, maybe on Saturday, as she will be teaching during the week. I need to pick her brain about organizing my classes," Jane replied. Her good friend Mary was a teacher at the four-room school at Grimstad and Sean had been courting her this past year and a half.

"Boy, yer takin' this teachin' thing real serious like," Ethan grinned.

"It's the next most important thing that ever happened to me after marrying you and having little Robbie." Jane smiled sweetly.

"Okay, I'll tell him," Ethan said with his usual grunting voice. "I won't be goin' till afternoon though. I gotta do some fencin' in the morning."

"That will be fine," Jane replied. "I'm getting frustrated. I need to teach them a little history, geography and science to go with their reading and writing. I'm a little shaky on those subjects."

"I weren't much on them myself," Ethan replied, "though I always was interested in the stars."

"Really Ethan, how much *do* you know about the stars?" Jane said eagerly as it suddenly occurred to her that basic astronomy could be part of her science class.

"I already told yuh about the big dipper and the pole star," he replied, eager to tell her about the stars. "Well, there's the littler dipper, Cassiopeia, Orion and Leo among the easy to find constellations and I know the names of the planets and how to find some of them."

"Oh, excellent Ethan," Jane beamed. "I must get this down as part of science, I bet Herman and Thomas will eat this information up. Oh, thank you dear." Jane leaned over and kissed Ethan.

"Gimme a piece of paper and I'll sketch some of them out for yuh," Ethan said getting caught up in Jane's enthusiasm.

Jane watched keenly as Ethan sketched out the big and little dippers on opposite sides of the pole star with the tip of the little dipper handle being Polaris and that the W shaped Cassiopeia was just beyond the little dipper. He also showed her that the stars on the outside of the bowl pointed to Polaris, and those on the inside pointed in the opposite direction to the heart of Leo. He drew Orion and showed the noticeable constellations around it such as Gemini, Taurus and the two dogs Canis Major and Minor, or the big dog and little dog as Ethan called them.

After dark he took Jane out into the middle of the barnyard for maximum horizon visibility and showed her the constellations, including the magnificent constellation of Leo. Looking at the star formations and letting her imagination take hold, Jane remarked, "Leo does sort of look like a lion in the sky."

Ethan smiled and pointed to a reddish looking star near to Leo and said, "That red star is actually Mars."

"Ho do you know all of this?" Jane asked, still astonished with certain aspects of his personality and depth of his knowledge.

"When yuh spend as much time outside as me, yuh learn things about nature including the stars," Ethan shrugged dismissively.

After looking up at the awesome canopy above them for a few moments Jane said, "Burr, I'm starting to get chilly lets go back."

"Yeah, I'm for that," Ethan replied. Every night that we're out after dark, I'll think of some more constellations to show you."

As they walked back to the house hand-in-hand Jane said, "At least my science class will at least get its share of astronomy."

"Yuh could also tell 'em all the kinds of animals, like the difference between snakes and frogs, and fish and warm-blooded animals like birds and mammals," Ethan replied, still caught up in Jane's proposed science curriculum.

"Yes, I could," Jane said enthusiastically, "you're a very good resource, dear. Maybe I won't need to pick Mary's brain," she added with a laugh.

"You'll still need her to tell yuh how ta run a class and such," Ethan replied as he opened the door for her.

"True, but you'll always be my greatest teacher." Jane smiled warmly at Ethan.

The following late Saturday morning, Sean brought Mary over and picked up Ethan as the two men would be spending the day working on the school. Since the time they first met, when they were asked to stand up for Ethan and Jane's wedding, Mary and Sean began courting but still had not formalized their relationship with marriage.

"Come in, come in," Jane beckoned from the doorway. "There is so much I need to ask you."

"I see your school is coming along fine," Mary smiled. "It looks like they're putting the roof on today."

"Yes. Everybody is coming for this big job," Jane bubbled.

"So you're making your dream come true." Mary smiled as she sat down by the table, setting the large handbag she brought along on the floor by her feet.

"Yes, I was hesitant at first, but all the neighbours talked me into it," Jane grinned. "Now I can't wait to get started."

"I hope they let you get away with it," Mary said gravely. "The school board that is."

Jane's face dropped with this sobering reality. "I hope so too," she replied. "Ethan promised there would be a major uproar if they try."

"I know school boards frown heavily on unauthorised schools and supposedly unqualified teachers," Mary replied.

"It is too far to go to Grimstad School for the neighbouring kids," Jane said, "and they say there aren't enough students to justify a school or teacher."

"That's the trouble with people living in remote areas," Mary continued. "Some of the kids slip through the cracks even though everyone is suppose to go to school."

"Well, these kids aren't going to slip through any cracks," Jane said resolutely. "Herman Kepler and Thomas Higgins, the two that I have been tutoring this past year are starved for knowledge. There is no way on God's green earth that I will let them grow up illiterate."

"I can see you are quite passionate about all this." Mary laughed as Jane poured her a cup of tea.

"You bet I am," Jane replied, still wound up about the subject. "Now all I need is a little advice from you on how to set up a curriculum, and how I can lay my hands on some readers and arithmetic books, even old worn-out ones will do. Oh, and anything on science, history and geography for the lower grades, and a couple of wall maps, one of Canada and one of the world would be gratefully appreciated."

"Wow, that's quite a shopping list you have there," Mary chuckled.

"Like I said, I'll take second-hand outdated stuff for now. Anything that will help me teach the kids the things they ought to know will do."

"I noticed that a few of the readers and at least one arithmetic book at the school are getting pretty tattered. I might be able to slip them to you. I know the maps are being replaced. If you take our world map it has the pre-war boundaries of the nations and a lot has changed in Europe and the Middle East."

"It will do nicely for the start, considering my pupils are beginners, so I won't need much detail on the world map."

"True, I'm sure I can stash some of the cast-off stuff from the school for you."

"Good, now let's discuss how to set up a program for teaching my pupils in an organized fashion. I have some rather copious notes on what I have planned to share with you," Jane said eagerly.

"Excellent. Get them out and let's see what you have," Mary replied. "I brought some curriculum material myself."

As Jane and Mary spent their day going over Jane's lesson plans, all of the workers including both Dave and Sean were building and shingling the roof at the school. They had just started when another vehicle drove into the school yard driven by Audi Dykstra. There was a brief grumble about why the notorious Dutchman had come. Audi had a bad reputation as an unscrupulous womanizer and was not completely trusted. Jane had a close brush as one of his victims two years ago. Audi looked apprehensively at Ethan, and Ethan chuckled to himself. He remembered when he had rescued Jane from Audi's clutches and left behind a death threat that he probably would have never carried out under any circumstance. Undaunted, Audi walked right up to where Wolf and Stan were measuring and cutting boards.

"Who is in charge here? I would like to volunteer my services."

"Zhey put me in charge," Wolf replied. "Are you a carpenter?"

"Why are you here? You don't have a wife, let alone kids." Ethan, who was working nearby, said with his rumbling voice.

"I am a firm believer in education," Audi continued evenly. "I came from a country that prizes education; nothing is more deplorable than illiteracy."

"Well that sounds reasonable," Stan added. "Back in Poland we praise education also." As a newcomer, Stan was unaware of Audi's reputation.

"Excuse me while I talk to Wolf for a moment," Audi said, sensing that he was somewhat less than welcome. He spoke to Wolf in Dutch, a language very similar to the north German dialect that Wolf spoke, and the two of them were able to communicate effectively. Audi explained that he owed Jane a major apology and since words alone could never suffice, helping set up her school would at least ease his conscience. The others were not to know this, especially Ethan. Wolf understood and agreed. When they resumed speaking English he assigned Audi the duty of finishing carpenter to install windows, build small tables for desks and a few other odds and ends, though his first assignment was to see if they could get a hold of a sheet or two of blackboard material.

Audi left the scene to look into the blackboard situation as Wolf wanted to discuss his participation with the others.

"So is the bloody Dutchman going to help us too?" Dave complained when they stopped for lunch.

"Vell, he has two good hands," Wolf replied. "Und we need ze help. He says he wants to do ze finishing work und put ze windows in. As far as I am concerned he is welcome to choin us. However, if you people don't feel comfortable mit him I will send him away."

"He sounded very interested in the school," Stan added. "And he speaks like somebody who is well educated."

"Bloody remittance man," Dave complained.

"A remittance man?" Stan was unfamiliar with the term.

"A remittance man is someone from a wealthy family who becomes an embarrassment to them, usually for scandalous behaviour, and is sent away," Dave explained.

"Out of sight, out of mind," Ethan added.

"Usually on a ruddy good stipend from his family to keep him away," Dave scoffed. "The Dutchman isn't starving by any means."

"So what to you zhink?" Wolf asked. "Should we let ze Dutchman work mit us?"

"Well, I don't see a problem in havin' him workin' with us," Sean added. "I'm not married with children meself and I'm a bloody Irishman."

"But you're working on it," Ethan said. The others

laughed and he continued, addressing the others. "Mary is over at our place today givin' Jane some pointers on how to teach yer kids."

"What do you think, Ethan?" Dave asked. "You had a run in with him concerning Jane."

"He's bin pretty quiet since I told him I'd put a bullet between his eyes," Ethan rumbled. "Let him help. Like Wolf said, we can use it."

"So does everybody want ze Dutchman to help us?" Wolf said.

Everyone agreed including Dave.

Chapter Three

It was the third week of August and the school was ready. The roof was finished, the windows and door installed, and even a brick chimney had been built. They managed to get three sheets of blackboard so the school would have a large front board and smaller side board. A box of chalk and two brushes were also part of the deal.

Leftover boards and slabs were used to build a shed for storing wood and coal. Audi had also built two outhouses at his place and brought them to the school in his wagon.

Since there was no way to get row desks without going through the school board, Audi also built low tables and chairs made from reinforced apple boxes for the students and a desk for Jane. The work crew also built a set of bookshelves at the back where Jane hoped to create a small library over time. Jane got a real chair from Kari Grimstad who in turn got it from Tom the station agent. He sequestered a genuine railway captain's chair from the station. Tom, the first person in Grimstad to meet Jane when she stepped off the train, collaborated knowing that the chair was a spare and that it was bound for Jane's school. Norton Topping conveniently decided he needed a new wood and coal heater for his house, so he donated his old one to the school while the lumber yard supplied the stove pipe.

Mary deliberately volunteered to do inventory on supplies at the Grimstad School. As she went through the books, she boxed discards that were presumably designated for the garbage. Mary was quite generous with the discards for Jane's sake, taking even a few books that were intact though dog-eared. Some of the other teachers helped her, suspecting these discards were bound for Jane's school.

They saw it as an opportunity to get new textbooks. As the new maps had arrived for the school, she also included the dated maps of the world and Canada. All discards were boxed then set by the garbage barrels outside the school and Sean came after dark to pick them up and take them to his place as the first step in getting them to Jane's school.

One evening, just after the school was built, the school committee held its first meeting inside the school house. As furnishings were Spartan, everyone had to bring their own chairs.

Jane and Ethan were the first to arrive as he grumbled about being hurried through supper and chores so they could be at the school early. Robbie was allowed to run free in the large space at the back of the school room as the tables to serve as desks were clustered around the teacher's desk at the far end of the room. As Robbie scampered around the room listening to his own echoes, Jane walked around in a dreamy state mulling over how she would set up the details of her classroom.

Jane commented on the pleasant odour of newly cut wood that permeated the room, and Ethan remarked with a teasing voice, "Kinda reminds me of the day you fumigated the house with resin."

"Only this time the odour isn't hiding anything," she replied with a twisted grin.

Ethan scowled briefly but made no comment.

Soon Sean and Mary arrived, carrying the book boxes and the rolled maps, "Look at what I have for you," Mary gasped as she set down a large box on one of the desk-tables. Mary began lifting out some items, there were the remains of three beginner readers whose pages were tied together with string, two more intermediate grade readers, dog-eared but in tact, a couple of raggedy but still bound arithmetic books, a spelling book and a couple of worn science books, one which was geared for beginners. Finally, Mary pulled out a Canadian history book designed for mid-elementary classes that focussed on the explorers. This was exactly as Jane had wished.

"Wonderful," Jane gasped as she handled the treasure. She put the books on the shelves at the back. "The ones that are falling apart I will let the students use first."

"Look, I have roll maps," Mary said eagerly. She drew open the map of Canada, apologizing that it was a bit out-of-date. While it was new enough to show Alberta and Saskatchewan as provinces, the boundaries of Manitoba, Ontario and Quebec were much smaller, though someone drew in their present boundaries with a heavy pencil. "I guess this map was made before 1912, but after 1905," Mary said.

Jane looked curiously at Mary and Mary continued. "As you must know, Alberta and Saskatchewan became provinces in 1905, and large areas of the Northwest Territories were given to Manitoba, Ontario and Quebec in 1912."

"It'll do," Jane said. Then turning to Ethan she said, "Ethan could you find a hammer and nails and can you and Sean can hang these maps up?"

"Oh, I guess," Ethan replied in his usual grumbling voice. He headed to the shed out back where the workmen kept their tools.

"These women never give ye a moments peace, do they now." Sean laughed as Ethan headed for the door.

"You can help him," Mary said, "and I also have a flag to hang up." She pulled out a folded up Union Jack from the box.

"That's where it stops," Sean said with a frown. "I'll help hang the maps and I'll even speak to the Englishman, but I will not be handling that flag."

"Oh Sean, get over it," both women said.

"I know that Canada is a willin' part of the British Empire and ye honour that flag, but it is the flag of oppression for Erin." Sean, an expatriate Irishman, harboured an almost fanatical hatred for the British and all they represented.

Ethan returned and Sean helped him hang up the maps. The Canadian map was directly behind the teacher's desk and the world map was beside it.

"We also have a flag to hang up," Jane said.

"Best be waitin' for someone else to come to help ye with that one, Ethan," Sean said.

Ethan looked from one to the other, and Mary replied with a tone of disgust, "Sean's living in the past again."

Ethan made the connection and said, "I can wait." Jane pulled down the world map and shook her head at the display of the now defunct empires of Austria-Hungary, the Ottoman Turks and Russia among other pre-war countries. Again someone had boldly penciled in the name Turkey below the Ottoman Empire name. This brought a brief discussion about the outdated map, but Jane said, "These children are just beginners and won't be interested in details. Just as long as I can show them where Canada is in relation to the world, or big countries like America, China, India and Russia."

Soon the others arrived with more comments about the still pulled down world map. Stan complained that it still showed Poland as parts of Austria, Germany and Russia. When Dave arrived he and Sean nodded a terse greeting and Ethan said, "Maybe you can help me with the flag." At Jane's suggestion the flag was hung centred along the front wall above the blackboard and maps.

They were about to sit down for the meeting with Sari using the teacher's desk for recording and Dave beside her to conduct the meeting when Audi walked in carrying two chairs. The words, "What's he doing here?" were on Sari's lips, and Jane spoke the same words quietly to Ethan with equal contempt.

"He has done a lot of work on the school and wants it to succeed," Ethan said out of the corner of his mouth, "so we invited him to come to the meeting. I don't think he'll cause any trouble here."

"Not with you here," Jane said with a crooked grin.

Although Audi sensed some hostile eyes present, he continued unconcerned. "I brought these two chairs from home as a donation to the school." He sat down on one of the chairs and since everyone else had brought chairs, his other one remained vacant. The children were all shooed outside with Helen taking Robbie by the hand. Dave brought the meeting to order with a slap of the yardstick that he had brought along. "Courtesy of the lumber yard," was his comment as he noticed the others looking at the yardstick. He laid it along the chalk ledge below the blackboard.

After the reading of the minutes and the meagre financial statement from the last meeting, the first order of business was to pick a name for the school. Several names were put forward such as Muskeg, Poplar Ridge, Aspen Ridge and Jane's school.

Finally, it was Audi who stood up and said, "Since Jane is the teacher and the inspiration for this whole project, let her pick a name."

"Yes, you pick a name Jane," several people cried out.

"Thank you for the honour," Jane blushed. "But we should vote on a name."

"Just pick one and we'll vote," Dave said amid chants for her to pick a name.

"Well, uh…" Jane thought for a moment. "Let's call it Opportunity School as it offers an opportunity for your children to become educated."

Cheers erupted and Dave called for order and for a vote from the list written on the blackboard. He called for a show of hands on Jane's suggestion and it received overwhelming approval. Stan volunteered to hand carve a sign bearing the name to be placed above the door on the outside of the school.

They moved on to discuss the need for a fundraising event in order to pay for basic supplies and hopefully more books, plus payment on the windows and door obtained on credit from the lumber yard.

After much discussion, they agreed on Dave's suggestion

that they hold a box social and dance the last Saturday night in August, as the second week following was designated the first day of school.

"Sari and I will organise the box social part," Jane volunteered.

"I vill speak to some of da Grimstads dat know how to play music. I tink I can get dem to play for free," Axel added.

"Very well, your offers are accepted," Dave replied. "If that is all let's adjourn the meeting as the coffee is on."

Hella had lugged along a large container of coffee and a big tray of raspberry strudels, while Sari brought cookies and Jane brought a cake. Now they could socialise and have the *real meeting* as Ethan had said. Sean spent a lot of time talking to Stan to get acquainted with his new neighbour and the women all wanted to talk to Jane as she got a final count of the names, ages and number of the students who would be attending the school. Raisa, who spoke virtually no English stated simply to Jane, "Two girls, Sonya and Tanya, dey seex years." She then stood back and let the other women continue chatting with Jane.

Audi meanwhile, stood by the bookshelf and looked over the books that Mary had brought, shaking his head at the state of their disrepair.

The neighbours of the area gathered for the box social and dance. Several couples made the twelve mile journey from Grimstad to attend as well as farmers and homesteaders along the road close to Grimstad, filling the school to near capacity. Like most husbands and male suitors, Ethan strove to get a glimpse of Jane's basket so he wouldn't bid for the wrong basket and in a feigned accident Sean also got a clear look at Mary's basket much to her chagrin. Also much to Mary's annoyance, Sean brought along a jug of moonshine to treat the men folk before the event got under way. Virtually all of the men involved in the construction of the school partook as the men gathered around Sean's

Model-T. Dave hung back, uncertain to whether Sean would invite him to have a swallow from his jug.

When everyone was called inside and seated on the rough wooden benches built that very day for this and future events at the school, Audi, who had no lady's lunch to bid for, was asked by Jane to be the auctioneer. For most, the bidding was a formality as many wives such as Sari and Hella left deliberate clues so their husbands would bid accordingly. However, as Hella's lunch was offered before Sari's, Dave deliberately bid it up before he allowed the frustrated Wolf to win. Dave laughed and said, "It's for the kids."

Having observed the little game, Ethan bid up Sari's lunch in turn before allowing Dave to win and he smiled offering the same comment.

The last two lunches to be offered were those of Jane and Mary. When the men were outside having a snort, the two women redid their boxes in such a way that neither Ethan nor Sean could be certain which box was which. So when Audi presented the first box lunch Ethan and Sean each thought it belonged to their respective partners and a bidding war ensued. Sean couldn't understand why Ethan wanted Mary's lunch, and dark thoughts of Sean's former yen for Jane began to surface in Ethan. Finally, as Sean had more money with him than Ethan, he was able to win the lunch.

This particular lunch belonged to Jane. When she went to collect it and take it to Sean, she smiled and winked at her husband who in turn glared at Sean. Ethan's mood lightened when he saw that the final box offered looked identical to the previous one. Sean's eyebrows rose and both men realized that the women had played a trick on them. Ethan offered what he considered to be a reasonable bid on the box and won it without contest. Sean motioned for Ethan and Mary to come and sit beside him and Jane, whereupon they all had a good laugh over the box confusion.

"Ye looked a wee bit worried when I outbid you Ethan me boy." Sean laughed.

"It was just my way of foolin' you into making a large donation to the school," Ethan replied in his usual grumbling voice though he had a twisted grin on his face.

"It goes to show you can't be trustin' the wiles of a woman," Sean added.

"If you hadn't *accidently* tripped and got a look at my lunch box, I wouldn't have conspired with Jane," Mary laughed.

"And you," Jane said to Ethan with a feigned scolding voice. "I saw you peeking at my box."

"Well, we wouldn't want the Dutchman to *accidently* outbid me for your lunch would we," Ethan said nonchalantly.

"That's why we made Audi auctioneer," Mary laughed. "So he wouldn't try to bid in on someone's lunch."

"What did I tell ye Ethan," Sean laughed, "women and their schemin' ways."

"I think the Dutchman would have more than his hands full if he tried anything fancy with these two," Ethan laughed.

"Truer words were never spoken," Sean replied. "Now that lunch is done we should be goin' outside for some air. Oh by-the-way Mary, it was a fine lunch indeed."

"Good idea," Ethan replied as both men stood up.

Jane frowned at Ethan with the comment, "Liquid air no doubt." She; however, did not try to stop him though she knew they were going for another nip of moonshine.

"Yers was a good lunch too," Ethan added to soothe her ruffled feathers.

"I will never understand this masculine need to consume spirits," Mary said to Jane sympathetically as they watched the men head for the door. She knew Jane was opposed to drinking.

"Me neither," Jane said tersely, though she loved Ethan too much to try to forbid him to drink.

Upon seeing Sean head outside, most of the men followed for that very reason. Dave again stayed behind with a despondent look on his face. Wolf came back into the school momentarily and fetched the reluctant Dave. Since they were all drinking to the completion of the schoolhouse on which they had laboured so hard, it was only fair to include Dave. Sean had no objection in view of the others insistence and even handed Dave the jug without comment when he arrived. Dave took it, also without comment and had a hearty swallow of the potent drink. As the men all chatted, Dave and Sean merely ignored each other except when the jug was passed again.

When the music started, signalling the beginning of the dance, the men all returned to the hall not wanting to face their spouse's wrath for spending too much time drinking. A donation box was set up as opposed to charging admission for all the late comers and others who didn't partake in the box social. Ethan noticed that Audi had put a handful of money into the box that included at least some paper currency.

The small band that provided the music consisted of a fiddler, a guitar player and an accordion player. They opened with a waltz that got nearly every adult couple on the floor. The waltz set was followed by a polka, which got everyone revved up. Sometime during the polka Ivan momentarily stepped out and came back with a mandolin and joined in with the band. After the tune finished the band members motioned for him to play lead and he began to play lively Gypsy flavoured Russian music. The fiddler listened intensely and soon caught on to his tune and most people stopped dancing to listen. His adrenalin aroused and sufficiently fuelled by alcohol, Ivan began to sing in Russian while most of the others began clapping to the beat of the music as he danced around. Having gotten the band attuned to Russian music, Ivan set his mandolin down and squatted with arms folded, kicking his legs out in rapid succession. The Cossack dance lasted only for a few moments before Ivan again sprang to his feet, grabbed Raisa and cried, "Everybody polka." The band finished out the Russian tune without him.

As darkness began to creep in, gas lanterns, brought by Dave and Wolf, were lit and the children began to come indoors. Infants, like Robbie, were put to bed under the tables while the older toddlers found their own way to a secure corner to sleep. Some of the children played tag on the dance floor between sets, but quickly got out of the way when the dancing started. By the time the dance ended around midnight, nearly all of the children were asleep and were gathered up from various secure places and carried out, still sleeping, to their parent's vehicles.

"Well, your school got properly broke in," Ethan said as they headed down the trail to their home. "There's nothing like a good old schoolhouse dance."

"Yes, it was quite a party," Jane said with a smile, and then with a more serious tone continued, "even though you drank your share of the moonshine."

"Havin' a snort or two is a man's thing," Ethan replied. "We were celebratin' havin' the school ready for yuh."

"Seems like you men always have an excuse to drink about something," Jane replied flatly.

"There weren't no harm in it," Ethan grumbled. "Even Sean behaved himself."

"Humph," Jane scoffed. She was too tired to offer further argument.

Chapter Four

The first day of school was the Monday of the first week in September. Jane came to the school the afternoon before, as Ethan dropped her and Robbie off on his way to see Axel Rutland about setting up the sawmill on his new quarter both as a means to help clear the land and use the lumber as a first step in relocating his farm. As Jane approached the doorway she noticed the sign hand-carved by Stan's deft hand above the doorway. She stood for a moment with a dreamy smile admiring the sign, Opportunity School, *my school,* she thought.

Jane went inside with Robbie following. He played inside the school while Jane did her fine tuning on getting ready for the first day of school. She organised the desk-tables in an arc around her desk, and was glad the pupils would be using the low tables instead of row desks so she could arrange them in this manner. This allowed plenty of room for her to stand directly in front of any given table. Jane labouriously scribed all the upper and lower case letters of the alphabet along the top of the front blackboard with single digit numbers following in proper sequence. She then printed her name *Mrs. Phillips* below the alphabet.

As Jane didn't have a proper register, she wrote the names of her nine students in a scribbler designated for that purpose, all in alphabetical order, and then she drew vertical lines so she could check off each day of the week that a pupil attended. They had made enough from the box social and dance to buy some supplies over and above school costs. Thus, she could issue each student two scribblers and three pencils to be doled out one at a time, one twelve inch ruler and one box of basic wax crayons for each of the seven younger children while Thomas and Herman, being older, would get a box of water colour paints to share. She held in reserve a straight pen and a bottle of ink for each of the older students to share. This would be issued to them when they were ready to start writing as opposed to printing. She laid everything out on a back table to be issued to each student when class started. Jane had amassed a bundle of scrap paper, white and brown alike, from both her house and the store in Grimstad. She cut it up with scissors to approximately page size as this paper would be used for rough work and art. She stored it on one of the shelves. Since the box social she had got the work bee to make three more tables. In addition, the school had received a few more discarded kitchen chairs in addition to those Audi had brought. They were all placed along the back. One table, designated as the learning table, would be by the bookshelves and another was to become a science table to display objects of a scientific nature. The third table would be general purpose and would be kept clear when possible and used for meetings and other adult functions.

Jane was just fussing over making superfluous final adjustments when Ethan came for her. Robbie raced to greet his dad and after picking him up Ethan looked around and said to Jane, "Do you think you can ever get it better than perfect?"

Jane sighed and replied, "I suppose I can't do anything more today. I just can't wait until tomorrow morning. I still think I'm missing something though."

"Well, nobody is perfect, it'll likely take a few days before you've figured what all yuh need. For now, it's best to get you home it's gettin' toward supper time," Ethan said. "Then you can get to bed early and rest up for the big day."

"Say Ethan, could you make me a small lock up cupboard for the school for stashing extra supplies?" Jane asked sweetly.

"Oh, I suppose," Ethan said with is usual grumpy voice.

"Thanks dear."

Jane had a fitful sleep that night as her mind was whirling in anticipation of the first day of school. Ethan grumbled of her restlessness during the night. At one point she sat up in bed wide awake saying, "I forgot to get a pencil sharpener and a garbage can."

"Wa- wha- at," Ethan grumbled as he woke up. "Why are you worrin' about that now?"

"How will the kids sharpen their pencils?" Jane worried.

"Use a knife, I guess," Ethan grunted. "Now go back to sleep."

"Can I borrow your pocket knife? I don't want the younger ones sharpening their own pencils."

"Oh, all right," Ethan grumbled.

He rolled over to try to get back to sleep and finally in frustration lit the lamp and swung out of bed. "Might as well make a cup a tea," he grumbled. "Seein' how you wrecked my sleep."

"Sorry dear," Jane apologised as she also swung out of bed. "Tea might make me settle down."

"I hope so," Ethan grumbled as he lit the fire. Jane checked on Robbie to make sure he was properly covered before she joined Ethan at the table.

While she was doing this, Ethan went over to the bedside and fumbled in his pants pocket for his clasp knife and handed it to her. "You can use it for now, when yuh see Hella tomorrow tell her to get Wolf to buy a pencil sharpener with the funds."

"Thanks love," Jane said as she kissed him. "I hate to deprive you of your knife."

"I still got my huntin' knife," he assured her. "I think there's an old pail in the shed you can use, if you don't mind a rusty-looking garbage can."

"As long as it'll hold the whittlings from all the pencils I'll be sharpening," Jane replied with a wry grin.

While they were having tea it occurred to Jane, "I don't

have a school bell either. How will I call the kids to class?"

Ethan thought for a moment and said, "Will a cow bell do? I think I got an extra one in the shed."

"A cow bell!" Jane exclaimed and then after a moments thought added, "Yes, that will do fine…maybe we can get a real school bell later."

"Now is that all, or are yuh gonna torment me all night with more stuff you forgot," Ethan grumbled.

"Sorry dear, but that should do it for now," Jane grinned. "I'll try not to disturb your sleep any more."

They had their tea and crawled back to bed, both going soundly to sleep.

Jane was at the school bright and early the next morning to make sure she was there to receive the first students. Ethan dropped her and Robbie off on his way to take a can of cream to Dave, who in turn would take it to Grimstad station to be shipped to Edmonton to the creamery.

When Jane entered the schoolhouse, she found a large cardboard box on her desk. She looked eagerly inside and gasped with utter astonishment. It was full of books. On top of the books was a large folded white paper. She opened it looking for a clue to whoever brought the box. Instead it turned out to be a large wall map of Europe with the postwar boundaries showing the multitude of small countries now existing in Eastern Europe. National Geographic Magazine was printed at the bottom of the map revealing its origin. She refolded it and put it on her desk thinking that later she could put it up on one end of the side blackboard. The books inside were for various ages, though not standard readers they would certainly help in making her pupils literate. There were a couple of vintage science books, which were in good shape. Jane took the box to the table by the bookshelves and placed the books upright on the shelves, dumbfounded as there was no clue to who her benefactor might be. Stan Gogowicz arrived some time after, bringing his three children as well as the Higgins' children. They were walking along the road when he picked them up. She told them all to leave their lunch pails and school bags on a designated bench along the back wall and go outside until she rang the bell, though Helen spoke to Robbie before going outside. Stan introduced his children as Lech, Lydia and Mark. Stan instructed them to say good morning Mrs. Phillips, which they said almost in unison.

"Good morning," Jane smiled. "Leave your things on the bench and go outside and play until I ring the bell." Lydia spoke momentarily to Robbie before heading outside. Stan wished Jane well and turned to leave.

Next to arrive was Ivan bringing his twin daughters, Sonya and Tanya. They were virtually identical and only distinguishable by the different coloured ribbons in their braided hair. Sonya had red ribbons and Tanya had blue ones. They smiled shyly at Jane, heads down with eyes rolled upward. "What you say to teacher," Ivan said to them.

"*Dobroe utro*," Tanya said.

"In English," Ivan said shaply.

"Good mornink, teacher," Sonya said.

Jane smiled and said, "Very good. You may play outside until I ring the bell."

They looked puzzled and Ivan explained to them in Russian. As they headed out, Ivan apologised. "Sorry dat my girls don't speak much English yet. But you feex dat and dey teach da Meesis."

"Yes, I will make sure they learn English." Jane smiled, but inside knew she had a potentially challenging task of having to teach the girls English. Ivan excused himself.

Finally, Hella showed up driving Wolf's car. Herman and Wilhelm didn't bother coming into the school. They went straight into playing with the others leaving their lunch pails by the door.

When Hella came into the school house to get Robbie, Jane asked her about the books, "When I came to school this morning I found a box full of books with a map of Europe on my desk. Did Wolf get them with left over money and bring them here last night?"

"No," Hella replied. "He vass home yesterday all day."

"Maybe Dave…," Jane wondered.

"No, Dave vass helping Wolf und zhey were cutting pigs."

"Now we do have a mystery," Jane sighed. "I don't suppose Mary or Sean brought them."

Hella shrugged then said, "I suppose I better take Robbie, I haff baking und vashing to do today." Turning to Robbie she smiled saying, "Come Robbie, come mit Aunty Hella." Jane bent down and kissed her son goodbye and also told him to go with Aunty Hella. Hella smiled again and extended her hand. Robbie clasped it and followed her.

With all nine of her pupils present, Jane went back to her desk to check the time. She had brought the alarm clock from home so she would know when to start and end the school day as well as manage recess breaks. It was nearly at the stroke of nine o'clock, the designated start time for classes, when Jane grabbed the bell and went to the door and rang for the students to come in. She stopped them from going directly to their desk-tables as she wanted to assign seats. She put the youngest, Sonya and Tanya, by the windows and next to them Mark Gogowicz, and then came Helen and Wilhelm, Lydia and Lech, and furthest from the windows were Herman and Thomas. Once they were seated, Jane did a proper roll call. Although it seemed superfluous for this tiny class, she wanted them to be accustomed to the procedure.

Jane stood up and introduced herself, "Good morning. As many of you know my name is Mrs. Phillips, the name you are to address me by." Led by Herman and Thomas they returned the greeting. Jane asked them to stand, bow their heads and repeat the Lord's Prayer after her. Then she had them stand at attention and salute the flag with a simple pledge to His Majesty, King George V of the British Empire and the Dominion of Canada. She informed them that every day would begin this way and then told the class to be seated.

On that first day, she trained her pupils how to print their full names and had the pupils print their first name in large print on a piece of paper. These were taped to the part of the table facing her, so she would have no trouble remembering the names of the Gogowicz children and distinguishing between the Malov twins as she was less familiar with them than the others. The pupils again printed their first names and these were placed on the wall along the back to designate a spot for each to hang their coat and such. She would ask Ethan to drive some nails in the wall by their names so they would be able to hang their coats until they could get proper coat hangers. All of this printing led to Jane spending much time sharpening pencils with Ethan's knife. Although all the boys, except Mark, had their own jack-knives, they had to sharpen their pencils into the garbage can under her close supervision so she could be sure they handled their knives safely.

The whole day was more or less orientation and how to behave as a class. Jane set up a roster on the side blackboard whereby the students of each family would have a duty, in turn, at the end of the day to clean those areas of the blackboard she wished to have erased and bang the chalk brushes clean. They would also take out the trash to the burn barrel as soon as she could get one and sweep the floor. When weather became colder they would also be required to bring in wood and coal for the heater. Jane set it up so one of the older boys would each have a turn working with the Malov twins when their turn came as they were not big enough for the heavier work.

At one point during the day, Jane took the two older Gogowicz children aside to test their reading and arithmetic skills. Lech was nearly as old as Thomas, but he could read or write only a few words beyond printing his name, having picked up his rudimentary reading skills from his parents. Lydia was likewise at the threshold of the reading stage.

Thus, Jane lumped them in the middle group with Helen and Wilhelm. Mark and the Malov twins were beginners, as all three were only six years old. The latter two having a language issue as well.

Jane decided that since there were so few students, and she had no training on how to grade them properly, she would simply teach each child at a rate that they could absorb the information. There would be no passing, failing, or marking system. She planned to send home a written note four times during the year and once at the end of the year to act as a report card stating their children's general progress both academically and socially.

Jane soon discovered that when the Malov girls became confused they lapsed into speaking Russian to each other. After sensing Jane's frustration, Lech offered to speak to them.

"Do you understand Russian?" Jane asked with a sigh of relief.

"No, but we sometimes speak Polish at home and I can tell some of their words are almost the same," Lech replied.

"Thank you Lech, you may speak to them," Jane smiled.

Lech spoke to the Malov girls in Polish and in spite the difference in some words and structure he was able to communicate with them. Jane appointed him as their helper whenever the language barrier got in the way. Lydia was asked to play with them at recess time when possible to try to get them to speak English.

During the lunch break, Jane had her first experience at checking the students' behaviour when she had to chase the three oldest boys, Herman, Thomas and Lech out of the slough at the edge of the school yard.

"Aw, but we had fun playing here during the meetings," Thomas complained.

"That was when you were in your parents' care," Jane said tersely. "When you are in my care during school time you will follow my rules."

"Yes, Mrs. Phillips," they said in unison with bowed heads.

Jane lined all nine pupils up at the back of the school and explained the perimeter of the school yard. "There will be no playing in the slough or creek, nor shall anyone go into the muskeg, or across the road. If necessary, I will ask Mr. Phillips to build a fence around the school yard to fence you in like the cows and pigs." There were a few snickers from the students and Jane continued. "I like to think of you as people, not farm animals. Besides, there might be hornets in the muskeg that will sting you. I got stung the first time I tried to enter a muskeg."

"And there could be a bear," Helen added.

"Yes, that's right," Jane replied.

"You could shoot it with your shotgun," Thomas audaciously stated. He was well aware of Jane's previous run-in with a bear two years ago.

Jane flushed with embarrassment. *Will the legend of me as a bear slayer ever die?*

This provoked questions from some of the others, directed at Thomas.

"Enough talk about bears," Jane said sharply. "I'll thank you Thomas not to talk about that incident."

"Yes Mrs. Phillips," Thomas replied dolefully. However, by the end of the day he had told all the boys in the class behind Jane's back since they demanded to know how Jane had killed a bear with a shotgun.

Jane finished the school day with some colouring and painting to take home. Lech complained that he had to use crayons, "Like the little kids." Jane promised to get him a paint brush as soon as possible, and he could share the paint set with Thomas and Herman. After class was dismissed she started a list on the side blackboard of the things they still needed: another paint set, another pen with nib, a pencil sharpener, some proper coat hangers and finally a soccer ball. She deemed that if the boys had a ball to play with, they might stay out of trouble. When Hella brought Robbie back, she also brought a pencil sharpener and some coat hangers as Wolf had gone to Grimstad during the day. Jane erased these items from her list.

When Ethan came for her at the end of the day, he asked the standard question, "Well, how did your first day of school go?"

"Very good," Jane bubbled. "I think I have them all organised so we can get into the real school work tomorrow."

Ethan grunted in acknowledgement and Jane carried on, "I had to chase the three oldest boys out of the slough and give them all a talk about staying in the school yard."

"Maybe we can get the crew together and fence it," Ethan wondered out loud.

"They'd just go through the fence if they wanted to," Jane replied, "unless you use pig wire."

"That'd be expensive," Ethan grunted. "But if keeping the kids in the school yard is a problem, then we'll take care of it." Then he added, "The sawmill will be setting up soon at the other end of the quarter and we don't want any of them coming over there."

"That's for sure," Jane replied. "Oh, Wolf got us a pencil sharpener and coat hangers today. Could you install them?"

"Oh I guess," he grumbled then added, "don't you have time?"

"They have mounting screws," Jane argued.

"So, I'll get you a screwdriver out of the shed. You seem like a good carpenter," he added with a twisted grin.

"Some things never change," Jane sighed. She was thinking of the time Ethan left her to build a screen door for the house. "If I want something done I have to do it myself."

"Maybe when I bring yuh tomorrow I'll install the hangers and sharpener, if I have time." Ethan relented.

"Don't let me get in the way of your busy schedule," Jane snapped.

Before Ethan could reply little Robbie started fussing and Jane spent the rest of the journey home tending to his concerns. Nonetheless, Ethan would install the sharpener and coat hangers in the morning without further comment.

Chapter Five

On the second day of school Jane began her classes in earnest. In setting her curriculum, Jane deemed that the two most mentally taxing subjects, language and arithmetic, would be taught in the morning when the student's minds were the fresh and most alert. She organised them in an alternating fashion; every second day language would come first until first recess, and then arithmetic would follow until lunch break. On the in-between days she switched the order to give her pupils variety.

In the afternoon, she taught either science or Canadian history and geography during the first part of the afternoon in the same alternating fashion. She knew that at a later date, as the pupils became more proficient, she would probably have to subdivide language into clearly defined subcomponents of reading, grammar and spelling, and would likely have to do the same with history and geography.

So by rote, Jane drilled her students on the alphabet letter sounds, moving on to words and later sentences. Since Herman and Thomas could already read at a basic level they were issued their readers to read silently while she dealt with the younger pupils, and then when their turn came, she had them read a passage aloud, though as time progressed she would assign them exercises in printing sentences. During arithmetic classes, the younger ones were drilled on their numbers and the concepts of quantity and grouping of numbers. Sometimes Jane used quantities of pebbles to illustrate the concept of adding and subtracting. While she worked with the younger students, Jane gave the older two more complex exercises on addition and subtraction.

Science, geography and history were taught in a more general way with each level absorbing what they could.

In science, she talked about animals by using familiar farm animals and wild animals of the area as examples, making occasional reference to more exotic animals such as elephants, lions and tigers. During the winter months she planned to teach them about the stars. History and geography concentrated almost entirely on Canada; they learned the names and later the capitals of all nine provinces, the territories and Newfoundland[1]. She told them about the main rivers and lakes, then for history she talked about the explorers. Names like Jacques Cartier, Alexander McKenzie, Anthony Hendy and David Thompson and the areas they explored became familiar to the students. As Jacques Cartier's name was both difficult to say and spell for some students, this led to talking about the French factor in Canadian history. Thomas Higgins, who was the most prolific reader among the students, sometimes bombarded Jane with questions that at times taxed her knowledge in these matters, just as Herman taxed her knowledge in science. Lech, with his own insatiable thirst for knowledge was catching up fast to Herman and Thomas in the complexity of questions he asked as well as in his reading and arithmetic skills. Lech, who quickly mastered the skill of basic reading, was trying his best to be one of the *older boys*.

When categorising animals such as mammals, birds, reptiles and such, Jane thought for simplicity sake to classify all creepy crawling things as insects or bugs until one day Herman asked, "Why do spiders have eight legs and other insects like flies, or ants have only six?" Jane scrambled to try to tell him that spiders were a special kind of bug. She had to look it up to find out that spiders were Arachnids, a creature as different from an insect as fish from a cow.

In geography class, Thomas wanted to know why Newfoundland wasn't part of Canada, and Jane was stuck for an answer and left lamely to say, "Because the people there didn't want to be part of Canada." But Thomas still wanted to know why.

General knowledge time was the last part of the

afternoon on Monday, Tuesday and Thursday, with this part of the day reserved for music on Wednesdays and art on Fridays. During general knowledge time the world map was often pulled down as Jane would show Canada in relation to the world and point out large countries like USA, China, Australia, or Brazil. Also, on the map of Europe that Jane had pinned to the wall, the homeland of her pupils' parents and familiar neighbours, places like England, Germany, Poland, Norway, Russia and Ireland were identified. Since this was a time for pupils to ask questions that were on their minds, geography and science were usually the subjects of choice as no one wanted to talk about language or arithmetic at this time of day.

The day after a globe and a soccer ball had mysteriously appeared on Jane's desk one morning, she unwittingly ran herself into a corner. Lech had asked what caused the seasons during general knowledge time. Jane stated that the Earth tilted on its axis one way for summer and the other way for winter, but stood straight up and down during spring and fall. She knew this was not correct, but thought it easier for the pupils to understand. She might have gotten away with it had it not been for Herman Kepler with his voracious appetite for scientific information. He argued that Jane's theory was not correct and she made the mistake of refuting his argument. He went quickly to the little library at the back and looked through the science text the benefactor had provided. He then showed her a page with a diagram that illustrated how the Earth's revolution around the sun caused the seasons and the axial tilt remained stationary. Jane was left stuttering for an answer. *That boy is too smart for his own good*, she thought. Jane's face flushed as she groped for words and attempted to explain that she was just trying to make things easier to understand for the younger ones. She then drew a diagram of the sun and Earth on the blackboard and explained to the class how the seasons were really caused. Jane had blundered badly, never again would she utter an untruth in the name of simplicity. She was dumbfounded that even this brilliant young man could fathom such things at the tender age of nine and half when last year he could hardly read.

If Jane was resolved to tell the truth even if it seemed complicated, she would be taxed again during another science class.

In her ongoing efforts to invite student participation in classifying animals into general groups, she had stated that mammals nursed their young with milk.

"Are people mammals?" Helen asked sincerely.

"Yes," Jane replied. "People are a very special kind of mammal."

"I remember when Maria was a baby," Lech piped in innocently. "Mommy nursed her like a calf."

There were snickers from some of the others and Jane's face turned beet red. Again she was lost for words. Knowing she had to quickly regain control of the situation, Jane replied sharply, "While you are correct Mr. Gogowicz, these things are not to be discussed when it comes to people. Nursing is very private, for the same reason that you don't take your clothes off in public. From now on people are to be left out of scientific discussion. When you are much older you will learn about the human race and how it fits into the scheme of things."

Silence followed. The younger ones did not comprehend her words, but sensed that Lech's statement was close to forbidden territory. Although it was ten minutes early Jane dismissed the class for recess. She desperately needed a breather. When the children had all dispersed outdoors, Jane placed her hands against the blackboard and braced herself. There were tears in the corners of her eyes as she muttered, "What am I going to do? These kids are too smart for me."

Regaining her composure, she added to her blackboard list one set of encyclopaedias and a great big dictionary. "Please, Mr. Benefactor, see this and deliver," she murmured. Feeling very weak, Jane went back to her desk and sat down.

She was glad the last segment of the day was dedicated to music, having the children sing should brighten things up.

Before the break was over, Lech came back into the school carefully approaching Jane as he felt troubled that he had upset his teacher. As he approached her desk, Jane smiled uncertainly and said, "Yes, Mr. Gogowicz?"

"Mrs. Phillips, uh… Mrs. Phillips, I'm sorry I upset you," he faltered. "Are you gonna tell Mom and Dad?"

Jane smiled radiantly and replied, "No, of course not. You meant well, it's just better that you don't make certain comparisons."

"Thank you Mrs. Phillips, I'll watch what I say."

"Go run along and play now, you still have ten minutes of recess."

Lech turned and bolted while Jane felt a load lift off her shoulders. She could now finish out the day with confidence.

If Jane was able to maintain a brave face for her students, later in the quiet of the evening when Robbie had been put to bed, she broke down and cried on Ethan's shoulder. "What am I going to do?" she sobbed. "These kids are outsmarting me. I was foolish to think I could be their teacher. Now I know why you need training to be a teacher." Ethan enveloped her with his huge forearm and stroked her hair, listening to her cry for a few moments. He was troubled; this did not sound like the fearless, indomitable Jane who had virtually brought him to his knees during their tumultuous courtship.

"Tell me what happened." he said quietly as Jane choked back a few sobs.

She first told Ethan about the incident with the rocking globe and the seasons. Although this incident happened a couple of days ago, Jane had not told Ethan of it previously for fear of ridicule. She also told him of the insects and the spiders. Then when she talked about Lech and human mammals, she was reduced to sobbing. "What am I going to do? I'm not prepared to answer the questions they ask, especially these two boy geniuses, Thomas and Herman, and now Lech is catching on."

"Hey, hey, there now Jane," Ethan said with a gentle firmness. He lifted up her hair and said, "Is the real Jane in there? The Jane who shot a bear, the Jane that fumigated the house with resin, or the Jane who smoked out the house to get rid of the flies?"

Jane smiled weakly with tear filled eyes as she recalled these incidents from their first few weeks together.

"Finally, where is the Jane that got so mad she walked ten miles down the road with two heavy suitcases and fended off the Dutchman all in one day?"

Jane laughed and wiped away her tears, "This is different." She said, getting serious.

"How so?" Ethan demanded. Then in a more gentle voice he continued, "No, Jane you woke up something inside these kids. They want to learn. They need you to teach them. Remember all those things you came up with when you were first with me? There was no problem to big for you to tackle Jane, and neither are these kids. If the Kepler and Higgins boys are all fired up on learning all this fancy scientific stuff, let them go ahead. Get them books to read. Don't be afraid to admit that you don't know everything. If they stump yuh tell 'em you'll find out the answers for them. Let them help you, if you think they know more than you about certain things. Sooner or later they'll trip up. They're just kids. They're not half as smart as they think they are. Just don't challenge them by sayin' things that'll back you into a corner."

"Oh Ethan, I love you," Jane choked. She hugged him fiercely and looked up into his craggy face with its deep lines and a day's growth of grey whiskers. It was the most beautiful thing in the world. "Maybe you should be the teacher," she said in a weak voice.

"Me!" Ethan exclaimed. "I don't know nothin'. I can't even talk properly."

"But you're the wisest man I've ever known," Jane kissed him.

After a moment or two of silence, Ethan said in a firm voice, "I want you to go straight into that school tomorrow and start askin' those two questions and find out how much they really know. Ask till they're stumped for an answer, but be sure you only ask about things you know the answer to." This time Ethan kissed her.

"Yes sir," she smiled weakly. "I can already see a brand new way to deal with these two shining stars in my classroom."

"I knew yuh could do it," Ethan assured her. "When yer back's against the wall I can count on you to come up with another brainwave. Now lets git to bed and sleep on it."

Jane went confidently to school the next morning planning a whole new tack for Herman and Thomas. She gave them a more intense grammar program and introduced them to multiplication and long division in arithmetic, or had them help drill the younger students in addition and subtraction with flash cards. In geography and history, she gave them reports to do on some explorers and to point out major Canadian river systems on the map. When they asked Jane questions about things she was unclear on, she promised to find out for them at the first opportunity.

Herman and Thomas dominated the general knowledge classes of late afternoon as Jane allowed them to spout their knowledge of science and geography. Often when one of the younger students asked a question she would in turn ask Herman or Thomas if they knew the answer, sometimes they didn't know or gave a misstatement, allowing Jane a small victory when she had to correct them. Every day she said a prayer hoping her benefactor would deliver the encyclopaedia soon. In spite of the confidence Ethan had reinstalled in her, she didn't know how much longer she could keep running ahead of these two.

One day in late fall a large Oxford dictionary mysteriously appeared on her desk when she came to school. There was much excitement among her three shining stars with this new reservoir of information available to them. Jane put the dictionary on the learning table beside the globe and before anyone was allowed to touch it she explained, "This is a very expensive and fragile book with thin pages that tear easily. No one is to use it without my permission and only then if their hands are clean."

Her three shining stars raised their hands simultaneously, each vying to be first to use the dictionary. Finally, she drew lots to see who would be first, allotting each person five minutes and declared, "The person using it, now and in the future, will have to sit at the learning table as the dictionary must not leave that table." Jane allowed each of her shining stars to use the dictionary during language class as she considered learning how to use a dictionary part of learning to read. As she taught the younger students in their reading lessons, she smiled as she watched Herman, Lech and Thomas pour over the dictionary in turn. It was an honour to have such students in her class. Tomorrow she would give them exercises in looking up specific words in the book.

On this very day during lunch hour the euphoria over her shining stars would fade rapidly over the issue of discipline. She was in the outhouse. Unbeknownst to them that Jane was nearby Herman, Thomas and Lech were walking by and Herman had to go to the outhouse as the boys' privy was only a few yards away. This triggered a string of foul language from the boys describing body waste and private parts of the male anatomy. They seemed to be having a contest on how many names could be applied to that area of the body. Jane was flushed with embarrassment and revulsion. These were her shining stars. *How could they stoop to this?* She waited inside the outhouse door until Herman came out of the other outhouse, before she stepped out wearing a deep frown. They froze in their tracks, mortified that Jane had overheard them. Their heads dropped in shame.

"Come with me to the schoolhouse at once," she said in a clipped voice. They meekly followed, terrified of the wrath that was about to descend upon them. Once inside she had them stand side-by-side beside her desk.

"I'm ashamed of the lot of you," she said in a choked voice. "I have never heard such filthy language in my entire life and coming from you, my shining stars."

There were tears in the corners of Thomas's eyes while the other two held a stoic calm, though with heads still bowed in shame.

"What am I going to do with you?" Jane continued relentlessly. "Should I tell your fathers?"

A look of abject terror swept over their faces. Each of them knew that if their father found out, his belt would be applied to their backside in such a way that they would have difficulty sitting for the next week.

"Or should I punish you?"

"*You* punish us," Herman trembled in a quavering voice. "Please don't tell." He in particular came from a home where discipline was rigidly enforced.

"All right, stick out your right hands with palms up." Jane said sharply. Each obeyed with trembling breath.

Jane took the yardstick and slapped them soundly three times on the hand, and then asked them to present the other hand for similar treatment. Herman and Lech cried out several times and Thomas started to cry.

"Now each of you will get some scrap paper and will write one hundred times, 'I will not use filthy language! You will start now and stop when class resumes, work on them during recess, and finish during general discussion time. If you finish before that time you will not be allowed to participate."

"Now, if I *ever* hear any of you use any sort of bad language again I will be sure to tell your fathers and will mention this incident as well," Jane said in a clipped tone. "That is a promise. Now get to work."

Not being able to participate in general discussion, especially for Herman and Thomas, would hurt almost as much as the physical punishment and the shame of getting caught. Herman and Thomas both finished their lines by the end of afternoon recess but Jane made them sit in silence at the back of the room. Part way through general discussion Lech finished his and was sent to join his cohorts.

The sheer terror of their parents getting wind of their misbehaviour and uncertainty about getting caught again made model students of her "shining stars" for the remainder of the year. Jane had the grim satisfaction that she again had the upper hand with these three, but wished it could have been accomplished through some venue other than punishment. When she told Ethan about the incident that night he shrugged and said, "Boys will be boys," then added, "but then, I'd probably give Robbie a hidin' if he was ever caught swearing."

(Footnotes)
[1] Newfoundland did not become part of Canada until 1949.

Chapter Six

It was early November when Jane finally got a chance to go to Grimstad. She hadn't been to town since mid-August as she was too busy setting up the school, taking off her garden, and other fall work around the farm. She would usually just make a list for Ethan to do the shopping. Now that the garden was in and the preserves put up, Ethan talked her into coming to Grimstad with him one Saturday. The trip usually took less than two hours with the buggy. As they headed out, Ethan insisted that Jane take the reins from time to time. When she was hesitant, he insisted.

"You gotta learn to drive sometime," Ethan said. "One-a these times, when I get that other team of horses I'm dealin' on you'll be taken yerself to school."

"Taking myself? Why, what are you going to do?"

"I won't have ta have my farm work interrupted all the time if you can drive yerself."

"Yes, but..." Jane faltered.

"It's okay, once yuh get the hang of it it'll be safe to take the buggy with Robbie," Ethan assured her.

"Where will I put the horses during the day?" Jane worried.

"There's a work bee goin' on at the school today and they're buildin' a barn so kids that are far away can bring horses when they are older. In good weather you can tie them by the trees and they can nibble all day."

"Do I have to unharness them?" Jane felt she could probably learn to drive a team without difficulty, but to hitch and harness them might be a problem.

"You could probably get away with leaving them harnessed all day though it would be better if you could take it off. I'll make sure you know how to hitch them to the buggy though."

"Thanks," Jane said without enthusiasm.

They came to the school where a work bee was in progress both in building a barn out of slabs and lumber tailings from the mill, and chinking the logs of the schoolhouse to shut out winter drafts. The squared logs fit together much more tightly than the round ones, but they still needed mortar. Jane noticed that the school door was open.

"Whoa," Jane cried, pulling on the reins as they came abreast to the entrance of the school yard.

"What are you stoppin' for?" Ethan said.

"Somebody's inside the schoolhouse, my schoolhouse," Jane said as she turned the buggy to go into the school yard.

"Well, yeah. There is a work bee goin' on," Ethan replied.

"I just want to see whose inside and what they're up to," Jane replied as she pulled up to the schoolhouse.

She stepped off the buggy leaving Ethan to manage the horses and Robbie. Inside, she found Audi, with Herman helping, calking the log joints from the inside. Curiously, she considered Audi to be trespassing and almost said something before she caught herself.

"Hello, Mrs. Phillips," Herman smiled.

Audi turned and grinned. "Good morning, Mrs. Phillips. We are going to make your school warmer for the winter time."

"Well, uh... I wish they would tell me when they're having a work bee."

"We didn't want to interrupt classes, so we decided to do this on a Saturday," Audi replied. "Don't worry, we won't disturb anything. Herman tells me how important everything is." He noticed that Jane frowned when she saw the map of Europe laying on one of the desk tables and added, "I had to take the map down to calk the logs behind it. If I have time after I'll make a frame for the map so it will stay up better."

"Thank you, Mr. Dykstra, that is very considerate of you," Jane said in a flat tone.

"Herman told me what a great teacher you are," Audi continued. "He was just showing me, on the blackboard, that he can already perform long division. I'm impressed."

Jane noticed that a long division calculation had been performed on the blackboard and replied, "Well, Herman is a very bright young man. I hope I can do him justice," Jane flushed.

"I'm sure you will," Audi replied. "Keep up the good work. We'll make sure we clean up when we're finished."

"Thank you. Well, we're heading to Grimstad," Jane said as she turned to leave. She felt strangely foolish for being so protective of her schoolhouse.

"Well, did they wreck anything?" Ethan chuckled as she climbed aboard the buggy. Jane glanced at him with a crooked grin and he added, "You'd think you owned this school."

"I do," Jane replied resolutely. "At least we do as it is on our land."

"Yes dear," Ethan chortled as he took the reins and headed his rig back down the road.

When they arrived at the Grimstad General Store, the proprietor Kari Grimstad and Jane exchanged warm greetings and hugs having not seen each other for several months. They had become good friends during the summer that Jane stayed in one of the rented rooms above the store. "It is about time you brought her out a da bush," Kari said to Ethan with her Norwegian accent.

"She wouldn't come," he grunted. "All she can think about is her school."

"I've been hearing some very good tings about Yane's school by yimminy. It's da talk of da town." Jane blushed and Kari continued, looking down at Robbie who was clinging to his mother's hand. "So dis is little Robbie, he is growing up fast. He vill be in school before you know it."

"Hello Jane," said a cheery voice. Jane turned and saw Mary coming out of the back of the store. "It's been a while."

"Mary!" Jane beamed as she hugged her friend. "You're just the person I'm looking for."

"What's on your mind?" Mary smiled.

"If you have time I'd like to discuss how to judge a student's knowledge level. I have two very bright pupils in my class and the others are catching on fast, but I don't know how to rate them. They may be at grade four or five, or maybe six. I just don't know."

"You have students advancing that fast, so soon?" Mary said incredulously.

"You don't know Herman Kepler or Thomas Higgins," Jane said breathlessly. "Once I taught them how to read and do numbers it was like opening a floodgate. Of course they are nearly ten years old, but still it is incredible and now I have another one, Lech Gogowicz trying his best to catch up. Some of the seven and eight year olds are also gaining ground."

"Sounds like you have a class full of gifted children," Mary laughed, "every teachers dream."

Jane's eyes rolled upward.

"She has to run to keep ahead of them," Ethan interjected. "She's afraid they'll catch up and pass her."

"Exactly," Jane added.

"Is that why they're taking up a collection for the encyclopaedia?" Mary said nodding toward the counter. For the first time, Jane noticed a large square box with a slot on top. A sign printed on the side of the box said, "Donations for Opportunity School Encyclopaedia."

"Who did this?" She said in disbelief, astonished that word about her request had gotten all the way to Grimstad.

"I tink it vas Wolf Kepler dat set it up," Kari said. "He vas saying dat Herman had told him dat you need von for da school."

"I hope that they get enough soon as Herman has an

insatiable appetite for knowledge. He's even taken to reading the dictionary that *someone* has given the school probably that same *someone* who has given us the books, the globe and the soccer ball."

"I guess this *someone* didn't have enough money to get the encyclopaedia," Ethan laughed.

"Anyway Jane, it looks like you need some assistance," Mary smiled. "If you've got time, come up to my room and we'll talk about how to assess the student's comprehension level."

Jane handed her grocery list to Ethan and said, "Do you mind, dear?"

"Oh, I guess," Ethan grumbled. "I bin doin' it all summer anyway."

"Oh, come on Etan," Kari scoffed. "You know dat Yane is doing a good ting vit da kids." To Jane she said, "Ve vill vatch Robbie too. So you yust go ahead Yane and don't vorry about us."

Ethan muttered indistinctly in apparent agreement as Jane and Mary left for Mary's room above the store.

Shortly thereafter, young Gary Topping came into the store, with wide-eyes and in an agitated state. "Mr. Phillips, am I glad to see you."

Ethan gave him a perplexed look and Gary continued breathlessly, "Have you seen Mr. O'Malley today?"

"No I haven't, what's goin' on?"

"The Goon Squad is here."

"The what?"

"The Goon Squad, they're here looking for moonshine," Gary continued breathlessly. "Dad barely had time to dump his out before they got to the stable."

"Is that so?" Ethan said calmly. Although he maintained a calm exterior he knew that if they caught Sean, or found his still, he would go to jail. "Thanks for tellin' me boy," he replied. "I'll pass it on to Sean." He had heard rumours of the Liquor Control Commission whose members were busy poking around looking for moonshine and being a general nuisance, often overstepping the law in their efforts to search private property. For their abrupt and callous methods they were often called the goon squads.

When Gary left Ethan said, "I better get out there and warn Sean to take down his still and get rid of any stash he brewed up."

"Ya, ve don't vant to see Sean go to yail," Kari replied. "You go now and varn him, I vill explain to Yane."

"Thanks," Ethan said hurriedly. He momentarily spoke to his young son, then turned and walked out the door.

The members of the special commission in collaboration with the Mounties – who were spread to thinly to mount an effective search were set up to stop illegal alcohol production and had the powers to search and seize homemade spirits and distilling equipment. Their efforts however, were mainly directed at those who produced and distributed moonshine. Word had got to them that a certain Sean O'Malley was operating a still in the area and they were seeking him out, as well as anyone who might be assisting him. As they checked around town, they were stonewalled everywhere as no one wanted to see Sean sent to prison. Ethan was about to head out of town when he was accosted by two members of the goon squad. One of them identified himself as Commissioner Alan Bates, head of the investigation team. Ethan noticed that his eyes scanned inside the buggy box as he spoke. This in itself put Ethan in a grumpy frame of mind.

"Do you know where Sean O'Malley lives?" Alan Bates demanded.

"Who wants to know?" Ethan replied with contempt.

"We do," Alan replied in a clipped tone. "He is suspected of making and selling illegal spirits."

"Is that so?" Ethan replied glibly with a mocking tone. "I wouldn't know because I don't touch the stuff. My wife is a temperance person."

"Why are all you people hiding this person? He is

breaking the law." Alan was now visibly annoyed at Ethan's contemptuous tone.

"Is that a fact?" Ethan sneered. "Maybe if they didn't have this stupid prohibition there wouldn't be moonshiners."

"Did you know that moonshine can be poisonous, or can make people blind?" Alan said trying a different tack.

"Wouldn't know," Ethan continued with his stone face. "Like I said, I don't drink it and I don't make it. Now, if you'll excuse me I gotta git home."

"Look, give us a clue and we'll leave you alone," Alan plead.

Realizing they were still going to badger him, or worse follow him, he sighed feigning great reluctance and said, "Did yuh go look along the river south a town, seems to me if a fellah wanted make shine, he'd wanna be near water."

"Good point," one of them said.

"If I was you, I'd check out some of them trails that head off down to the river." Ethan knew most of those trails and knew they lead either to river flat fields, or locally designated picnic areas and fishing holes. He slowly nudged his horses forward and they watched him pull away, discussing taking up Ethan's suggestion.

Ethan drove his rig slowly out of town and across the bridge so to not attract suspicion, and once he was sure he was out of sight, he drove the horses at full gallop as much as he dared all the way to Sean's place. Sean was just leaving his building site with his car and a few jugs of homebrew for customers when Ethan stopped him. His face betrayed great anxiety.

"What's happening me friend?" Sean grinned. "Ye look as if ye had a fright."

"Ye gotta get rid of the stuff and the still. The Goon Squad is here."

"The Goon Squad?"

"Yeah, the busy-bodies that are after the moonshiners. They're in town askin' questions," Ethan said. "They were askin' me how to find you. I put 'em off by tellin' 'em ta look by the river, but sooner or later they'll find out where yuh live."

"Thanks for helpin' me." Sean smiled, "Best get rid of the evidence."

Sean got out of his car and reluctantly poured the contents of his jugs on the ground complaining, "A waste a good whiskey."

"Now what are yuh gonna do about yer still. They'll put yuh in the slammer for sure if they find it."

"Hmmm…," Sean thought for a moment. "I'll take it down and hide it along with the other jugs I have." He thought again and added, "I'll hide it in Dead Man's Muskeg."

"I'll help yuh," Ethan said. "Oh, and get rid of any yuh have in the house for personal use."

"I'll meet ye at the still then," Sean said.

Fortunately, Sean had not used the still for several hours so his distilling equipment consisting of a pressure pot and a length of coiled copper tubing could be quickly dismantled. The components were put in the back of Ethan's buggy along with a tub of fermenting mash of chopped potatoes. They covered it with a tarp that Sean had, while Sean put the bottles of hooch in the trunk of his car. They were about to head out when Ethan suggested, "Let's go up the road to my place and go into Dead Man's Muskeg from there."

"Why would you be wantin' to do that?"

"It'll throw them off the trail. Sooner or later they'll come to your place and will be snoopin' around with a fine toothed comb. If they see tracks leadin' off into the bush, they'll follow 'em."

"Now what would yer temperance missus be sayin' about you helpin' out a moonshiner," Sean chuckled.

"I left her in Grimstad at the store, but even if she don't like drinkin' I'm sure she don't want yuh goin' to jail. Best we get movin' though."

Ethan and Sean quickly headed up the road with Sean in the lead, but frequently looking over their shoulders for anyone following. As they passed the school, Ethan stopped and hastily drew Wolf aside to explain the situation involving the Goon Squad, and if any of them came by not to breathe a word about their passing. Once out of sight of the school Ethan stopped and dumped the tub of mash by the side of the road. When Sean came out of the car to see what Ethan was doing, Ethan merely commented, "Destroyin' the evidence."

"Well at least all the mice and squirrels will get drunk at me expense," Sean laughed.

Upon arriving at Ethan's place, they went directly to the garden area along the fence near the trail that led to Sean's place. They carried the still components the quarter mile to the muskeg then struggled their way through the willow tangles, and placed the equipment deep within the muskeg. The full jugs were also taken to the muskeg and everything was buried in the moss save one jug. As they hid the jugs, they noticed a crude wooden cross nearby standing in the moss.

"Heaven forbid, its Black Pete's grave," Sean said crossing himself.

"So it must be," Ethan replied. "Well, I hope his ghost doesn't get too drunk on your 'shine," he added with laugh.

"A drunken ghost, now that would be a sight for a meddlin' Goon Squad to see." Sean laughed in turn. They each took a swallow from the jug that Sean had kept and then turned to head back.

Once back at his car, they each had another swallow and Sean said, "I'll stop and give the men workin' at the school a wee nip. It might be the last for a wee while."

"Better not be passin' the stuff around till the Goon Squad is gone," Ethan rumbled.

"The Goon Squad, ye say," Sean said in a low voice. "I've seen them before." He had a flashback to a bad memory of the Black and Tans, a brutal auxiliary police force used by the British to try to crush the Irish rebellion, searching houses back in Ireland without warrants or respect for the dignity of the occupants.

"Best I be gettin' back to me home then," Sean said as he started his car. "Thanks for bein' a friend."

"That's what bein' a neighbour is all about," Ethan replied. He then drove his own team down the hill to the well to give them a drink of water before heading back for Jane.

Chapter Seven

When Jane came back downstairs, armed with the information on how to judge the competence level of her students, she was surprised to find that Ethan was no longer there. Robbie was behind the counter where Kari was allowing him to use tinned goods for building blocks. Her grocery order was on the counter, placed in a cardboard box, save for the sacks of flour and sugar leaning against the front of the counter.

"Where is Ethan?" Jane asked, surprised but not concerned.

"He had to run a very important errand," Kari said mysteriously, and then looking around to make sure no one else was in the store she added, "he vent to help Sean."

"Help Sean? With what?" Jane was perplexed.

Just then Alan Bates and two members of the liquor commission came into the store. He hastily introduced himself and announced their intention to search the store for moonshine. Their brusque manner terrified Robbie, and he fled to his mother crying.

"What's going on?" Jane scowled at the intruders who were now busy poking through various areas of the store where it might be possible to hide a jug or two of moonshine.

"Vhat gives you da right to search my store," Kari protested. "Coming in here and scaring a child oy, yoy, yoy, you should be a shamed of yourself."

"What's down there," Alan demanded as he pointed to a trapdoor in front of the counter.

"Vhy don't you open it and see, maybe dere is a still down dere," Kari said with scorn.

Alan scowled at her and opened the trapdoor and his

62

men went down to investigate. He turned to the women and said with a sneer, "Why is everyone in this town so uncooperative. We are officers searching for illegal spirits, surely you ladies would appreciate that."

"Well, I am a temperance person," Jane retorted as she tried to calm the howling Robbie. "I don't approve of drinking and never have. But I also believe here in Canada we have due process. A real policeman would not simply barge in. No wonder they call you the Goon Squad."

"Sometimes we have to use tough measures to catch these people that otherwise law abiding citizens seem to want to hide," he shot back. "What's in here?" He added as he was about to look in Jane's grocery box.

"What do you think you're doing?" Jane demanded. "That's my groceries and none of your business!" She grabbed a top flap on the box and pulled it away from him as she wore an indignant scowl.

"Searching for illegal liquor is our business," Alan said harshly, "and non co-operation is a punishable offense by law."

"What law?" Jane's eyes glowered with contempt. "I always thought that you had to have a search warrant to search private property."

"Vhen I came to dis country I vas told dat you have laws and courts," Kari added in a scolding tone. "Dis is trespassing."

"We have special powers to search for illegal spirits," Alan insisted. However, he made no further attempt to paw through Jane's groceries in the face of her truculence. He turned instead to the donation box saying, "What is this?"

"Keep your hands of dat," Kari said as she snatched the box away from him.

"Unless you wish to make a donation," Jane sneered. "And by the way you've been acting it should be a rather large one."

Alan scowled at her in turn but offered no comment.

Just then, Kari's husband Hal entered the store with his

daughter Linda. "Vhat is going on?" he demanded.

"Dey are searching da store for moonshine," Kari said. "Dey have no warrant."

"Den get out of my store," Hal demanded.

"Here, take Robbie," Jane said to Linda. Handing her child to Linda, she said in a calm voice trying her best to smile. "You go with Linda now, and she will play with you."

Swallowing her fright, Linda took the howling Robbie to the living quarters.

"What's back there?" Alan demanded.

"My living quarters and if you go back dere I'll break your skull," Hal said belligerently. He picked up an axe handle that was in the bin beside him and stood in the doorway leading to the living quarters.

"You can't stop us," the commissioner challenged.

"You don't go into da house vhere I live vitout a real policeman and a varrent."

Jane could not believe this was happening; here, in Canada, where everything was peaceful and according to law.

The two men emerged from the cellar saying there was nothing of interest down there. The three of them were about to advance on the ever defiant Halvar when Jane grabbed a broom from behind the counter and moved to Halvar's side. Kari took the wet mop from the bucket used for washing the floor and stood on Halvar's other side. Both women bore determined scowls.

"You ladies should stay out of dis," Halvar said gravely.

"Ve vill see if dese men are *shicken* enough to hurt a lady," Kari's eyes blazed with defiance. Jane likewise bore an unwavering glare holding the broom up, ready to attack.

Mary came up behind them, asking what was happening. Jane replied out of the corner of her mouth, "Get yourself a club. No way are these goons going to invade Hal and Kari's living quarters."

"I'll have you all arrested for obstructing justice," Alan shouted in a desperate tone.

"This isn't justice," Jane said harshly. "You are a Goon Squad intimidating innocent people. Everyone knows I am opposed to drinking and especially moonshine. You people are exceeding the law."

"It vould be something if Etan walked into da store now," Kari said feeling more confident as Alan was reconsidering his ploy.

"He'd shoot the lot of you down like a pack of wild dogs," Jane spat. "Because that's what you are."

"Etan should be back soon anyvay," Kari added sardonically. She was now convinced that they had the upper hand since the Goon Squad was unarmed.

There was indistinct mumbling among the Goon Squad members, perhaps realizing that they had overstepped their authority. Then Alan finally said, "We will go now, but we'll be back with a constable if we even suspect there is one drop of moonshine anywhere in this building."

The commission members turned and retreated out the door. Once they were outside, Alan declared to the others, "I guess we overdone it a little. Boy, are these people hostile."

"You never want to rile up a Norwegian," one of the others said. "But that other woman, the one with the nose," he said in snide reference to Jane. "I don't think I want to tangle with her again either."

"They're hiding this moonshiner, this Sean character," Alan retorted. "Let's do some more snooping. Sooner or later someone will spill the beans on how we can find him."

As Bessie was taking a long drink of cold water she began to tremble and falter. Ethan tried to soothe her but the horse began to buckle and breathe very coarsely, then she collapsed.

"Oh no, don't die on me Bessie. I promise I won't make you run so much again," Ethan said desperately as he tried to massage the old horse. "I'll let you rest a while, Jane will understand." Bessie stirred and tried to get up looking at her master with doleful eyes.

Ethan began to undo Bessie's harness and managed to move her around enough to get it undone and half off before Bessie collapsed again. This time she did not move.

"Rest in peace Bessie," Ethan said sadly as he looked at his fallen horse. She was an old horse when he bought her seven years ago, and a very gentle, faithful one since. Clyde also looked morosely at his fallen companion. Ethan wrestled to get the remaining harness out from under Bessie, and then found a rope and tied Bessie's hind legs together. Hitching the rope to Clyde, he dragged Bessie's body over the hill past the garden, opening the fence so he could drag her all the way to Dead Man's Muskeg over top of the path that he and Sean made in stashing his contraband. Bessie's body was left by the willow tangles. "You did one last service old girl," he said sadly. "If them snoopy Goon Squads come around here they'll find the trails go to yer corpse and will be satisfied." He chuckled to himself with the thought, *I hope, if they come, it is in a couple a days time when your carcass starts to stink to high heaven.*

Once he got back to the barnyard to where his buggy was, a sobering thought came to him. *How am I gonna get Jane? My buggy doesn't have a hitch for only one horse.* Looking at the position of the sun, he reckoned that the work bee would be winding down and the people working would likely have gone home for chores by the time he could ride Clyde out to the school. Ethan decided instead to go over to Sean's place. While it might not be wise for Sean to go into town, Sean still had his horse and trap and Ethan could take that into town to retrieve his family.

Jane was in a stew after an hour had passed and the sun was getting low in the early November afternoon. Ethan had failed to show up. "What if they caught him and Sean in the act of trying to hide his moonshine operation?" She fretted,

"They'd both get put in jail."

"I don't tink dat happened," Kari assured her. "Dey are too busy boddering everybody in town to go to Sean's place. If dey can even find somevon to tell dem where it is at."

"I don't even know vhere his place is and I have known Sean for years," Hal added.

"Besides, Etan asked me to ask you if you could bring Yane and Robbie home if he didn't come back soon."

"I'll wait for a while yet," Jane sighed. "If I go home and he's not there we may miss each other on the road."

"I vill make supper for everybody," Kari said.

They had just sat down to supper when Ethan arrived, harried and somewhat dishevelled.

"Daddy, Daddy!" Robbie cried as he ran to his father. Even though the tumultuous events of the afternoon were beyond his immediate comprehension, he seemed relieved to see his father.

"Come in and yoin us," Kari smiled. "Ve are yust sitting down to supper."

"You look like da Goon Squad has been *shasing* you," Hal added.

"It was one hell of an afternoon. I helped Sean hide his operation and old Bessie died on me."

"Bessie, oh no," Jane gasped. She was quite fond of the gentle old mare.

"I guess I just ran her too much and her old heart couldn't take it anymore so she laid down in the barnyard and dropped dead, poor old girl. So I rode Clyde over to Sean's place and borrow his trap to fetch you and Robbie home," Ethan said as he sat down to the table.

"You should have seen what happened here," Jane said. "The goons, as you call them, came to the store and started searching. I gave them a piece of my mind, but they were still going to search the living quarters."

"I can just hear you tear into them," Ethan chuckled.

"Then Hal came along and stood in the doorway with an

axe handle ready to brain them," Jane continued.

"Den da two vomans yoined me," Hal laughed. "Vit Yane on one side holding a broom and Kari on da udder vit a mop, no vay dey vhere going to get into da house by yimminy."

"I told them that if you came along you'd shoot them down like a pack of mad dogs," Jane added. "After that, they backed down and left."

"I can just see you women standing in the doorway, ready to club them down." Ethan laughed and then more ominously added, "If they'd a hurt you or Robbie, I'd a made good on your threat."

That night, when they left the store driving the horse and trap, they were watched. Alan saw Ethan return with another rig, and later noticed that the formidable woman *the one with the nose*, they had encountered in the store got into the trap with him when they headed north out of town. Now more than ever, Alan was convinced that Ethan either knew the whereabouts of Sean, or might even be in cahoots with him.

Their investigative prowess did not stop there; Alan found out through stealth that Mary, a teacher at Grimstad School, was being courted by Sean. Mary was accosted by Alan on her way home from church the following day.

"Don't you people believe in the Lord's Day," she protested.

"Not when it comes to stamping out the works of the devil," Alan replied. "And you, being a Christian woman, has to admit that moon shining *is* the devil's work."

"So why are you bothering me? I'm a teacher not a whiskey trader." She snapped.

"We understand that a certain Sean O'Malley has been courting you these past two years," Alan continued relentlessly.

"He's a friend, yes," Mary said tersely. "What business is that of yours?"

"What do you think the school board would say if they heard your boyfriend was a moonshiner?" He sneered. "If you tell us where he lives your part in this will never be mentioned."

"Go to hell," she said vehemently. "You can't connect me to this...this ugly rumour about Sean."

"We can do a lot more than that," he said smugly. "How much do you enjoy teaching?"

"I will tell you this once, everybody in town is ready to charge you with harassment. If I am reprimanded or fired for something you can't prove, I am sure there is a way to contact your superior or the real law enforcement and have you charged with harassment and overstepping your bounds. If you think you can blackmail me you can...go to hell again." Mary walked away with her face frozen in a frown but inside she was very disturbed at the possibility of losing the job she loved so much.

The following day the Goon Squad found their way to Sean's place. He smiled and invited them to search his place then sat smugly in his cabin and smoked his pipe while they scoured his buildings and surrounding forest. They even followed the trail part way to Ethan's place for any evidence; however, coming up completely empty handed. They gave up when they found that the trail crossed a stream and the edge of a slough that showed no signs that it had been recently used. Sean stood by his cabin door watching their return with an impish grin on his face. They stopped to speak to him and when they tried to grill Sean about the nearly hidden little cabin that was set apart from the other buildings he shrugged and said, "It is me guest house."

"Guest house indeed," Alan snorted. "Why would you need a guest house?"

"For guests," Sean stated. "Why else would I be needin' a guest house? I have people come to help me with me the praties."

"Look you Irish rabble," Alan threatened, "we can use

other means to get to the bottom of this."

"Irish rabble is it," Sean said sharply. As he was standing by the doorway to his cabin when they began to question him, he reached in and grabbed his shotgun. Pointing it at them he said, "I'll be thankin' you to be leaven' me property now. I've seen the likes of you over in the Old Country bullying innocent folk. I swear by me mother's grave that it won't be happenin' to me again. Now be off with ye."

"We can have you arrested for threatening us," Alan stated.

"That you could, but the way you've been treatin' folk around here I think that I would have the upper hand in court. I'm tellin' ye again, get off me land yer Tresspassin'."

The Goon Squad turned and left. Any thought Alan had of using strong arm tactics evaporated in the face of a loaded shotgun.

Yet Alan and his boys seemed to need one more act of humiliation to finish their day, which occurred when they visited Audi Dykstra.

"Good day gentlemen," Audi said pleasantly as he stood in the doorway of his house watching them approach. "What brings you to my humble abode?"

"I am Alan Bates of the Liquor Commission," Alan said evenly. "We are searching for illegal spirits, especially the production of them."

"Do you think I am a moonshiner?" Audi replied indignantly.

"Not necessarily, but we would like to look around," Alan replied. "It is our job."

"Do you have a search warrant?"

"We have wide powers of search and seizure when it comes to moonshine," Alan said smugly.

"Indeed, I always thought we had due process in Canada," Audi replied. "No, you may not search my property. I don't want you going through everything and messing things up especially when I am innocent."

"We could just search without your cooperation," Alan said defiantly.

"You could, just as I could and would consult my lawyer if you tried," Audi retorted.

"What is it with you people?" Alan said with a sigh. "You refuse to cooperate with the law, and I don't suppose you'll tell me anything about Sean O'Malley either."

"What is there to tell?" Audi shrugged. Then after a moment of thought he added with a heavy sigh, "You know I was just reading a newspaper I get from back home and it was talking about the situation in Italy since the country was taken over by Mussolini, and the strong arm tactics used by his goons. Fascism is the word used to describe his society. And gentlemen, that is what you remind me of, fascists. They wear black shirts. What colour is your shirt?" Audi mocked as he attempted to open Alan's coat. Alan stepped back with an indignant frown. "Now gentlemen, if you come back with a peace officer and a proper search warrant you'll have my every cooperation, but until then I will ask you to get off my property."

Alan Bates' mouth quivered for an answer and he finally replied, "We will leave now, but we may very well be back."

"Just remember what I said," Audi called after him.

Finally, the next time Sean came to Grimstad, Mary refused to see him and when he finally cornered her a few days later Mary informed him.

"Don't talk to me Sean O'Malley. Don't touch me and don't even be on the same side of the street with me. Until you can promise me that you are through with making moonshine for all time, I don't know you."

Mary turned and walked away, leaving the hapless Sean stuttering and trying to find words to counter. Even though they could find no evidence to charge Sean with illegal liquor production and distribution, she lived in fear of being dismissed from her job by association.

Chapter Eight

The first snow came in mid-November. The Goon Squad had left after being stonewalled and outright threatened by the community and without a shred of evidence to arrest Sean. Sean nonetheless kept a low profile. Over time he carefully sold off the remaining stock of moonshine he had stashed in the muskeg and took a winter job at Axel Rutland's sawmill that was now operating on the school quarter.

The sawmill was far enough away from the school without being a noise hazard, but when outside on the grounds the students could clearly hear the whine of the saw, the falling of trees, or the puffing of the steam engine driving the mill. Finally, the older boys in their ongoing thirst for knowledge badgered Jane into taking them over to the mill as a field trip. She agreed and took her class to the mill one afternoon in lieu of their regular science class. They carefully approached the mill and stopped at what Jane considered a safe distance. She held onto the three younger children while the others clustered around her. They were fascinated with the machinery from the great puffing steam tractor with its visibly moving pistons and big rotating pulley that connected it to the actual mill via a long belt. They could see the great circular saw ripping along a log while two men manned the levers that controlled the thickness of the boards being cut. Further back, men were cutting long logs into manageable lengths with hand-operated cross-cut saws.

"There's Mr. O'Malley," Herman cried as he saw Sean working the winch that drew logs up on the deck for sawing. Sean noticed the class and waved.

"There's Mr. Phillips," Helen cried. In the distance they

could see Ethan skidding a log from the cutting area with Clyde. Now that the snow had fallen, Ethan hired out Clyde to skid logs for the mill. He hoped to earn enough to buy a companion horse to replace Bessie. Her loss had set back his plans to buy a second team.

Presently, Axel came over to greet them, wearing a smile at the sight of the children.

"I hope you don't mind us watching the sawing, Mr. Rutland." Jane said. "But the kids wanted to see the mill up close."

"Not at all," Axel replied. "It is good for da kids to see tings like dis. I vill bring you in a little closer vhere it vill still be safe."

Axel took them up beside the mill but still kept them back several yards and invited them to ask questions. The boys wanted to know about the workings of the machinery while Jane asked what kinds of trees they were sawing. Axel explained that the spruce trees were cut into planks and wall studding, while the poplar was cut into boards for sheeting. Jane told her students to pay attention, as they would be tested on their field trip when they got back to school.

After an hour, the class returned to the school feeling chilled from their outing. They huddled around the heater and Jane put a kettle on to make them cocoa. While they waited and warmed up, Jane asked the students questions about their outing.

They remembered the two kinds of trees spruce and poplar, that were being sawed and that the saw blade was called a ripsaw. Later that afternoon they had a special art class where each student was asked to draw the sawmill. She got a wide variety of interesting results and the artwork was hung along the bottom of the side blackboard.

When Jane did her mid-November assessment of her pupils, she decided to do one better than merely send her makeshift report cards home; she invited the parents to come to the school for an afternoon where she would have the students demonstrate their learning prowess. All parents eagerly participated, bringing with them lunch and snacks of sandwiches, cakes and cookies that were set on a back table. A kettle was put on for tea and hot cocoa along with the coffee pot. The parents all sat on benches along the back. When Hella brought Robbie with her, the tot raced to be with his mother.

"Hi sweetheart," Jane smiled as she picked Robbie up. She held him in her arms as she walked around trying to organise things. Then Robbie cried, "Daddy, Daddy."

Jane looked up surprised to see that Ethan had just walked in the door. She set Robbie down and he raced to his father.

"What are you doing here?" Jane smiled radiantly.

"I took the afternoon off so I could see for myself if you're doing any good here," he replied with a twisted grin and his usual gravelly voice.

"Good, you can watch Robbie then," Jane replied.

Just then Audi walked in.

"Did you come for ze free lunch," Wolf said making light of his arrival.

"Well, as a member of the Opportunity school board I wanted to see first hand the fine job that our teacher is doing with your children."

The students were squirming anxiously in their seats, nervous about having to demonstrate their knowledge to their parents.

Jane rang her cow bell to get everyone's attention and then thanked all the parents for coming out. "It means so much to me to see how much you care for your children's education and they are doing very well. It means so much to the students to show you what they have learned. We will begin with their reading skills."

The younger students each read a simple passage out of their readers, and the reading demonstration grew more complex with the middle students. Finally, Thomas Higgins recited a short poem of deep philosophical significance called *Abou Ben Adhem,* found in one of the donated books. While he offered to recite, Jane was surprised that he had picked that particular poem. After the applause, she asked him to explain the meaning of the poem.

"It tells us we will be rewarded for loving our fellow man," Thomas said directly.

"Bravo!" Audi exclaimed and started to slowly clap. Jane smiled in astonishment and Thomas wondered why everyone was so in awe. Finally, she said, "It is a pleasure, or should I say an honour, to teach a student like Thomas."

More clapping erupted.

Next came the arithmetic with the younger students shouting out answers to simple addition and subtraction equations Jane called out, then she had them add columns of three and four single digit numbers on the blackboard. The older ones did multiplication and long division. It was Herman's turn to shine when he solved a long division equation involving decimals. In the science demonstration, Herman again took command by drawing the sun and the planets on the blackboard, calling out their names in proper sequence.

"Now you know why I say I have to run to keep up to some of my pupils." Jane beamed, "We weren't going to start talking about the stars until next month." A ripple of laughter went through the crowd at the back.

For a history demonstration, Lech stood up and pulled down the world map and taking the yardstick, he said, "The first two explorers that came to Canada were John Cabot," he used the yardstick to trace the path from England to Newfoundland, "and Jacques Cartier" pronouncing Jacques as Jack. He traced his journey from France to the St. Lawrence River. "Some say the Vikings came before them," he added as he traced a line from Norway to Newfoundland skimming past Iceland and Greenland, "but the Vikings didn't know how to write so nobody knows for sure." This brought on a few chuckles from that audience.

Jane asked him, "How did Newfoundland get its

name?"

Lech shrugged and replied, "Because it was a new found land and nobody could think of a better name." Again there were chuckles.

"Out of the mouths of children," Jane laughed, "straight simple answers."

"Very good Lech, you may sit down."

Everyone clapped as Lech took his seat.

Next came geography, Jane asked Sonya which country has tigers. She replied in a faltering voice, "India."

"Can you point to it?" Jane asked. Sonya used the yardstick to point to India. Helen was asked to show and tell where elephants lived and she identified Africa. Thomas interjected saying, "And India."

"Thank you Thomas, since you are so good at geography, which country is shaped like a carrot?" Jane asked.

Thomas belted out, "Czechoslovakia," without difficulty. There were murmurs among the parents' as some had never heard of this awkward to pronounce country that had been created since the Great War. Jane closed the demonstration by saying, "Now you know why I want a set of encyclopaedias for the school." Everyone laughed.

After the geography demonstration, the students were dismissed and lunch was served. "Well, am I doing any good dear?" Jane said to Ethan with fluttering eyes.

"Them kids know a lot of stuff, a hell of a lot more than I do." Ethan replied in his usual rasping voice.

"Your wife is an exceptional teacher," Audi said as he came over to speak to Jane.

"You're tellin' me," Ethan said.

"Don't blame me," Jane replied. "I have some very bright students here. All I did was open the door to the secret of letters and numbers and they ran through it with open arms."

"How is it possible for that Kepler boy and Higgins boy to know so much so quickly, and even the Gogowicz boy, when you've only been teaching them since September?" Audi asked.

"Well, I had been tutoring Thomas and Herman in my home for over a year, so they already had a good grasp of reading and arithmetic and Lech learned some reading from his parents, and ever since school started he has been trying to catch up to them."

"Yes, of course. Poland was one of the first countries in Europe to adopt universal education," Audi stated.

"Once those three got their hands on all those donated books," she raised her eyebrows, "there was no stopping them. They're forever in that dictionary looking for things," Jane said with great enthusiasm. "Since I am not up on grade structure or standard curriculums, I allow the students to learn at their own speed and those three seem to have a very fast speed. Also, they're older and can grasp ideas more quickly."

"In view of the situation," Audi continued, "perhaps your system is better. Too much structure can hold a child back."

"For a bachelor, you seem awfully interested in this school," Jane queried.

"Well, I'll let you in on a little secret," Audi smiled. "I have been corresponding with a woman from back home and have her nearly convinced to come over here in the spring to be my bride."

"Another mail-order bride," Jane replied with a crooked grin.

"If all goes well and if in a few years we have children of our own, I will want you to teach them."

"Thank you," Jane blushed.

Presently, Ivan, followed by a very shy looking Raisa, whose hair was covered with a babushka, came over to speak to Jane. Audi said, "Keep up the good work," and moved away.

"Tank you Messis Phillips," Ivan said with his broken

English. "My cheeldren don't speak Roshyn hardly at all anymore."

"Dey even teachink me," Raisa faltered.

"They are both very bright, well-behaved students. It was no trouble at all to teach them to speak English. Actually, the Gogowicz children helped as Lech told me that Polish people can understand Russian."

"Da, language is at little bit seemilar," Ivan said. "But eet is you dat teach dem."

"Sonya and Tanya love teacher," Raisa smiled.

"This may be a foolish question, but can you write in Russian?" Jane asked as an idea suddenly occurred to her.

"*Da*, I can write, but Raisa don't know how. Why you ask?"

"I know that you have a different alphabet than ours, and it might be interesting for you to print it on the backboard sometime with equivalent letters from our alphabet." Jane said eagerly, "Just a way of showing the children different types of writing."

"Eet would be pleasure," Ivan replied.

After socialising began to taper off and people were getting ready to go home, Jane thanked the parents and students alike. The Gogowicz children, whose turn it was to be monitors, quickly moved to do their chores.

"You don't have to do them today. Today is a special day." Jane smiled at them.

They were about to turn and get ready to go home when Stan spoke up, "Let them do their chores. Children must have responsibility." Then to his three children he said firmly, "Go do the chores that teacher wants. Be quick about it."

Mark took a brush and wiped the areas of the blackboard that Jane wanted wiped clean, and then stepped outside to bang the chalk dust out of the brush. Lydia grabbed a broom and began to sweep the floor, while Lech lugged in wood and coal for the morning.

Jane thanked them and praised Lech for his innovative presentation. Then to Stan and Ludy she said, "It was entirely his doing. Lech did not even tell me exactly what he had in mind for a history presentation."

"You are a great motivator Jane," Ludy said with her Polish inflected, but clear English. "I hope you are here for as long as my children go to school."

"I'll try," Jane smiled. Deep inside; however, she was worried that the school board would find out about her little school. "Whatever happens make sure your children, especially Lech, get as much education as they can."

"We praise education," Stan said, "even though I need the boys to help on the farm."

"Both of you speak English rather well," Jane said.

"I was born and raised in Silesia, the part of Poland that belonged to Germany before the war. Even though they tried to make Germans out of us we did get access to education. I came to Canada just before the war, so had a few years to learn English." Stan said.

"I was born in Galicia, the part of Poland that belonged to Austria," Ludy added, pronouncing the country as *Owstria*. "I was also in Canada before the war."

"We met in an internment camp," Stan said gravely.

"Internment camp?" Jane asked, puzzled at the term.

"Yes. We were considered enemy aliens because we both came from countries that Canada was fighting against," Stan replied. "I would have joined up if I would have been allowed."

"Crazy isn't it," Ludy added. "Now we have Germans, English and Russians for neighbours. Our children go to the same school."

"This is what Canada is all about," Jane said with pride. "People come here from other countries to forget about the past and build new lives."

"Yes, they're all good neighbours," Stan said. Then he noticed that his children had finished their school chores, "Well, we must go. Now that our children have done their chores, they have plenty more at home."

As they drove home that day, riding on a stone-boat pulled by Clyde and dodging snowballs kicked up by his hooves, Jane said, "You need to adapt the cutter for one horse," as a snowball whizzed by her.

Ethan laughed and slowed Clyde to a walk, "I thought of it, but plan to have a new mare in a week or so." Then he continued with a wry grin, "I see you were talking to the Dutchman."

"Yes, he is very interested in the school."

"Yeah, he seems to be." Then with a chuckle Ethan continued, "Ain't you afraid to be near him any more?"

"With you there?" Jane laughed. "He's probably worried that you had your rifle nearby. Actually, he seems quite sincere, though I still don't entirely trust him and would not want to be alone with him."

"Good precaution," Ethan replied. "Though he seems to be behavin' himself lately and like you say, is interested in the school."

"He said he is sending for his own mail-order bride all the way from Holland and hopes that I am still teaching should they have children."

"He scared all the Canadian women away," Ethan said with his usual rumbling voice. "Maybe one of his own kind knows how to handle him."

"Maybe being threatened with a gun changed him."

"Maybe."

"Like I said, I'm still wary of him and always will be," Jane replied and then with a grin added, "just like he'll always be wary of you."

As daylight was fading, Ethan nudged Clyde to a trot again saying with his grumbling voice, "Wanna get home before dark."

A clod of snow landed on Jane's coat. "You really need a front board on this thing," she complained, brushing the snow off.

Jane wrote in her diary that night:

I believe today went quite successfully. The students performed admirably, especially my three shining stars of Herman, Lech and Thomas. I pray that I can do their inquisitive minds justice. I am pleased that the parents also seem to have given me a passing grade.

Chapter Nine

The cold days of winter were upon them. For Jane it meant getting up in a cold house, riding for two miles in a cold sleigh, and arriving at a cold school. Often though, Axel or Sean, on their way to the mill, would stop and light a fire in the school heater, which at least made that end of the journey for Jane more bearable.

Jane insisted that the older pupils play outside as much as possible, particularly during the longer noon break though on the coldest days they got to stay indoors. She drew chalk squares on the floor at the back of the room so the girls could play hop scotch, other times the students played tick-tac-toe or hangman on the blackboard.

One morning in early December, Wolf appeared at the school just before lunch break. He carried a large, heavy box into the school and set it on one of the back tables.

"I haff a surprise for you und ze children," he grinned.

Eagerly Jane tore the box open, undeterred by the ice-cold cardboard. "The encyclopaedia!" she gasped. The students all turned and craned to see what was in the box. It was a twelve volume set of the Book of Knowledge. She lifted one out and thumbed through it noticing full-colour photographs on a few of the pages. "They finally got enough collected to buy the set," Jane breathed again.

"It looked like it might take a long time to get ze money, but somehow in zis last week zere vas lots of money in ze collection box," Wolf stated.

The mysterious benefactor, Jane thought and then she said, "Well, this is a godsend. It is perfect for the students. Who made the actual purchase?"

"It vas Audi, he vas at ze store vhen ze money vas counted yesterday und since he vas going to Edmonton on ze train, he offered to get ze encyclopaedia."

"It is perfect," Jane gasped as she continued to take the individual volumes out of the box and stack them on the table. At the bottom of the box was a large single book. Lifting it out, she exclaimed, "Oh my God an atlas." She opened it to the map of Europe and added, "And it's up-to-date as well!"

By now the class was quite noisy as all interest in studies had vanished. As it was near to lunch time, Jane dismissed the class. They all rushed over to see the encyclopaedia, but Jane stopped them from actually touching any of the books with a hand gesture.

"First, you must eat your lunch, and then you may help me put the books away. After that, we will establish rules about using it." She informed them, "These are very special books that cost a lot of money."

A moan of disappointment rippled through the class, and they retrieved their lunch pails and went to their desks to eat.

"Well, I vhill leave you to enchoy your treasure," Wolf grinned.

"Thank you very much," Jane smiled radiantly. "And thank Audi when you see him."

"I will," Wolf replied as he headed for the door.

Jane went to her own desk to eat her lunch, eying the bookshelves at the back while she ate, trying to decide exactly where to put the encyclopaedia. The students were all in a very excited mood about the books, especially her shining stars.

Thomas, who gulped down his lunch first asked, "Can I help you start putting them away, Mrs. Phillips?"

Before she could answer Herman swallowed his last morsel and asked, "When can we look at them?"

Jane smiled as she knew that her shining stars were desperate to start devouring this reservoir of knowledge. "First, you must wash your hands before you can even touch them, and you can't start reading them until they are put away and I have made the rules," Jane smiled.

"Can we at least wash our hands now?" Lech asked in an anxious tone.

"Yes, you may," Jane grinned.

The students all clamoured to the washstand at the back, while the older students ladled hot water from a large pot on the top of the heater and then diluted it with the cold water from the cream can at the back that held their drinking water. They all jostled for a spot at the wash basin creating shoving matches for both the wash water and the common towel until Jane threatened to put the books away herself if they didn't settle down. Her shining stars stood at the table and looked longingly at the books, but none touched them before Jane was ready.

Jane had each student carefully carry one volume at a time over to the bookshelves where she placed them in numerical order along the bottom shelf. The atlas was placed on the learning table beside the dictionary and the globe.

"Now class," Jane began as she addressed her students. "As with the dictionary, you must have clean hands when handling the encyclopaedia and atlas. You must sit here when using them unless I give special permission for you to take a volume to your desks and, like the dictionary, you must be extremely careful while handling the volumes as the pages will tear easily."

"Can we look at them now, Mrs. Phillips?" Lech asked anxiously. She noted the same anxious look on Thomas and Herman's faces.

"You, Thomas and Herman will be allowed to each take a volume to your desks, but only one at a time because you are older and more responsible. Younger students will have to sit here at the table to look at them."

The youngest pupils lost interest after a few moments as the information in the encyclopaedia was beyond their comprehension and attractive pictures were few and far between. As expected; however, her shining stars devoured the information offered as the Book of Knowledge encyclopaedia was geared for late elementary or junior high school level. In the days that followed her shining stars Herman, Lech and Thomas spent every spare moment pouring through the books. Jane had to practically chase them outside during mild weather. Now, when they stumped her with difficult questions, Jane could invite them to find their answers in the Book of Knowledge.

Zachery Smith was the school superintendent for the area. He was rigid and doctrinaire, believing firmly that teaching must follow the curriculum to the letter. He was tall and lean with a balding head with paled features that suggested he spent too little time in the sun, and his face was set in a humourless expression to match his rigid manner in matters of his job. As a result, most teachers were apprehensive about his periodic visits to their schools and extremely cautious about any innovative methods used in the classroom lest he disapprove, which he often did. Journeys from school board headquarters for him were awkward, requiring either a trip by train with an overnight stay in Grimstad if lodgings could be found, or a torturous journey by automobile. Thus, the teachers of remote schools like Grimstad were fortunate to only have to endure two visits per school year, except for special circumstances.

On a cold early December day, Zachery showed up at the Grimstad School in the course of his regular rounds, but also with a couple of other issues on his mind. He spent some time observing each class in progress, and then had a meeting with the four teachers that the school board employed. He gave each teacher a passing grade in their overall classroom performance, though not without some minor criticism, and then turned to the other issues. He began by asking what had become of the old readers and maps.

Mary swallowed with resolve and said, "I put them in the garbage. They were ruined."

"They are suppose to be sent back to our headquarters

and *we* will decide what is to be trashed," Zachery replied sharply.

"But they were garbage," Mary insisted. "The pages were soiled and torn, covers were missing and the maps were out-of-date. I didn't think you would want maps that were no longer accurate."

"So you just trashed the lot?" the Superintendent said brusquely.

"Yes sir," Mary replied meekly. She was essentially telling the truth since she carefully placed the lot near the outdoor garbage bin so Sean could later remove them to take to Jane's school.

"I concur with Mary," said James Jones, the teacher who was the defacto principal of Grimstad School. "While I apologise for not sending them back, they *were* in pretty bad shape."

"Well, from now on any textbook or outdated map, no matter the condition, must be sent back to the school board office for proper disposal. In some of the more remote schools and with money in short supply, we use dated maps until new ones can be purchased and even worn textbooks if they can be fixed."

"From now on we will send them back," James replied. Although he and the other teachers suspected the ultimate fate of the discards, they held their tongues.

Zachery continued relentlessly, "Have any of you heard of this Opportunity School, I believe it is called, operating somewhere in this vicinity?"

He looked carefully around until James finally said, "I've also heard of that rumour. What is the problem, if I may ask?"

"It is an illegal school that is not sanctioned by the board, and to my understanding the teacher has no training and thus has no business teaching."

"No training," the other teachers murmured among themselves in feigned surprise. They were all aware of Jane's school and supported it in principle, but knew that sooner or later she would be found out.

"I would like to see this school and its so-called teacher," Zachery said strongly. "A teacher without training...that's not good," James said.

"Without training this so-called teacher can neither grade, nor properly teach these children. I know there were some parents at the board last spring requesting a school somewhere north of here, but there weren't enough students to justify one. Do you have any students from very far north out here?"

James thought and said, "No, I think the furthest one has three miles to come."

"It's mainly old bachelors who live up in the bush beyond that," Mary added.

"Like Sean O'Malley," one of the teachers added and both Mary and Zachery glanced at her.

Another teacher was about to mention that some new families had moved up north, but Mary bumped her foot and she clammed up.

Finally, Zachery said, "I'll have to make a trip up that road before I go back to see if I can find that school."

"You will need a horse and cutter, as the snow is too deep for an automobile," James added.

"Where there's a will there's a way," he replied.

When the meeting was dismissed, the superintendent asked Mary to stay back as he wished a private word with her. Mary braced for the worst.

"It has come to my attention that you have been seeing a certain Sean O'Malley," Zachery stated.

Mary swallowed and said, "That is in past tense, sir."

"I hope so," he continued. "It is said, though not yet proven, that he manufactures and sells illegal spirits."

"So I've heard," Mary replied evenly. *The commissioner must have tipped off the superintendent,* she thought. *Thank God I broke up with Sean.*

"It would not do well for a teacher, a supposed pillar

of the community, to be seen in the company of a man suspected of criminal activity."

"That's why I broke it off with him," Mary said in a flat tone. "Not that it is anyone else's business who I choose to associate with."

"My dear lady," Zachery replied in a resolute tone. "If you should be found to be courted by a known criminal you could and probably would be dismissed from your job. It's just a thought should you ever decide to resume the relationship."

"Yes sir," Mary replied with a hint of contempt.

"Oh, and one more thing, are you acquainted with this so-called teacher at this...this Opportunity School?"

"I've met her," Mary said as she swallowed.

"What is her name?"

Mary was cornered, but admitting she knew Jane she could not decline to reveal her name and risk her job.

"Jane, her name is Jane, sir."

"Jane who? Doesn't she have a last name?"

"Jane Phillips."

"Is she a friend of yours?"

"I know her," Mary said tightly. "Why are you asking me all of this?"

"I need to find her and shut this illegal operation down," he said with a scowl. "I hope you, or any of the other teachers here haven't been helping her."

"Why would we do that?" Mary said evenly. "Like you said, she is unqualified and wouldn't be able to instruct the pupils properly."

"I'm glad you realise that," he said sharply. "You don't suppose she got a hold of that school stuff you threw out did she?"

"I wouldn't know sir," Mary swallowed. "Why am I being grilled about this?"

"Because there is something going on here, I can't help but have a feeling that the others, especially you, are hiding her," Zachery continued unremittingly. "If you or the others have been aiding her in setting up this…this school, you will be in a lot of trouble. That will be all for now, Mary."

When Mary returned to the store, she was visibly relieved to find Dave Higgins there. She spoke hastily addressing both him and Kari in a whisper, "The school superintendent is in town and he is looking for Jane. You must warn her and tell her she got the old supplies out of the garbage if he should find her school. He will be going up the road looking for it, so tell all the neighbours not to give him directions."

"Righto," Dave replied. "It's a bloody good thing we decided to build it off the road. There is no way in hell that ruddy superintendent is going to find Jane."

"I vill spread vord around town," Kari added. "Ve just got rid of da Goon Squad and ve don't need anudder busybody around. Even dough I rented him a room upstairs not knowing."

"Well, let him stay and collect his money for lodgings," Dave laughed. "That way you can keep an eye on him."

"I have to stay in a room beside him," Mary complained.

"If you don't vant to eat vit him, I vill send your supper up to your room." Kari offered.

"That's too much trouble," Mary said. "I'll grin and bear it and have my supper downstairs at the regular time."

"I better get going and spread the word," Dave replied as he picked up his purchase and headed for the door.

The following morning when Zachery tried to get a team and cutter from Norton, he lapsed into speaking Norwegian which was incomprehensible to the superintendent. Finally, using Kari, who could not deny her knowledge of English, as interpreter, he managed to get a horse and cutter and headed up the road.

Since the school was invisible from the main road, Zachery drove nearly all the way to Rocky Ridge before turning back without finding the school. When he stopped at various households to seek directions they either plead ignorance or stonewalled him. During his enquiries Zachery made the mistake of identifying himself as the school superintendent, which immediately gave away his purpose.

At the Kepler farm he was met at the door by Hella. She deliberately lapsed into very broken English that was mixed with German making the conversation almost impossible.

At the Higgins' household, Sari let him inside, but as soon as he identified himself she declined to offer him a chair or let him stand near the stove to warm up and looked at him through hostile eyes.

"Do you know Jane Phillips?" he asked.

"So what if I do?" Sari said sharply.

"It is my understanding that she is running an illegal school around here somewhere."

"What Jane does with her time is her own ruddy business and should be none of yours."

"As a school superintendent it is my business," he continued undaunted. "Do you have school age children?"

"And what bloody business is that of yours?" Her tone was decidedly hostile.

Just then Dave entered the house; he nodded a greeting and appeared outwardly friendly until Sari identified Zachery. "This bloke is the school superintendent, and he's been asking all sorts of questions. You'd think he was the ruddy police."

"I am concerned about the education of your children," Zachery said mildly.

"My children are no concern of yours," Dave said sharply. "I'll thank you to be on your way."

He opened the door to the superintendent and nodded with his head.

As the superintendent stepped outside he said, "I'm only concerned for their educational welfare." As the door was shut in his face.

Finally, he made one last stop. The side trail he chose from the many that led off the main road took him to Audi's doorstep.

Audi let him in and allowed Zachery to stand by his stove to warm up even after he identified himself.

"And how may I help the superintendent of schools?" Audi asked politely though he knew full well why Zachery was at his doorstep.

"Perhaps you could direct me to the whereabouts of Opportunity School?" Zachery said evenly, feeling he might get somewhere with the less hostile appearing Audi.

"Afraid not," Audi smiled. "As you see, I am a bachelor without either wife or child, so schools don't interest me."

"You appear a learned man," Zachery said with a smile. "You must appreciate the value of a proper education."

"Oh, I do," Audi replied. "I hold a Bachelor of Arts from the University of Amsterdam. The educational system back in Holland is of the highest order."

"Then surely you must oppose the idea of an unsanctioned school presided over by an unqualified teacher."

"How do you mean unqualified?"

"Well, this Jane Phillips has no formal training and takes it upon herself to set up a school and devise her own curriculum. What kind of an education will those students get?"

"It is my learned opinion, Mr. Superintendent, that a mere piece of paper does not entail qualification, but that lie in the teacher, in her ability to conduct an orderly classroom and to effectively convey vital knowledge to her pupils." Audi smiled sardonically.

"Yes, but she cannot grade her students and she surely has very limited resources," Zachery insisted. "How can she teach them with no knowledge of a curriculum?"

"Perhaps she has a natural gift for teaching," Audi said smoothly. "Just like some people have a gift for music or art."

"But, but..." the superintendent stuttered then composed himself, "why do I have the feeling that you know a lot more about this school and its teacher than you are letting on?"

"Perhaps you have the gift of intuition," Audi chuckled. Then glancing outside at the closing darkness he continued, "I'd love to have you stay and debate what makes a teacher qualified, but I have chores to do, and you should get back to Grimstad before dark." Audi opened the door for him.

Of all the encounters with the uncooperative neighbourhood he found Audi the most exasperating. *Why would this polished intellectual curiously living in the backwoods want to hide that illegal school?*

Tired and nearly frozen, he returned to Grimstad at the end of a long day convinced that there was a conspiracy afoot to hide Jane and her school. He caught the morning train home, resolved to wait until later winter or spring when the weather was better. In the meantime, he could devise a new plan to find out the location of this illicit school.

As for Mary, although she was still quite fond of Sean and valued her friendship with Jane, she was terrified of the superintendent.

Chapter Ten

Jane decided that her school would host a Christmas concert on the last day before Christmas break. Her school would have its break to coincide with the Christmas break at the Grimstad School. For the month of December, general discussion time was devoted to preparing for the concert.

One day, at Jane's request, Ethan brought in a large well-formed jack pine to serve as the school Christmas tree. It was set along the far wall just past the side blackboard. With the arrival of the tree and the concert fast approaching, art class was now devoted to making paper Christmas decorations. Jane showed them how to make paper ropes and snowflakes and had them draw and paint pictures of angels, stars and images of Santa to hang on the tree. Helen and Lydia crafted a well-designed star from cardboard to put on the top.

In music class, Jane taught them to sing familiar carols and she included *O' Christmas Tree* among them. Herman informed her that this was actually a German carol called *Tannin Baum.*

"Do you know how to sing it in German?" Jane asked.

"Well...uh, yes," Herman said reluctantly, fearing Jane would ask him to sing.

"Mom taught us," Wilhelm volunteered. Herman scowled at him.

"Would you two like to sing it together at the concert?"

Wilhelm grinned, but Herman shuffled uneasily.

"I think your parents would be proud to hear you sing that carol in German and the other parents would be entertained."

"Did you know that *Silent Night* is also German?" Wilhelm announced, "and Christmas trees."

"Willy," as of late Wilhelm was called Willy, "stop it!" Herman said sharply. He feared that they might be asked to sing *Silent Night* in German as well.

A novel idea came to Jane, "Herman why don't you make a presentation at the concert telling everyone all the aspects of Christmas that we celebrate in Canada that came from Germany?"

"I will do that rather than sing," Herman said.

"I was hoping you'd do both. You and Willy could both sing after you read your report."

"I can sing it alone," Willy said.

Jane thought for a moment, Willy was a clear and enthusiastic singer during music class. "Sing us a verse?" she asked.

Willy looked shyly around, wondering what he'd gotten himself into.

"Come on Willy, sing for us," Thomas grinned.

"Yes, let's hear you sing in German," Lech added.

So, with reluctance, but full of encouragement from both Jane and his classmates, Willy sang in his child's voice, which could still hold a tune, a couple of lines from *Tannin Baum*. This brought applause from everyone and a momentary hug from Jane. Jane decided that Herman would give his report on the German factor in Christmas and Willy would follow with a solo version of *Tannin Baum*.

"Now if I only had music for back up," Jane mused aloud. She thought of Ethan but dismissed the idea immediately. A fiddle wasn't the ideal backup instrument even if Ethan would play in public.

"Dad can play an accordion," Herman piped up.

"Would he play at the concert?" Jane wondered out loud.

"I'll ask him," Herman volunteered

"*I'll* ask him," Jane stated.

When Wolf came for his children and to deliver Robbie, Jane approached him on the matter.

"Well, I haff never played in public," Wolf flustered.

"Your young son Willy is going to sing *Tannin Baum*," Jane said enthusiastically, "and the other carols also sound better with music."

"I will haff to zink about zat one," Wolf replied.

Jane added, "I am thinking of hanging a curtain rope across the front of where I'll put the stage, and you can sit behind the curtain so no one will see you play."

"Zhat makes it a little better," Wolf replied. "I'll let you know tomorrow."

The following Saturday, while Jane was at the store looking for items that she could use as Christmas presents for her students, Mary came in from the back then retreated to her room after exchanging a brief greeting.

"What is the matter with Mary?" Jane asked Kari with a knitted brow.

"It vas dat school inspector. He has all da teachers terrified." Kari replied gravely.

"Why?" Jane demanded.

"He is looking for you and your school. He vent up da road von day nearly all da vay to Rocky Ridge looking for your school."

Jane laughed and replied, "There was a reason they built it on the road to our place rather than along the main road. It was pretty smart thinking on Ethan's and Dave's part."

"Ya, he vas very disappointed vhen he couldn't find it," Kari added, "and very cold riding all day in da cutter."

"I am aware that the superintendent was out and asking about my school," Jane said seriously. "But what's that got to do with Mary?"

"I tink dat you should go up to her room and have a vord vit her," Kari replied. "It vill do her good and it vill be more private. I vill bring up a cup of tea."

"Thank you Kari, you are a real friend," Jane smiled. "I'll do that. When Ethan comes back from his errands you can tell him what is happening. I'll take Robbie with me so you can mind the store."

"Leave him here, he vill be no trouble," Kari assured her. "Linda vill be along soon anyhow and she can look after Robbie."

When Jane knocked on Mary's door, Mary glanced up and down the hallway before letting her in.

"Hello Mary," Jane said with a friendly grin. "You look worried."

"I am worried for you," Mary replied in an anxious tone. "The superintendent was looking for your school."

"He didn't find it though."

"Oh Jane, he'll shut you down. He also asked about the school books and maps that I threw out. If he should come to your school and find them…"

"You'll be in trouble," Jane cut her off. "Don't worry. If it comes to that I will tell them I fished them out of the garbage."

"He really grilled us about the books," Mary said in a morose tone. "James stuck up for me though, but we got a lecture about how all discarded school supplies must be sent to the head office. If he sees the maps on the wall of your school, or the textbooks he'll confiscate them."

"He can try, but he won't get them without a fight." Jane's jaw was set in a determined line.

Mary momentarily smiled as Jane had a reputation of standing her ground. A confrontation between her and the superintendent would be an interesting prospect.

"Then he singled me out, warning me that I would lose my job if I resumed seeing Sean."

"He sounds like a real ogre just like that commissioner fellow from the Goon Squad," Jane said. "He has no right."

"Oh, Jane…between him and the Goon Squad I don't know what to do," Mary said tearfully.

"Well, at least the Goon Squad is gone and probably won't be back now that Sean has quit making moonshine," Jane assured her.

"Has he really quit?" Mary asked anxiously.

"He's working at the sawmill," Jane replied. "He was over for a visit last week and said he wasn't going to make moonshine any more. How about you, have you spoken to Sean recently?"

"I broke off with him because I was threatened with losing my job," Mary said sadly. "And I love teaching."

"But, personally, do you care for Sean?"

"But…"

"You know Mary, if you still care for Sean and I know he still cares for you, you guys should really get together and talk things out."

"But the superintendent said…"

"Hang the superintendent. Your personal life is none of his business, especially now that Sean has reformed," Jane declared. "You know the good people of Grimstad will stand behind you as they think well of you as a teacher."

"Just like you," Mary said with a watery-eyed grin. "They will all stand behind you as they think it is wonderful that you are providing an education for those children up there."

"Together we will muddle through this," Jane smiled confidently. "As Ethan would say, to hell with the authorities," she put an arm around Mary.

Mary began to sob and tightly hugged Jane. "Forgive me my dear friend, I will never turn and walk away again. I am so proud to know you, proud of what you are doing with your school and proud to have you as my friend."

"That's better," Jane said, looking Mary in the eye. "My school is having a concert the Saturday after school is out. I would like you to come. You can stay over with us if you like. I would also like you to have Christmas dinner with us."

"Is there room for me to stay over in your tiny house?"

"Ethan has built a lean-to for our bedroom and is installing a staircase to the loft from inside. You can sleep on the couch."

"Then yes on both counts, though I'll need a ride out there."

"I'll send Ethan to get you." Jane smiled as she stood up. "I'm sure he won't mind. Speaking of Ethan, he is probably downstairs waiting for me now."

"Thank you again my dear friend Jane," Mary said tearfully as she stood up and hugged Jane again.

As Jane opened the door to leave, Kari was coming down the hall with her tea service.

"Is Ethan back?" Jane asked.

"He is downstairs vatching Robbie, I vas yust bringing your tea."

Mary appeared in the doorway and said, "Let's have it downstairs in the kitchen and Ethan can join us. I would like to see Robbie."

Kari turned and they followed her back downstairs.

"That is about the stupidest thing I ever heard," Ethan railed when Jane explained to him how the superintendent had all but forbidden Mary to associate with Sean. "Who in the hell does he think he is?"

"Mary says he'll shut my school down if he ever finds it and me," Jane said.

"Like hell he will," Ethan roared. "That school is on private property and since it doesn't have the school board's blessing it's a private school."

"I never thought of it that way," Mary said.

"I'm still not looking forward to dealing with him," Jane said gravely.

"Well, I'd like to meet him and give him a piece of my mind," Ethan rumbled. Then he looked at Jane and smiled. "I'd like to watch him have a set-to with you though. I think he'd come out the worst of it."

Mary laughed.

"Say, I invited Mary to come to my concert and to stay over Christmas," Jane said. "You won't mind getting her on Saturday?"

"Sure, not a problem," Ethan smiled at Mary. "We got more room in the house now, yer more than welcome."

"Thank you," Mary smiled.

"Or did he also forbid you to be seen with us?" Ethan grunted.

"In a round about way," Mary said gravely. "He forbade me to help Jane in any way."

"He's just like that commissioner for the Goon Squad," Ethan replied. "Give 'em a little authority and it goes to their heads." Then as he looked out the window at the gathering darkness he replied, "We should be going, it'll be dark before we get home."

As Jane stood and gathered up Robbie, Mary followed them and thanked them again. Ethan said he would come by on Saturday afternoon to pick Mary up for the concert.

The night of the concert was a cold one. Ethan went for Mary in the early afternoon and left Jane and Robbie at the school, as Jane wanted to get everything ready. Dave had brought Sari over to help her and brought Helen to entertain Robbie and keep him out of the way. Jane and Sari strung a rope across the width of the school just in front of the teacher's desk and hung blankets from it to serve as curtains for the stage. All of the students' desk tables were bunched together to serve as a stage beside the teachers desk and the benches and chairs were set out for the audience.

It was nearly dark when Ethan returned with Mary and Dave had just left with Sari. Jane proudly showed Mary around her school, which looked impressive even in its current altered state, while Ethan brought in more coal and stoked the heater. There were large pictures on the wall of exotic animals such as elephants and tigers, and the now framed map of Europe. Most impressive was the small library at the back with the encyclopaedia and the books donated by the mysterious benefactor.

"You know, I have to envy you," Mary said as she looked around. "Your own little school run exactly the way you want it to run, with nobody looking over your shoulder telling you how you should run it."

"Like that superintendent," Ethan rumbled as he closed the heater's fire door.

"Exactly," Mary replied.

"Well, I don't get paid like you do."

"But you are doing it because you want to see these children educated," Mary replied.

"Yes, and that's payment enough for me. Just to know that if my three shining stars go on to bigger and brighter things, as I sincerely hope they do, I'll know that I had a hand in giving them their start."

"Speaking of shining stars, they're out now and we ought a get home for supper and chores before coming back for the concert."

"Yes dear," Jane said as she began to bundle Robbie up for the cold two-mile journey home.

They all huddled in the cutter under a horse blanket; the night was clear and the moon was not yet out and their way was dimly lit by an awesome canopy of twinkling stars. As they journeyed through the darkness, Jane was able to point out to Mary the constellations of Gemini, Taurus and Orion along with his two hunting dogs of Canis Major and Minor.

"Gosh, how do you know so much about the stars?" Mary asked.

"Ethan taught me, and after Christmas break my science class will focus on astronomy for most of the winter."

"Look up at Taurus," Ethan said. "See that bright star?"

"Yes," both Jane and Mary said together.

"That's the planet Jupiter." Ethan replied.

"How do you know that?" Mary asked with fascination.

"The constellations like Taurus and Gemini are of the zodiac and that's where the planets are."

"Amazing," Mary gasped. "I should have you come and give my class astronomy lessons."

"The stars aren't out in the daytime," Ethan said with his grumbling voice as they broke over the hill near to the farmstead.

The house was still warm when they got there as the large lumps of coal in the stove had not yet burned out. Ethan poked at the coals and soon had the fire blazing, while Jane lit the wick lamp. "Well, I better get to the chores," Ethan said as he turned to go outside.

"I'll have supper ready by the time you get back," Jane replied as she pumped up their Aladdin lamp. "Ah, that's much better," she said as she lit the coal oil driven lamp which had one large mantle. It gave off a soft white light that was much brighter than the wick lamp.

As Jane rustled in the food box, located along the north wall, for some items she could use to make a quick supper, Mary looked around the house and helped Robbie remove his coat and boots.

"Your house has a lot more room since you built that annex," Mary said.

"Yes, the bedroom is big enough not only for Ethan and I, but Robbie for the time being. It allows us space for a bit of a living room." Noticing the bearskin rug in front of the couch, she added, "I like the bearskin. Is it the one you shot?"

"Yes," Jane sighed. "It seems the bear incident will haunt me for the rest of my life. Even the kids at school mentioned it."

"Well, it was quite an event. I think I would have run for my life," Mary said.

"I was too scared to run and in my panic I pulled both triggers and nearly tore my shoulder off," Jane replied.

"I see you've even installed a ladder to the loft," Mary said as she looked at the ladder like stairs leading to the loft with the trapdoor presently closed.

"Yes, Ethan built the stairs and put a window where the outside entrance to the loft used to be. He says Robbie will eventually sleep up there as will any future children we might have."

"I'll bet it's cold up there," Mary said.

"Actually it's not that bad," Jane replied. "The floor has a mud plaster coating which absorbs heat from the stove, and of course the stovepipe runs through there as well. I'll show you later."

An hour later Ethan returned from chores and Jane had prepared a throw-together supper of eggs, bacon and potatoes all mixed together in the frying pan which they later washed down with coffee and raspberry preserves. All too soon it was time to bundle up again and head out into the darkness to the concert. As the others came outside and got nestled in the cutter, Ethan loaded the stove with large a lump coal that would burn until they got back a few hours hence. He brought a small bundle, wrapped in a blanket, and slid it under the seat with an off-hand comment, "A little something extra for the concert."

"What is it?" Jane asked.

"A surprise," Ethan replied as he nudged the horses forward.

Chapter Eleven

The Phillips' were the first to arrive for the concert and Ethan was thus assured a place for his team in the school barn, which only had limited space for shelter from the cold night. He lugged in extra coal and banked up the fire in the heater. He also brought in the bundle wrapped in an old blanket and placed it under a table at the back. When Jane asked him again about the bundle, he again replied mysteriously that it was a surprise. Jane lit the wick coal oil lamps that belonged to the school and Ethan's lantern to provide lighting. When the Higgins family, who were next to arrive came along Dave also brought in his lantern. Wolf did likewise when the Kepler family arrived. Two of the lanterns were hung above the makeshift stage as this was where most lighting would be needed. A large kettle of water and a coffee pot were put on the heater and prepared lunches set on a back table. Soon other families began to arrive, including a few with only pre-school age children and Axel with his wife and children who made the long, cold journey from Grimstad.

The room was soon full of noisy people with children scampering about in an agitated state and the recently arrived adults huddling around the heater for warmth. Jane gathered her pupils and took them to the front to prep them for the concert. Then she asked Audi if he would be master of ceremonies, presenting him with her program. Just as the lights in the main part of the school were being turned off, Mary noticed the arrival of Sean. She braced for the possibility that he may try to speak to her. For the present though, he stood by the heater to warm up. As soon as Wolf's accordion was warmed up enough to function properly, he took his place behind the curtain. Audi stood up on the stage and announced, "Ladies, gentlemen and children, the first Christmas concert of Opportunity School is about to begin. May it be the first of many to follow?" Cheers erupted from the audience and he continued, "Our very astute teacher, Mrs. Jane Phillips, has put together what I am sure will be an impressive entertainment for us." Again there were cheers. He then announced the first event.

Jane's class was assembled on stage and with Wolf's accompaniment they sang *Away in the Manger* and *The First Noel,* as Jane conducted them. After the carols, several of the smaller children did brief recitations in their thin childhood voices, while Lech belted out *The Night Before Christmas* in a clear voice. The Malov twins followed with a quiet presentation about Christmas in Russia. Jane then had her class enact the Nativity Scene, with Lydia as the Virgin Mary, Willy as Joseph and her three shining stars fittingly played the three wise men. The others were shepherds and a rag doll served as baby Jesus. Jane read the appropriate biblical passages as the scene unfolded. Wolf closed the scene with an accordion rendition of *Hark the Herald Angels Sing.*

Finally, Herman and Willy Kepler were called on stage. Herman made his presentation of all the things that Germany contributed to Christmas, such as Christmas trees and the familiar carols, *Tannin Baum* and *Silent Night,* the latter he explained was called *Stille Nacht* in German. Then as an extra surprise, he mentioned how the carol *Silent Night* almost stopped the Great War in its tracks. He described how the German and British soldiers heard each other singing the carol while in the trenches and how they all came out, shook hands and wished each other Merry Christmas. This stirred murmurs among the others as many had not heard of this incident that took place during the first Christmas of the war.

"Leave it to Herman to come up with something like that," Jane muttered.

Following the presentation, Willy sang *Tannin Baum* and when he began to falter, Hella, who was near the front, helped out in her rich voice while Wolf smiled and played his accordion.

Next, Jane lined up all of her pupils and each held one of the letters that spelled out the word Christmas, though the Malov twins had theirs in the reverse order. This went unnoticed by Jane until the recitation in which each pupil described how their letter had a Christmas meaning. As they represented the H and R it was too late to change but to the amusement of the audience the twins recited in the right order, not realising they each held the wrong letter.

Audi made an amusing comment about Jane's spelling class when the recitation was complete. As a finale, the audience was invited to sing along with the children for the closing carols of *God Rest Ye Merry Gentlemen* and *Silent Night*. Hella, who did not know the words of *God Rest Ye Merry Gentlemen*, hummed the carol, but when they sang *Silent Night* she sang it in German, not knowing the English version and her clear voice stood out. On the third verse everyone stopped singing to hear her finish, both for the quality of her voice and the curiosity of hearing the carol sung in German. Though she was embarrassed that everyone had stopped to listen, she received a very strong round of applause.

Audi stood up on stage with the closing comment, "We would all like to thank Mrs. Phillips for the excellent concert she has put on as testament to the incredible job she is doing in providing an education for your children." This brought a thunderous round of applause and left Jane blushing. Mary was smiling broadly. Here was Jane in blatant defiance of the system providing a Christmas concert of the first order, by a well-disciplined class. She was thinking of how insignificant the overbearing superintendent was for the first time. She did not for a moment regret helping Jane with her school and would continue to do so in the future.

The children had been kept on stage until the door opened and in stepped the familiar red suited symbol of Christmas. They were; however, required to sing *Here*

Comes Santa Claus before being dismissed. As they sang, Santa moved through the audience with the large sack on his back speaking to the adults and other children before taking his seat by the Christmas tree. The children all clamoured around him, though Herman and Thomas, both almost too old for public association with Santa Claus hung back. He reached in his pack and called out each child one at a time, whereupon they got to sit on Santa's knee as he presented them with a small candy bag. A last minute head count of the extra children had been made and names assigned to the extra candy bags so no one would be left out.

When Thomas's turn came and Santa spoke to him he said, "You are really Mr. O'Malley aren't you?"

"Now what would make you be sayin' a thing like that?" Santa replied with an Irish brogue.

"You talk like him and I know your beard is a fake," Thomas replied though he spoke in a low voice so the others wouldn't hear.

"Well, Santa was busy tonight," Sean said. "Did ye not know that his right-hand man is an Irishman?"

Thomas sighed raising his eyebrows as he got up.

"Now don't be tellin' the little ones," Sean asked.

"I'll keep yer secret," he assured Santa.

Most of the older ones guessed that Sean played Santa and some younger ones commented that Santa either had a funny accent or talked like Mr. O'Malley, leaving parents to scramble for a plausible answer.

Finally, after the last candy bag was handed out, Santa called for Mary McKay. She was flustered that Santa would call her and then she noticed that Sean was not present in the crowd. Jane winked at her. So, with a coy smile Mary went up to Santa and sat on his knee, noticing he had his hand deep within his sack.

"I have a wee present for Mary McKay from the North Pole," he said as he presented her with a small wrapped present. "For all the support she has been givin' to our teacher."

Mary flustered and said with a smile, "Since when did Santa acquire an Irish brogue?"

"Everyone knows that Santa is an Irishman," Sean replied with a laugh. "Do ye think that yer school inspector will condemn ye for sittin' on Santa's knee?"

"He might if he knew that Santa was an Irish moonshiner," Mary teased.

"Ex-moonshiner," Sean replied. "I'll not be makin' that stuff again. I have a real job now."

"That's what I hear," she replied. "But somehow tonight the superintendent seems so far away."

"May he stay far away," Sean said. "It would please me to be courtin' you again."

"I'll think about that one," Mary said with a grin as she rose to her feet. "Thank you Santa for the present."

"I have but one wee present left," Sean called. "Would our teacher Mrs. Phillips come over to speak with Santa?"

Jane smiled and set herself down easily on Santa's knee. "Here is a present for you, for all that you have done." He handed Jane a present identical in size to that of Mary's gift.

"Thank you Santa, you shouldn't have."

"Well, it's only fittin' for the occasion don't ye think? Not only for the kids but for bringin' Mary along."

"She's speaking to you is she?" Jane asked.

"At least through the beard," Sean replied. "It's a wee start in the right direction."

"I hope you two get back together and thanks for playing Santa Claus tonight," Jane said as she got up. Then with a wink she turned and added, "Come and grace our table for Christmas dinner. Mary will be there."

"I'll be puttin' me reindeer in Ethan's barn then," he laughed.

With that Santa got up with his empty sack and wished everyone Merry Christmas as he headed for the door. Everyone cheered and clapped.

Thomas, Herman and Lech gave each other knowing

glances as Sean came into the school, shivering from the cold a few minutes later. They; however, kept their promises not to reveal Santa's identity to the younger children.

"I say there my good friend and former foe," Dave said to Wolf as he approached his neighbour, who was standing at the back near the door, "that was quite a presentation your sons did. Did you have any input into it per chance?"

"Oh, you mean ze bit about ze first Christmas of ze war?"

"I heard a story about that, but it seemed hard to believe."

"I vas zhere und I remember shaking hands mit English soldiers. Vhere you not in ze war yet?"

"I didn't get to the front until the next year. There was no Christmas fraternizing when I was at the front."

"I zink ze chenerals made sure it didn't happen again."

"You guys should have went back to Berlin and shot the Kaiser and we should have went back to London and shot his cousin," Ethan said as he joined the conversation, "instead of us shooting at each other."

"Were you zhere?" Wolf asked Ethan.

"No, I wasn't in the war 'til 1916; I helped kick the hell out of you guys at Vimy the following year."

"The bloody war is over," Sari said as she joined them. "It's Christmas and you should be talking about something nice, like this marvellous concert Jane put on."

"Yes, it was an excellent show thanks to your talented wife," Dave said.

"Yeah, well…I hear that school superintendent is lookin' for her so he can try to shut her down," Ethan rumbled.

"He'll have a ruddy fight on his hands if he tries that," Dave said resolutely.

"Dat is one war where we will be on ze same side," Wolf added.

"This school is on private property. He can't close it or stop Jane," Ethan rumbled. "Or there will be hell to pay."

"I think I'll call a meeting of our board right after

Christmas," Dave said, "so we can have a contingency plan should they try to shut this school down."

"*Javoul*," Wolf said quietly.

After lunch was served with coffee and tea for the adults and hot cocoa for the children a dance was held. Wolf played his accordion and Ivan had brought his mandolin; they attuned to each other and began to play a curious mixture of German and Russian music which soon had the adults dancing to the polka. Since Wolf was playing, Hella induced a reluctant Herman to dance with her. Sean approached Mary saying, "Would ye dare to dance with Santa without the beard?"

"I'll take a chance this one time." She smiled and accepted, noticing that he was only a few steps ahead of Audi who also aspired to dance with Mary. Thwarted in his bid to dance with Mary, Audi settled for dancing with Raisa since her partner was also playing in the band.

After the first round of music, Ethan gestured for the makeshift band to refrain from playing as he went to the back and reached for the bundle he had brought. As all eyes were on Ethan, Jane said breathlessly, "Oh my god he brought his fiddle!"

Ethan calmly took his fiddle from the case and walked to the stage with a steely eyed calm, avoiding even the adoring gaze of his wife.

"I didn't know Ethan could play," Mary gasped. That thought was on nearly everyone's mind. While some of his neighbours had heard he could fiddle, none heard him play save for Sean.

"Aye, he's a good fiddler, but he's not one to be playin' in public," Sean replied. "There must be a special reason."

On his way to the stage Ethan plucked the strings to assure they were in tune, and then stepped up on stage and faced the anxiously waiting crowd.

"Not many people ever heard me play," he said in his usual gravelly voice. "And I told Jane long ago that I only play on special occasions for special people. Well, both conditions apply tonight." With that he began to play. Tears flowed from Jane's eyes as he played the opening strains of her special tune, *Never-Ending Road*. After the first refrain he said, "I would like to ask the beautiful lady who stole my heart with this song to join me and show our good friends and neighbours one more of her many talents."

He extended his hand to the faltering and teary-eyed Jane while the crowd chanted for her to join him. After initial reluctance, Jane joined him on stage feeling that if Ethan could bring himself to play before a crowd she could not deny him. The crowd, children included, stood in awed silence as Jane belted out a powerful rendition of *Never-Ending Road* in her rich soprano voice. At one point, Robbie toddled over to his mother even though Helen tried to stop him. Jane picked him up in her arms without missing a chord even as he tried to reach for Ethan's fiddle.

The song ended with a thunderous round of applause and Jane hugged Ethan tightly saying softly to him, "Thank you my darling. I love you so much." Sari, Hella and Mary all wiped tears from the corners of their eyes.

Holding Jane with one arm, Ethan declared in a loud voice, "To hell with the school board! This is our school, our teacher and my wife. God bless her soul."

There was a massive outcry of agreement from the others.

"I could have never done it without him," Jane declared. "He is my rock, my anchor and my beloved husband, and I thank God for the day I answered his letter asking me to be his mail-order bride."

Again there was a massive outburst from the crowd. She kissed Ethan briefly on the lips, turned and said, "I'll leave him to entertain you now." She stepped off the stage still holding Robbie.

Ethan then said, "One more tune before I put this away and let the real musicians play. This one's for Santa." He fiddled out the lively Irish tune called *Rakes of Killdare*.

"If he keeps this up, he'll have me dancin' a jig," Sean commented to Mary.

"Why don't you?" Mary teased.

"Well, I think there are some things best left the way they are," Sean replied.

After the tune, Ethan was about to leave the stage when the others asked him to play a waltz. He attuned himself to the other two musicians and played *Casey's Waltz*.

Helen had once again taken charge of little Robbie when a friendly voice asked Jane, "May I have this dance, Mrs. Phillips?"

Jane turned and there stood Audi with extended hand. She swallowed with resolve and then accepted, thinking that it was perfectly safe in this situation.

"It was a superb concert you put on tonight," Audi said as he whirled her around the floor. "I should have guessed that you are such a beautiful singer."

"I sing for Ethan," she replied defensively. "I live and breathe for him. Everything I said when I was up beside him, I meant."

"He is indeed a remarkable man of many surprises," Audi replied.

"Tell me about it," Jane replied. "He surprises me every day and tonight was one of the biggest ones he's pulled in a long time."

"You didn't know he was going to play?"

"Not a hint, when he brought that bundle into the school he wouldn't tell me what was in it."

"He did it to honour you as you should be honoured," Audi said in his smooth manner.

"And I sang to honour him."

After the tune was over, Ethan stepped from the stage and Jane excused herself to join him. She was still unsure as to whether Audi was sincere, or still angling for her favour.

Chapter Twelve

The Phillips family were the last to leave the school. As each of her pupils left Jane gave them a small present and invited them to take any of the decorations they had made from the Christmas tree home. Any that remained after all the others had gone; Jane removed for her own Christmas tree, a tree that Ethan had yet to get.

The fire in the heater had been allowed to burn low before they left so that it would safely burn itself out during the night. With all in order, they bundled into the cutter for the cold, dark ride home. The old horse blanket was drawn over them and Robbie, snuggled in between his parents, was completely covered. The small semi-enclosed sleigh offered the illusion of cosiness as the team, Clyde and the new mare Nelly, trudged through the darkness with the sleigh runners crunching the snow.

"Gosh, it's like travelling through a tunnel," Mary observed as the night was now overcast and even the snow could not reflect any light.

"It's a good thing the horses know their way home," Ethan remarked.

"What made you decide to bring your fiddle tonight?" Jane asked Ethan. "I just about fell over when I saw you take your fiddle case out of the bundle."

"I just thought it seemed like the thing to do," he replied in an off-hand way. "I knew they'd be heapin' praise on you for puttin' on such a good concert so I thought I'd add a little of my own."

"It was a wonderful thing you did, Ethan," Mary added. "You are a good player."

"She is the talented one," Ethan replied modestly. "Did you ever hear anyone sing like Jane?"

"That was a beautiful song you sang Jane," Mary replied.

"I remember hearing it the second day we were together when she was plantin' the garden," Ethan interjected, "if I needed anythin' to remind me that Jane was for me that was it."

"It's just an old Celtic tune I learned somewhere along the way," Jane replied diffidently, "but it has become my song for Ethan. I sing it only to him or for him."

"And I play my fiddle only for special people like Jane, and although everyone got to hear me tonight I was thinking only of Jane."

"How sweet," Mary replied.

"Now you know why I love him," Jane said snuggling up to Ethan, "though he put me through the mill the first month we were together."

"I was testin' yuh to see if you were the one for me and yuh passed with flyin' colours," Ethan replied. Then changing the subject he said to Mary, "I see you got a present from Santa Claus."

Mary smiled and replied, "I'll bet Jane's school is the only place where Santa talks like an Irishman."

"I saw you dancing with the Irishman," Jane teased.

"I was being polite," Mary said coyly. "But I saw you dancing with the Dutchman."

"I was also being polite," Jane replied. "I knew it was safe to do so in a crowded room with Ethan close by."

"Oh, I think yer startin' to like him," Ethan teased.

"He seems to have changed, but I still don't trust him," Jane replied resolutely.

They continued on in silence as the cold night air nipped at their cheeks. Only Robbie was comfortably asleep on the straw covered floor under the horse blanket where he had slid down to their feet.

Soon they arrived home to a cold, dark house. Ethan lit the wick lamp and then after lighting his lantern he announced he was going to put the horses away in the barn. After laying the still sleeping Robbie on the couch, Jane opened the stove lid and poked the large lump of coal that was still burning. "Brr, it's cold in here," she said as she primed the fire with wood.

Jane soon had a blazing fire and Mary exclaimed, "Ah, that feels better already!" as she stretched her hands over the stove.

"As soon as the house warms up a bit more, I'll put Robbie to bed properly," Jane said as she put a few lumps of coal into the blazing fire. She then lit the Aladdin lamp to give them a brighter light. Mary looked around the house observing the frost in the upper corners of the walls while Jane opened the bedroom door to allow the heat to get in there.

As the house began to warm up enough for them to take off their coats, Mary again looked at the stairs and the trapdoor saying, "You say it's not too cold up in the loft?"

"Yes, it's surprisingly warm especially with the trapdoor open. The mud plaster coating on the floor of the loft absorbs a lot of heat. Why do you ask?"

"I just got an idea. Is it too much trouble to open the trapdoor?"

"Not at all," Jane replied as she went over and climbed the ladder pushing the trapdoor open and securing it with a hook. A wave of cool air came down at them. Turning to Mary she said, "Light the wick lamp and bring it up. I'll show you the loft."

Mary carefully climbed the ladder-like stairs with lamp in hand, handing it to Jane when she reached the top. Although the rafters glistened with frost, it was not unduly cold and they could feel some warmth radiating from the stovepipe on the far side.

Noticing Ethan's old pallet on the floor Mary mused, "Maybe I should sleep up here instead of on your couch. That was my idea."

"If you like lying on a pallet," Jane replied.

"Sure, I was wondering if you had anything you could use for a bed up here. It's more private for me, and you won't have to worry about disturbing me when you get up in the morning."

Just then they heard Ethan come in, stamping the snow off his feet. He watched them emerge from the loft as he undid his outerwear.

"You forgot the trapdoor," he said when both women were back downstairs.

"Mary wants to sleep up there," Jane said.

"This time of year she's nuts," Ethan said gruffly.

"It's quite nice up there," Mary replied. "Once the house warms up it'll be quite toasty."

"Yer still nuts," Ethan said.

"Go see for yourself," Jane added.

Ethan climbed the ladder to the loft without a lamp and as he walked around they could hear him mumbling in agreement.

As he came back down Mary continued, "It will give both of us more privacy."

"Besides, what better way to find out if the loft will be suitable for Robbie than to have an adult test it out on a cold winter night?" Jane added.

"Okay, okay do whatever," Ethan sighed. "I suppose you'll want my lantern?"

"Or the wick lamp," Jane added.

"Nah, the lantern's safer. If yer still snorin' when I go out for chores in the morning, I'll just go up and get it. There'll be a light on downstairs by that time anyway."

"You do that, Ethan. I'll probably make my bed near the trapdoor."

With that, Mary and Jane both went upstairs to make Mary's bed on the pallet using the lantern for light, while Ethan checked the fire. Once back downstairs, Jane put the kettle on for tea, put Robbie properly to bed, and then served everyone a cup of tea before turning in. Jane took out the small present she got from Santa, handled it for a moment and finally said, "No, I'll put it under the tree and open it with the rest on Christmas morning."

"Good idea, I'll do the same," Mary said in agreement.

The loft was cool the following morning when Mary awakened. The layer of frost on the roof boards and rafters was thicker than ever. Though her face was cool the floor was warm as its plaster coating, as Jane had said, was a good heat retainer. She was glad that she was beside the trapdoor though, as a wave of heat was emanating from below. She noticed that the light was on, and she could hear the muffled voices of Ethan and Jane talking. She heard a door open and close then silence.

"Jane," she called down leaning over the edge of the hatchway.

"Yes Mary," Jane replied, coming to the foot of the stairs.

"Has Ethan gone out?"

"Yes, he went to do chores."

"Good, I'll come down to get dressed then."

"Is it cold up there?"

"It's warm under the covers but cool on my face."

"It's nice and warm by the stove. Come on down. The coffee is on."

Mary braved the chill when she flipped off her covers. She slipped on her slippers, grabbed her clothes, and quickly came down stairs. Jane slipped the inside bolt on the door lest Ethan suddenly barge in on them while Mary was dressing.

"Ah, this feels good." Mary stood by the cook stove absorbing the heat. Sniffing the air she said, "Smells good too." The coffee was starting to boil with its warm aroma filling the air as was that of the oatmeal in the pot.

"Did you guys eat?" Mary asked.

"No, we generally don't have breakfast till after the milking," Jane replied.

"So this is the day before Christmas," Mary said as she

looked around the room. "Where is your tree?"

"Ethan will get us one right after chores and once it is light out. Our big project of the day will be decorating it."

"Sounds like fun."

Just then Robbie emerged from the bedroom still holding his teddy bear.

"Good morning Robbie," Mary smiled.

"Santa come tonight?" Robbie asked as Jane picked him up.

"Yes, this is the night."

"Daddy get Christmas tree?"

"Yes, he'll get one after the sun comes up."

"What do you want for Christmas, Robbie?" Mary asked.

"I want rocking horse and train."

"Ooh, if you have been a good boy maybe Santa will bring them," Mary said with a warm smile.

"Would you like a cup of coffee before breakfast?" Jane offered. "It'll be another half hour before Ethan gets back from milking."

"Sounds good," Mary replied. "That'll finish warming me up." She sat down on one of the chairs. Jane poured her coffee and then stirred the fire and put in a couple of lumps of coal.

After a time, they heard the stamping of feet outside the door. A wave of cold air swept in as the door opened, and Ethan stepped in carrying two pails of milk. They were balanced at either end of a notched pole across one shoulder so he could carry his lantern with his other hand. He was covered with snow.

"I guess it's snowing out," Mary said.

"Snowing out!" Ethan exclaimed. "It is falling so thick that I could barely find the barn."

"Daddy a snowman," Robbie said observing his snow covered father.

"Yeah, Daddy's a snowman," Ethan laughed as he began

to peel off his outerwear to hang it on a peg by the door. Ethan stepped out into the tiny porch lean-to outside the door and turned off his lantern.

"Umm, that coffee smells good," he said as he settled into his chair by the table. Robbie came over and climbed onto his knee. "Gonna get Christmas tree, Daddy?"

"When the sun comes up and the chores are all done." Ethan smiled as he bounced Robbie on his knee.

"Now if I would have asked him, he would have grumbled about it," Jane laughed, glancing at Mary as she poured coffee for Ethan. Ethan ignored the comment and continued playing with his son while Mary only smiled.

"Well come and get it," Jane said as she stirred the pot of oatmeal on the stove. "The porridge is ready."

As daylight slowly crept through the windows, Jane opened the curtains and all they could see was a mass of large falling snowflakes gently coming down.

"Good thing you're already here," Ethan said to Mary. "Today wouldn't be a good day to be travelling. I could get lost and miss my road."

"You won't be checking your traps then either," Jane added.

"No way, I'd get lost in the bush for sure." Ethan replied.

"I hope you can find your way far enough to get us a tree for the house," Jane said with a slightly worried tone.

"Yeah, there's lots of young spruce around the clearing to the east of the house. I should be able to get that far without getting lost. I'll take care of it after I feed the pigs and chickens."

It was just before noon when Ethan brought the tree in and affixed a stand to hold it up. It was placed in the corner under the stairs and Jane and Mary had an enjoyable afternoon decorating it. They used the leftover decorations from the school tree and manufactured a few more of their own. Jane put on some popcorn, some of which was for eating and the rest for popcorn strings. Ethan, who stayed indoors due to the snowfall, kept Robbie out of Mary and Jane's way while they ate a generous share of popcorn smothered in butter.

Jane handed him a spool of thread with a needle sticking out of it saying, "Why don't you pull off a long piece of thread and put it through the needle, and make some popcorn strings for the tree."

Ethan grumbled indistinctly as he threaded the needle and fed it through the individual pieces of popcorn, muttering, "Seems like a waste of popcorn."

"But it looks good for the tree," Jane replied.

"Daddy want more popcorn," Robbie said as he handed Ethan a handful of popcorn with his tiny hand.

"See even Robbie wants you to make strings," Jane laughed.

"Daddy make strings," Robbie mimicked.

"Oh, all right," Ethan grumbled as he carried on with Robbie getting him the popcorn.

As the afternoon wore on and the snowfall let up allowing the low December sun to shine, Ethan excused himself to do chores. "Looks like the wood box is getting empty," he muttered as he got up.

"Thanks dear," Jane said as he handed her the string. "It's about long enough."

When he brought in a pail of coal, Jane was putting on her coat. "Where are you going?" he asked.

"I thought I'd go out to the root cellar to get some things for tomorrow's dinner," Jane replied. "Want to come along and help?"

"I could a done that," Ethan said. "I'm doin' all the outside stuff anyway."

"I need the fresh air," Jane said with a wink then added, "you can light and hold the lantern for me as it will be dark in there."

"Oh, all right." Ethan grumbled as he lifted down the

lantern from its hook in the lean-to by the door.

"Robbie and I will finish the tree," Mary said cheerily.

Ethan held the lantern as they entered the dark dugout. They walked past the front part of the root cellar that was partially above ground, where the meat hung in a frozen state. This included the turkey they got from Wolf.

"We'll have to take that turkey back in with us so it will thaw out in time for tomorrow morning," Jane said.

"Yes dear," Ethan replied.

Deeper within the root cellar through the second door was the cellar where the temperature stayed just above freezing for most of the year, they kept the root crops and preserves. The former was buried in sand and moss while the latter was on low shelves.

As they gathered stuff for tomorrow's feast, Ethan said, "Does Mary know you invited Sean for dinner tomorrow?"

"No, I left that as a surprise. Although he knows that she is here."

"Those busy-body inspectors ruined a perfectly good courtship," Ethan added.

"Sometime after dinner tomorrow we'll have to find a reason to get out of the house for a bit so they can talk," Jane stated.

"Yeah, I'll try to think of somethun," Ethan replied.

Chapter Thirteen

The snow stopped falling in the night and they awoke to a glorious Christmas morning of bright sunshine. When Ethan returned from chores the gifts were opened. Robbie received a hand-made rocking horse and a set of building blocks from his parents. These gifts, addressed from Santa, kept Robbie amused for much of the remainder of the day and he spent most of his time playing on the bearskin rug in front of the couch. Mary gave him a toy train consisting of the engine and two cars also made from wood.

Ethan gave Jane a leather covered diary. "Thank you dear," she gasped upon handling the leather covered book with its rich creamy pages. Along with the diary was another small package. Jane opened it. "A fountain pen, I've always wanted one of them. Look Ethan, you can load this pen with ink and not have to keep dipping it all the time or change the nib."

"I know you probably got lots of pages left in yer diary," Ethan said, "but I thought yuh might want somethun for recording stuff at yer school. I seen these pens in the catalogue and they looked a lot less messy than a straight pen," Ethan added modestly.

"I was thinking of having a diary just for school records, but a fountain pen...! Thank you dear," Jane beamed, "I'll have a record of this year's events at school no matter what may happen to my teaching career in the long run." She grabbed Ethan and planted a big mushy kiss on his lips.

"Don't you worry none," Ethan assured her, "there ain't nothing goin' to stop you from teachin' at that school for as long a you want."

"I wish I had his confidence," Jane said to Mary.

"Don't you worry neither," Ethan said to Mary. "You have

a right to live your own life and be courted by whoever you choose. It's that superintendent that needs to be educated."

"Here's my gift to you, Jane," Mary said handing her a modest sized present. "We'll deal with tomorrow when tomorrow comes." Jane eagerly opened the present from Mary and let out a gasp. "A Collection of Great Poetry!" As she quickly thumbed through the pages, she said in a breathless tone. "It has the poems of Shelley, Keats and other famous poets. Oh wonderful, I love poetry as do some of my students. I'll take this to school and read from it to my class." She read the opening lines from *The Highway Man* and said, "We'll definitely discuss this one first thing in the new year."

Ethan and Mary both grinned broadly at Jane's ecstatic reaction to the gift.

"Oh Mary, what a dear, dear friend you are." She grabbed Mary and hugged her fiercely.

"You've given me so much in the way of friendship," Mary replied modestly. "It's only fair I give some of it back. I knew the poetry was something that you'd enjoy personally and would share with your class." Turning to Ethan she said, "And I have something for you."

He opened the small present she handed him and held up a new smoking pipe and a packet of tobacco. "Thanks Mary, I needed a new pipe."

"And for you my dear," Jane smiled, handing Ethan a large, soft present. "I made it myself."

Ethan eagerly opened the present and held up a colourful hand-knitted sweater. "You made this?" he gasped, "but when?"

"I worked on it at times when you were out on your trap line or at school during lunch hour and during silent learning sessions. I even taught Helen and Lydia a few stitches."

"This is too good to wear around here for chores. I'll put it on for Christmas dinner and other special occasions." He said to Mary, "There is just no end to this woman's talents."

122

"I know, Ethan," Mary grinned, "believe me I know."

Mary received her own diary and fountain pen, wrapped together as a joint present from the Phillips'. She hugged them both in appreciation.

"Now let's see what Santa gave us from the concert," Jane said anxiously as she lifted the two small presents from their places on the boughs of the tree and handed Mary her gift. They eagerly tore them open and found that they had received identical presents, a small box with a single row of chocolate covered wafers.

"At least Santa thinks of the women," Ethan said in his usual grumpy voice.

"He was probably thinking of both of us as he knows we'll share," Jane replied and grinned. "Here dear, have the first one." She held the opened box out to him.

"Have one of mine too," Mary teased, holding out her box as well.

Ethan was left momentarily speechless, and Robbie toddled over. Noticing that treats were being offered he asked innocently, "Can I have a cookie?"

"Have one of mine." Mary offered holding her box down to him. As Robbie took one of Mary's wafers, Ethan took one of Jane's.

Finally, Jane said, "Let's put them altogether in a bowl." She stepped over to the kitchen cupboard to retrieve one.

It was just after noon and the turkey was simmering in the oven when they noticed another figure go by the window swaddled in winter clothing and walking on snowshoes. They heard stamping in the porch and when Ethan answered the knock on the door, it was Sean. Mary looked at Jane in surprise and apprehension as if to say, "Did you invite him to Christmas dinner as well?"

Sean looked around with a wink and a grin, his elfin features red from the cold. "Well, Merry Christmas to ye all."

Jane and Ethan repeated the greeting, but Mary only

smiled.

"I see ye come to spend Christmas a way out in the bush," Sean said to Mary as he unbuttoned his coat.

"I'm staying for a few days," Mary replied nonchalantly.

After hanging his coat, he said with a smile, "It's a wee bit roomier in here since Ethan fixed the place up."

"Quite cozy actually," Mary replied.

Sean reached into his coat pocket and presented Jane with a small box containing four delicate wine glasses. "This is for the lady of the house for invintin' me to partake in her Christmas dinner." Jane was about to ask what the glasses were for, but Robbie toddled over and looked at Sean expectantly who winked at the toddler saying, "And I've not forgotten the wee man of the house." Sean presented Robbie with a jack-in-the-box.

"Thank you, Mr. Malley," Robbie said as he turned to take his newest toy to the bearskin rug.

The toddler was first startled by the character that popped out of the box, but soon found it amusing and would find particular delight in having Jack pop out right in the faces of the various adults laughing at their reaction.

Jane was about to ask again about the glasses when Sean pulled out a bottle of homemade wine causing looks of consternation from both Jane and Mary. "Don't worry, I didn't make it. I got it from Velma to grace yer Christmas table."

"Now I know why you brought the glasses," Jane said wryly.

"It wouldn't be a proper Christmas dinner without a glass of wine," Sean grinned.

"I suppose not," Jane sighed. As she and Mary set the table, they put one of the glasses in front of each adult setting.

"If I could a got a bottle of whiskey, I would a had a drink for us after dinner," Ethan said to Sean with a grin.

"Oh, brother," Jane groaned.

"Men!" Mary added.

Noticing the sweater Ethan had put on for dinner, Sean remarked, "A fine lookin' sweater you got there Ethan."

"From my many talented wife," Ethan grinned.

"Why am I not surprised that she could knit a sweater like that," Sean replied with a grin.

With the table set, Jane called for everyone to be seated. The four of them, along with Robbie, sat down to a scrumptious Christmas dinner of turkey, potatoes and a carrot pea mixture served in a white sauce. Ethan carved the turkey while Sean poured wine for the adults. Jane was about to say no, but Sean grinned and said, "Surely you'll be wantin' to make a toast for Christmas."

"But I...," Jane faltered.

"Don't be givin' me that temperance nonsense," Sean grinned. "I know ye better than that Jane Phillips. I've seen ye have a wee nip of wine a time or two in the time I've known you."

"During the time that Sean tried to court me," Jane said with a crooked grin, "he was always trying to feed me wine."

"And ye sampled it and it didn't kill you, did it now," Sean laughed.

"You men always seem to need alcohol to have a good time," Mary added.

"I always said a drink or two never hurt anybody," Ethan rasped as he finished carving the turkey.

When Sean proposed a toast to the feast and to Jane for providing it, all raised their glasses and watched Jane take a sip and grimace. They then tucked in and devoured the succulent meal with many quiet sounds expressing culinary pleasure.

After they devoured her blueberry pie, which was smothered in whipped cream, Sean pushed back his chair and said with a grin, "Now that's a meal worth wadin' two miles through the snow. I think I'll need a wee rest before tryin' to go back."

"Amen to that," Mary said.

"Yes dear, once again you've shown everybody that yer one hell of a cook." Ethan added.

"You men go sit on the couch while Mary and I clean up and get the kettle boiling for tea," Jane suggested.

"Tea!" Ethan exclaimed. "We got this." He picked up the wine bottle and his glass as he and Sean got up, "Unless you ladies would like another nip."

"No thanks for me," Mary said brusquely, "one drink at the meal was plenty."

"Since you men seem to need a drink so badly, you might as well finish it off," Jane scoffed.

"We'll let you women be the tea totters." Ethan grinned as he poured another glassful for both Sean and himself.

Jane shot a dark look at him but made no comment. When Ethan and Sean retired to the couch to settle their meal, Ethan pulled out his new pipe and lit it and the cabin was filled with the odour of his scented tobacco.

When the women came to join them Ethan moved tight to one end, but Mary tried to insist that Jane sit on the couch between Ethan and Sean. Ethan got up to allow both women to sit, and Jane made sure she took his place obliging Mary to sit between Ethan and Sean. The four of them visited for a time and then Jane said abruptly, putting her hand on her forehead and contorting her face, "I'm getting a splitting headache. I should go lie down a while." She struggled to her feet as she held her head. Mary was about to help her, but Ethan moved first.

"Here, let me help you to your bed," Ethan said, taking her arm.

When he got her to the bed, she smiled and said, "I really could use a lie down, so I'll stay in here a while so they can talk."

"Matchmaker," Ethan grinned. "Yeah, I'll need to go out and get some more wood and coal, and maybe check the animals."

Ethan came back to join the others and repacked his pipe. While lighting it, he commented, "I think the strain of Jane makin' her first big Christmas dinner must a caught up to her." Sean and Mary both agreed.

After he finished his pipe and banged it out into a tin can that served as ashtray, Ethan announced, "I need to fetch in some more coal and wood, and I should check on the critters in the barn. If I could ask you two to keep an eye on Robbie for a bit."

"No problem," Mary assured him. "I'll even have some fresh hot coffee on for when you come back in."

"That's a good idea," Ethan said buttoning up his parka.

"Is there any way I can give ye hand there, Ethan?" Sean asked as he was about to get up.

"Nah, I can handle it. You can help Mary keep an eye on Robbie," Ethan replied as he opened the door and stepped out.

Sean finished his drink and set down his glass, turning to Mary. "Well Mary McKay, have ye been thinking things over?"

"What things?" Mary said flatly.

"About us," Sean replied carefully. "We were courtin' until all those busy-bodies stuck their noses into it."

"I'm thinking about it," Mary replied.

"Surely he can't be firin' you for seein' me when I'm not guilty of any crime?"

"You were making moonshine and that's against the law," Mary said flatly.

"I quit the business as ye well know. It was gettin' a little hot for me. It is not me intent to be goin' to jail."

"How do I know you won't start up again once you're sure the heat is off?" Mary asked. "Even if you are never caught, I don't want to be courted by a man who is breaking the law."

"That's why I took an honest job at the sawmill. I did it

for you as much as to keep meself out of jail."

"Have you still got your distilling equipment stashed away somewhere?"

"I'll be givin' it to Ivan Malov in the spring when the muskeg thaws out."

"Is he taking over as the moonshine provider for this area?" Mary said tersely.

"He wants to make it mainly for himself with maybe a wee bit for close friends or neighbours. As ye may well know, Russians are fond of their vodka and moonshine is homemade vodka," Sean said in a matter-of-fact tone.

"Well then, Sean O'Malley, as long as the distilling equipment is still in your possession, I can't be seen courting you. You could still be caught and I'd be out of both a beau and a job."

"It is stashed off me property in a place where no one can find it," Sean said with an almost pleading voice.

"Well, as long as you have it the courtship is suspended. When you can demonstrate that your equipment is in Ivan's hands and that your next year's potato crop is grown entirely for legitimate purposes, you can ask for my hand in courtship. I am sorry Sean, but that's the way it has to be."

"So, there will be no sleigh rides or winter dances then?" Sean said with doleful expression.

"I'm afraid not. If our paths cross in public as it was with the concert or in private as it was today, we can be cordial and even pleasant to each other. But please, when you see me on the streets of Grimstad treat me as a casual acquaintance."

"That bugger must have really put the fear of God into ye then," Sean added.

"He did that, but that superintendent also made me come to grips with the problem of your lifestyle. You see Sean, I was never comfortable being courted by a person whose livelihood was outside the law."

"Well, I guess I can't be faultin' ye for that," Sean said with a watery-eyed smile. "I just hope you will give me a period of grace to prove I'm a changed man. For ye know Mary, I hold ye dear to me heart."

"As I am fond of you," she smiled. "Ask me again in the spring and we'll take it from there." She said as Sean stood up and offered her his hand.

Mary clasped it and pulled herself up. Then with sudden impulse she leaned forward and kissed him on the cheek. She looked Sean in the eye for a long moment then turned saying, "It feels like I should put some more coal in the fire."

"Maybe I should be helpin' Ethan. It's takin' him a good wee while to get the wood and such."

"Do you think they left us alone on purpose?" Mary grinned as she lifted a stove lid.

"I'd bet me next years praties crop on it." Sean winked. "Just like we both got invited here for Christmas."

"That's good friends for you," Mary added. "I am glad though that we had this talk."

"Me too," Sean said as he buttoned up his parka. "It put me mind a bit at ease, but it'll be a long, lonely winter."

"Well you can always hope for an early spring," Mary said with a twisted grin.

"Aye, there is that," Sean replied as he opened the door letting in an icy blast of cold air.

Mary started to prepare a pot of coffee. A short while later Jane emerged from the bedroom saying in an innocent tone, "My headache is gone down. I can face the rest of the day now."

Mary gave Jane a crooked smile thinking, *it's okay Jane, you don't have to make excuses*. As Jane looked around about to ask about Sean, Mary said, "Sean went outside to help Ethan."

"I see," Jane said carefully.

"We had a very good talk," Mary said, "and we both thank you for arranging for us to be alone."

"What are friends for?" Jane smiled. "So how did it go, if I may ask?"

"We agreed to put our courtship on hold until some issues are resolved, mainly the fate of his distilling equipment," Mary replied.

"A prudent decision, but I trust you are still fond of him?"

"Yes, very much so, but don't you dare breathe a word to him or even Ethan."

"I won't," Jane assured her. Then with a laugh she added, "This is all so much like a scenario I played out a couple of years ago. It seems you and I like to torture the men who care for us."

"It worked out for you though," Mary laughed.

"As I'm sure it will for you my dear friend," Jane replied.

Chapter Fourteen

It was a bitterly cold night in early March, and Ethan had loaded up the fire for the night letting it burn hot. Around midnight he was awakened by Fluffy and could hear a roaring sound coming from the area of the stove. It also seemed warmer than expected in the room. Quickly, he sprang out of bed and went to the main room. Not only was the roaring sound louder, but the stovepipe was glowing red hot. Outside, Spot was barking frantically trying to warn his masters of the peril they faced.

"Oh my God, a chimney fire!" he exclaimed. He raced over to the stove and turned the damper on the stovepipe fully closed. He cried out and shook his hand from touching the red hot damper handle.

Jane awoke with a foreboding that something was wrong. She too sprang out of bed and nearly collided with Ethan in the doorway of the bedroom.

"Glad you're awake," he said urgently. "We got a chimney fire. Oh ow, my hand!" It was still smarting from the burns.

"Oh no, is the house on fire?" Jane asked worriedly. Then noticing Ethan's discomfort she added, "What happened to your hand?"

"I burned it turning down the damper, but haven't got time to worry about it now. I'll have to slip outside and see if the house is burning," Ethan replied breathlessly as he hastily drew on his clothing. "Meanwhile, get yourself dressed. Bundle up Robbie and the pair of you come through to the main room in case we have to run."

Ethan turned and quickly put on his coat and winter boots before stepping outside. He withdrew the mitt from the hand that was smarting and scooped up a handful of snow to cool the burns while he investigated the exterior. Jane dressed herself and rolled Robbie up in his blanket, along with a set of his clothing, and brought him to the couch while quieting his protests about being disturbed. He quickly went back to sleep while she lit the lamp.

Meanwhile, as Ethan looked up at the stovepipe protruding through the roof, flames were roaring out the end of it as if it were a blowtorch. It generated enough light that he could see that the snow had melted from the roof in a wide area around the stovepipe while sparks and black flakes of soot rained down all around. Spot was still barking though his barks were mixed with whines as he sniffed Ethan over.

"It's okay boy," Ethan said, petting the dog with his mitt. "Everybody is safe."

He stepped back inside to update his anxiously waiting wife. "So far the roof isn't on fire," he said fretfully, "but I'll have to stay outside and watch. If I can find the ladder in the snow, I'll carry buckets of snow up there to keep the bare part of the roof wet so it won't catch. Meanwhile, be ready to head for the barn in a moment's notice."

"We're ready," Jane assured him.

"That's good," Ethan said with a fleeting grin and then sniffing the air he said, "Better check the loft."

Ethan strode over and climbed the stairs pushing the trapdoor open as he did so. The air was warm and somewhat steamy from the frost having melted from the rafters and it carried the strong odour of overheated metal. The stovepipe, running through the loft, was glowing red. He quickly went over to it and pulled away several boxes and other clutter that had gotten hot from being too close. He called out to Jane for water. She handed him up the water pail and he doused the area around the stovepipe causing a hissing sound from the water hitting the flash plate and falling through onto the stove.

When he came back down, Ethan told the anxious looking Jane, "I'll bring in a bucket of snow. Keep an eye on the upstairs. I'm going back out to check the roof and throw some more snow up there."

Ethan quickly scooped the water bucket full of snow, and reaching through the doorway he set it inside for Jane. He went back out and pulled the ladder out of the snow bank behind the house. He climbed up to where the stovepipe protruded through the roof and threw snow on the roof where it had melted using a milk bucket.

After a time the fire began to die down and the flames retreated back down inside the stovepipe and its red glow began to turn dark. Ethan came back down the ladder and watched the dying chimney fire for several minutes before coming back inside. He brought both milk buckets full of snow in with him.

"Whew, that was a close one," Ethan said as he undid his parka.

"The danger has passed then?" Jane asked anxiously.

"Yeah, there are no more flames shooting out of the chimney and the pipes ain't glowin' red anymore," Ethan replied as he stepped out of his felt boots. "I'll check the loft again, though it should be safe."

"I'll put on a cup of tea, if I dare stir up the fire."

"Yeah, you can stir it up; the stovepipe is all clean now."

"I'll be afraid to go to sleep now," Jane said, "for fear the house might burn down. What causes a chimney fire anyway?"

"We been burnin' too much black poplar lately," Ethan replied as they sat and had tea. "It's full of stuff they call creosote, it can build up in the chimney then a spark can set it off. From now on I'll try to mix the spruce with poplar."

"The coal will be safe then?" Jane asked anxiously.

As the excitement of the fire was now wearing down Ethan again became painfully aware of the burns on his hand where he had grabbed the damper. He plunged his still stinging hand into a pail full of snow letting out a great sigh of relief, then noticing Jane's look of concern he replied,

"It'll be okay when it cools down, just surface burns."

"You're going to be all right?" she worried.

"Once the snow cools my hand down, I'll be okay. It'll be sore for a while and I'll be branded, but I'll survive." He assured her and then continued, "In regards to yer earlier question, yeah, coal's safe. There must a been a piece a spruce wood that wasn't burned and it popped open. I should a cleaned the pipes last fall like I meant to."

"Is a brick chimney safer?" Jane asked.

"Yeah, a lot safer, but they can catch on fire too if they ain't cleaned," Ethan replied.

"Maybe you should install one in the spring," Jane replied.

"I thought about it, but it all depends how long we stay here before buildin' the new place. That house for sure will have a brick chimney."

"Look at Robbie, sleeping so peacefully, unaware that the house almost burned down around him." Jane said.

"Yeah, he could-a woke up in the barn if the house went up," Ethan said. "I see you were gonna make sure the fiddle and your diary didn't get burned. You sure think of everything."

"Well, they are two things that can't be replaced." Jane replied as Fluffy jumped up onto her lap. "Would it have been cold in the barn?"

"Nah, drafty maybe, but with the cows and horses kept in there overnight and the loft full of hay to hold the heat in, it is generally quite warm," Ethan replied. "I usually have to take my parka off when I milk cows." Then looking at the cat purring on Jane's lap he added, "It was Fluffy that woke me yuh know," Ethan said. "Animals seem to have a sixth sense about danger, especially when we are snorin' away."

Jane cuddled Fluffy praising her for being such a good cat. Then she added, "So is that why Spot was barking so much?"

"Yeah, he was also tryin' to warn us of the danger."

Ethan got up and stirred the fire, putting in a couple

lumps of coal. Satisfied that all was in order he suggested with a yawn, "Well, everythun is under control now so we might as well go back to bed and catch the rest of our sleep." Although Jane noticed that he winced when he withdrew his hand from the snow in the pail.

On a bright clear morning two weeks later, when Ethan started out in the cutter taking Jane to school, they had both commented on how spring was just around the corner. As they approached the school; however, Ethan noticed a change in the sky.

"Somethun's gonna happen with the weather soon," he said pointing at the sky. A storm front was sharply dividing the sky into the clear eastern half and a dark cloudy western half. "It's gonna storm soon."

"Do you think anyone will send their kids?" Jane wondered.

"Dunno. I'll just be at the mill, so if nobody comes you can come there and I'll take time to drive yuh home."

"Sounds good," Jane replied as she and Robbie climbed out of the cutter.

All nine pupils came to school that morning, though some of the other parents had reservations about the weather. Jane assured them that they could take their children home early if they sky looked too threatening.

By mid-morning the sky had turned dark with a massive cloud cover, and by noon a brisk wind had picked up, blowing up sheets of snow causing a near white-out. Only the older boys ventured outside for noon break and they soon came back in although Jane managed to persuade them to fill the coal buckets first. The wind was so ferocious by the start of afternoon class that it seemed to make the school shudder and the drafts made it colder in spite of the blazing fire in the heater. Jane had everyone move their desks closer to the heater for warmth, while she sat on a chair by the side blackboard with a lesson plan in her hand. About midway between noon break and recess the door opened letting a blast of swirling snow in and this created a dramatic increase in the sound of the howling wind. Ethan stumbled in and quickly closed the door behind him. His face was beet red. Jane looked at him in surprise and he explained, "The sawmill shut down on account of the weather. I hope yuh don't mind an extra student this afternoon. No use goin' home then turn around and come back in this blizzard."

"Glad you're here," Jane said. "You can keep the coal bucket full and the heater blazing. It's cool in here."

"Yes ma'am," he replied, "as soon as I put the horses in the school barn out of the weather."

By the end of afternoon recess, the sky was quite dark from the ongoing storm and the howling wind seemed more threatening than usual. Ethan filled the school lamps with coal oil and lit them.

"Are we gonna have to stay here all night?" Helen worried. "I don't want to walk home in this."

"Oh, the storm will pass," Jane assured her. "Nobody will send you home in this blizzard. I won't leave this school until I am sure all of you have a ride home. Meanwhile, I'll put some water on and make you all a nice cup of cocoa."

"Too bad yuh didn't have coffee," Ethan grumbled.

Ivan Malov arrived with his team and bobsled, and pulled up along the east side of the school to keep his horses out of the wind. He stumbled into the school half frozen with the edges of his parka hood and his beard covered in ice from his breath. "Just like wedder in Roshya," he said stretching his hands over the heater, "I vait for storm and geeve ride to da Gogowicz cheeldren as well."

Jane smiled and said, "I made some cocoa."

"Sounds like good idea," he replied as he opened his parka and flipped back the hood, though he kept his sheepskin hat on. Jane ladled him a cup of cocoa. The icicle on his beard began to melt enough to fall off.

"Mr. Malov looks like Jack Frost," Willy observed.

"A fellah needs them whiskers in this weather," Ethan remarked in reference to Ivan's beard.

"It don't help much in dis wedder, son-of-a-bitch," he replied. Then noticing Jane scowling at his use of the expletive in front of the children, he added, "Sorry, forgot kids have big ears."

Jane gave him a fleeting smile, realizing his relative unfamiliarity with the English language sometimes caused him to say things out-of-line unintentionally.

"Will you be able to find your way home in this weather?" Ethan asked.

"It's not bad on a bush trail, but in open by da fields blow like son-of-a..." he caught himself this time and Jane smiled. "I vait a bit and see eef vind go down."

"Good idea," Ethan said.

"We better go soon before it geets darker," Ivan said after finishing his cocoa. "You too," he indicated to the Gogowicz children. "I geeve ride."

"But it's our turn to be monitors," Lydia protested.

"Don't worry about that," Jane assured her. "It's more important that you go home now with Mr. Malov." Then turning to Ivan she asked in a concerned tone, "Are you sure the children will be warm enough out in that weather?"

"Oh ya, I put plenty straw in da sleigh and a blanket so da kids can cuddle down. It will be me dat freezes," Ivan assured her.

"Driving into the wind on the way back, is that a good idea?" Ethan wondered out loud. "You'll freeze to death for sure."

Ivan was about to leave when Dave arrived. He entered the schoolhouse stamping his feet. He was carrying a big soup kettle. "Bloody awful weather to be out in, is it not?" he remarked as he set the kettle on the heater. Then looking at Ethan he continued, "I say Ethan, have you been here all day? I see your horses are in the barn."

"The mill shut down earlier so I came over here," Ethan replied. "No use letting the horses freeze when there is shelter."

"What's in the pot?" Jane asked.

"Soup, Sari made a big pot of ham and pea soup in case we got stuck at the school."

"That was very thoughtful of her. There's still a little cocoa left, Dave," Jane offered as Dave opened his parka to allow the heat in and pulled off his mittens to warm his hands.

"Cocoa! I brought some tea," Dave replied. He nonetheless, took the cup of cocoa saying, "This will warm my hands and insides while the kettle boils." Holding his cup in one hand he fished a small packet of tea out of his pocket, while Jane put the kettle on the heater.

"You haven't seen Wolf along the way have you?" Ethan asked in a worried tone.

"Actually, I was about to tell you. I will be taking their children home too. Hella had the good sense to realise that Robbie shouldn't be out in this weather so she'll keep him for the night."

"Smart thinking on her part," Jane said with relief. "I wouldn't want him out in this storm either."

"We'll miss the little tyke though," Ethan rumbled.

"Just think, the two of you all alone in that cabin on a stormy winter night, no telling what you could get up to," Dave said with a wink.

Jane flushed with embarrassment, while Ethan grinned wryly.

"Well, children," Dave said, "We're going to stay for a cup of soup and see if this wind will die down before heading out. That goes for your lot too Ivan."

"I got cows to milk," Ivan said.

"So do I, but they're all safe and warm in the barn." Dave replied.

"*Da* mine too, put dem dare just before leaving."

"Wish mine were," Ethan said in a small voice. "But they should be okay standing by the side of the barn away from the wind."

"Then do please stay," Jane said. "The soup is nearly ready and it is all ready dark."

"I'll erase your blackboard then," Lydia said.

"And I'll clean the brush," Helen offered even though it was not her turn to monitor.

"Want me to get coal Mrs. Phillips?" Lech offered.

"No, there are enough adults here to take care of that." Jane smiled.

They all sat down to enjoy their cup of soup and tea and by the time they were finished it seemed the wind wasn't howling quite so badly. Ethan got up and looked out, observing, "The wind is dying down."

Ivan and Dave also looked out through the doorway and could see the moon trying to shine through a thin veil of cloud as the blizzard had passed though it was still bitterly cold.

"I tink ve can be going now," Ivan said.

"Yeah, it's calm enough to take our chances, but it'll still be a bloody cold ride."

"Will there be school tomorrow, Mrs. Phillips?" Thomas asked.

"It depends on the weather," Jane replied addressing them all. "If there is a blizzard blowing, or if it is too cold there won't be. Your dad will know whether it is safe to bring you to school or not."

As the children put on their outerwear, Jane fussed over them to make sure everything was buttoned up properly and their mittens securely in place.

"Goodnight Mrs. Phillips," they all called as they went out the door into the bitter cold.

With the last of the children gone the school held a ringing silence. Jane began mopping up around the heater where the snow had melted from both Ivan and Dave's clothing.

"I'll go hitch up the team so we can head home to our cold, quiet house," Ethan remarked also noticing the sudden silence.

"I'll load up the heater and shut everything down in here," Jane replied as she moved to do the tasks.

Soon they were off with the horses, ploughing through snowdrifts in the bitter cold. The frozen landscape had a strange beauty of its own with the snow sparkling in the moonlight and the snow hanging from the spruce trees making their great boughs sag considerably. Jane paid scant attention to the frozen beauty, as the frost nipped at her nose and her cheeks felt papery from the threat of encroaching frostbite while she constantly worked her toes to try to keep her feet warm. They arrived home to a frozen house and had to shovel a snow drift away from the front of the doorway to get the door open. Jane soon had a roaring fire blazing in the stove and could almost hear the groan of relief from the house as the heat began to reach the frosty walls. She was too cold to worry whether or not the roaring inferno within the stove would trigger another chimney fire. She was glad she didn't have to bring little Robbie home to this cold. Although the house felt empty without Robbie, she knew he was warm and safe with the care of Hella.

Chapter Fifteen

Spring had come. By early April the snow was fast melting turning the trails to mud. Every low spot was full of water, and the evening air was filled with the mating calls of innumerable frogs and toads. Ethan had felled some logs on the home quarter and was now dragging them to the mill for sawing. With his share of the lumber cut from logs on both quarters, he could build a new house and start relocating to the school quarter. This move would please Jane. She would get a better and bigger house and be less than a half mile from the school, within easy walking distance even in bad weather.

Spring also brought the return of the Goon Squad. Alan Bates was going to make one last attempt to catch Sean O'Malley as there were still rumours of moonshine being available in the area. The total non-cooperation and often outright hostility to his efforts among the people of Grimstad did not deter him. Alan Bates was also unaware that Sean had quit making homebrew.

The Goon Squad didn't bother with any searches within the village, but went straight to Sean's place armed with a warrant that declared they had reasonable suspicion that he was producing and distributing illegal spirits. Sean was away at the mill working when they arrived and since he never locked his cabin door, they had an easy time of scouring his property but were unable to find more than a few empty liquor bottles. As they sat eating their lunch in their car, which was parked in Sean's yard, his first deputy Arnold Watkins recommended that they go home or to look elsewhere as there was no evidence of a still.

"Maybe we scared him off and he went out of business," the second deputy Jesse Jones suggested.

"Yeah," Alan sighed reluctantly. Then something occurred to him. "Wasn't there a well travelled trail going over the hill past that shack where he probably had his still? It seemed to head toward the northeast."

"We walked part of that trail," Arnold said, "until we came to a slough that cuts it off. No evidence of anything out there."

"Maybe in dryer weather you can go further and his still might be way back in the bush," Alan mused. "I'm positive he had a still in that building he called the guest house but moved it before we got there last fall. We should have followed the trail all the way then."

"We could still walk it, just skirt around the slough and pick up on the trail on the other side," Arnold said eagerly. "We all brought rubber boots."

"Good idea, I'll just drive the car over the hill so he won't see it if he comes home before we're done," Alan said as he started up the car.

They drove along the trail for about a half a mile before coming to the slough. They then continued on foot, wearing their rubber boots and wading through puddles and streams left from the spring thaw. Jesse carried a shovel in case Sean had buried the evidence of his stash or operation while Alan and Arnold each carried sacks to collect potential evidence. They were encouraged to see that the trail was well used. Sean almost always used it when he went over to Ethan's place, even driving his car right up to Ethan's fence in dry weather. Ethan even used it on occasion as it was the shorter route to Grimstad.

The Goon Squad slogged on. At every ridge they scoured, sometimes with binoculars, for any evidence of an old shack or such structure that would allow for a still, but came to no avail. Finally, they came to the ridge overlooking Dead Man's Muskeg.

"There's a good place to hide a still," Alan observed as he looked over the muskeg that consisted of a dense growth of swamp spruce surrounded by sprawling willow tangles. "Let's keep walking and look for any evidence of a trail going down into there. It may not be the ideal place for a still, but it would be excellent for stashing the hooch."

They heard a cow bawling in the distance. "We must be near another homestead," Jesse commented. Trudging on they came to a trail of sorts leading down to the muskeg and following it, they came to the partial skeletal remains of a horse just outside the willow tangles. Beyond that were fresh human footprints and some broken willow to suggest recent passage. Feeling hot on the trail, they ventured into the muskeg through dense thickets and scattered dead and broken spruce trees, some standing, some fallen over, making walking exceedingly difficult. The whole place was dark and forbidding with tall spindly trees and weirdly shaped dead trees that both stood and fell over. They found an open area where the moss had been recently upturned.

"Someone dug something up," Arnold observed.

"I'll bet he hid the still here when the heat was on and now that spring is here he moved it out to set up business again," Arnold observed.

"Looks like it," Alan replied.

"Look over here!" Jesse exclaimed. "There's a crude-looking cross marking a spot."

The others quickly went over to where Jesse was standing and Arnold said, "Maybe a marker for a stash."

"Dig it up and see," Alan said.

Jesse started digging in the wet moss and soon struck something hard. Exposing the hard object he let out a cry. The others looked and Alan cried, "Oh my God, it's a human skull."

"With a bullet hole in it!" Arnold exclaimed seeing a small round hole in the forehead.

Being squeamish about the whole thing, Jesse turned and moved away. "We should get out of here," he trembled. "If this is how they get rid of people like us for investigating to closely…"

"Nonsense," Alan said. "There is a murder mystery here, and that might help us get a warrant to turn this whole area upside down. Let's go back and report this to the RCMP."

They emerged quickly from the muskeg and looking up the hill from whence they had came, Alan studied the rough trail as it headed north along the hill from the muskeg. "It looks like it has been used recently all right." They heard a cow bawl again and Alan added, "There is a farm near here, lets follow it there."

They soon came to Ethan's fence and they could see a clearing ahead. "See the rails," the commissioner said, they're not nailed to the posts but held with wire so they can be removed like a gate."

"Ah, the plot thickens," Arnold grinned.

They went through the fence and came out at Jane's garden patch. It was a large area of bare ground with a pea vine net running up the middle. There was evidence of last year's rhubarb and horseradish growth near the base of the hill. From their hilltop position they could see the whole of Ethan's farmstead and all its various buildings.

"There's a good place for a still," Jesse said, pointing to Ethan's smoke house which was half hidden in the poplars at the base of the hill below the house.

"Yeah," Alan said. "I think we ought to check it out."

"Think anybody's home?" Arnold asked. "If we go sneaking around we're liable to get shot. It happened before."

"Yeah, I don't wanna join that other corpse in the muskeg," Jesse fretted.

"You have a point there," Alan said scratching his head.

"We should go back and look for the road into here," Arnold suggested. "It should be the next lead-off trail to the east from the main road."

"That would be more legitimate, and if this homestead owner resists our search requests we can back away quietly then tell the Mounties everything. They'll crawl all over this area looking for evidence regarding that skull we dug up with the bullet hole in it."

They trudged their way back to the car at Sean's place and upon checking the area map they discovered the farm belonged to Ethan Phillips and that he also owned another quarter next to the main road. They breathed easily when they were back on the main road without having encountered Sean. They went up the main road to the next trail heading east. They turned in and soon came upon the school.

"I didn't know they had a school way out here," Alan remarked.

"Wait a minute," Arnold said. "My brother-in-law is the school superintendent for this area. He asked me to keep an eye out for an unsanctioned school run by an untrained teacher. I think he said it was called Opportunity School."

"Let's check it out," Alan said. "After all, in our business we leave no stone unturned."

They drove up to the school and barely had time to read the hand-carved sign that said Opportunity School before the door opened and Jane stepped out closing the door behind her. She had seen the car pull up and was braced for a possible confrontation with the superintendent. It was the last segment of the day and she had her students do silent reading while she went out to meet their guests.

"May I help you gentlemen?" Jane asked in a flat tone.

"I'm Alan Bates, the commissioner for investigating the illegal production and distribution of homemade spirits," Alan smiled.

"You!" She exclaimed, suddenly recognising him from the incident at the store the previous autumn. "What do you want with my school?"

"We check everywhere for moonshine," he smiled artificially.

"She's from that time at the Grimstad store," Arnold said.

"I helped block a doorway to where you had no business then and I'm doing it again," Jane said defiantly.

145

"Feisty isn't she?" Jesse said.

"My dear lady, we can search anywhere we want if we suspect anyone hiding moonshine." Alan said smugly.

"This is a school not a distillery," Jane said ever tersely. "It'll be over my dead body that you'll go barging in there upsetting my class. Now, I'll thank you to get off the school grounds. You're on private property and you're trespassing," she turned and went back inside slamming the door behind her.

"Do you wanna go in there and search?" Arnold laughed.

"Not when school's still in," Alan replied. "We've already earned the enmity of the people around here with our work. If we barge in there and upset all those kids the manure will really hit the fan. Let's follow this trail and see if it leads to that farmstead we saw." Then with a glint in his eye Alan said, "So this is that illegal school with the untrained teacher. Interesting, we may be able to use this to our advantage."

"I don't think I want to mess with her anyway," Jessie added. "She looks pretty formidable."

They went up the trail past the sawmill for another mile when they met Ethan with his team that was pulling two large long saw logs. He was standing on the logs holding the reins. His Winchester was slung across his shoulder and he stopped directly in front of them. He recognised the commissioner when he stepped from his car and walked right up to him, scowling.

"What are you doin' way out here," Ethan growled.

"I recognise you from somewhere," Alan said with a knitted brow.

"I recognise you and we don't take kindly to Goon Squads pokin' around where they got no business."

"Are you Ethan Phillips?" Alan asked undaunted.

"What if I am?" Ethan growled.

"We'd like to search your place for evidence of moonshine production."

"You got a warrant?"

"We have wide powers of search and seizure," Alan said ever smugly.

"I don't care what you got, you ain't comin' on my place without a warrant and a Mountie and that's a fact," Ethan rumbled.

"Is your place the only one at the end of this trail?" Alan asked.

"What if it is?" Ethan said truculently.

"We were already there," Arnold sneered.

"What!" Ethan cried. He made a movement that suggested he was about to unsling his rifle. The deputies stepped back with frightened looks in their eyes.

"We followed a trail from that Irishman's place back to yours and one from the muskeg south of you. We decided; however, to seek permission before searching your place."

"What the hell you doin' way back in the bush?"

"Looking for a still, and we see strong evidence of one around here somewhere. Why is there a well-worn trail between your place and Sean O'Malley's?"

"What business is it of yours?" Ethan snarled. "They ain't no law against cuttin' trails through the bush between neighbours, is there?"

"So, you're not gonna let us search your place then?" Alan persisted.

"No, I ain't gonna let yuh. Not without a paper sayin' why you want to and a Mountie with yuh. Now turn that car around yer in my way. I have to get back to the school and get my wife."

"Your wife is the teacher?" Alan said carefully.

"Yeah, what of it," Ethan rumbled. Then after a moment he added in an ominous tone. "Were you at the school harrassin' her? Because if you were…"

"I understand her school is unsanctioned and she has no certificate to teach." Alan continued in bold defiance to Ethan's menacing glare.

"What of it? She's teachin' ain't she and those kids are

learnin' things. And it ain't none a yer business anyhow." Ethan moved closer to him, with a threatening scowl.

"It is the business of the school board though, and I could make the whereabouts of this school known to them."

He had barely finished his sentence when Ethan's fist shot out and smashed into Alan's jaw, knocking him to the ground. "You leave Jane and her school out of it or there will be hell to pay and I don't mean maybe."

"I can have you arrested for this, and maybe I will when I bring a Mountie out to your place." Alan threatened as he crawled to his feet brushing the mud from his clothes. His words were somewhat slurred from the excruciating pain in his jaw.

"Hah," Ethan spat.

Just then they heard the hoof beats of several horses coming from the east. Lakota[1] and several other First Nations men came down the trail and stopped as they surrounded Ethan and his adversaries. All of the natives bore rifles whether slung on their backs like Ethan or in slip holsters under their saddles.

Ethan grinned and said with a laugh, "I always thought it was the cavalry that arrived to save people from Indians, not the other way around."

"Were they giving you trouble Brother Ethan?" Lakota said with his Cree accent. "We were just on our way to Grimstad to trade some furs before going west on our spring hunt. Now I know why no one was at home."

Ethan spoke to them in Cree explaining his situation and the Goon Squad threat against Jane. Alan who was cocky a few moments ago was now decidedly uncomfortable as were his men since they were surrounded by a dozen armed native men who looked upon the Goon Squad with sombre expressionless eyes. They found the ongoing conversation in Cree, which none of them could understand, quite disturbing. Sometimes Ethan and Lakota would looked at them and laugh as they spoke.

Finally, Lakota said to them, "Ethan is our brother and

both he and his wife are honourary members of our band. Jane is a good woman of strong medicine. Their friends are our friends and their enemies are our enemies." He turned and spoke again to Ethan in Cree.

Then Ethan said, "These gentlemen would like to accompany you back to Grimstad since they are going there anyway."

"No thanks," the Commissioner replied in a small voice. Then to his deputies he added with a sigh, "We might as well go back to Grimstad our business here is finished for now." To Ethan he added in a belligerent tone, "We'll be back."

"As long as you bring the police," Ethan replied in a taunting voice.

The Goon Squad turned their car around and headed back. Lakota and the others stayed with them all the way back to Grimstad. Alan and his cohorts were thoroughly humiliated to have a First Nations escort.

As he nursed his tender jaw that night, the normally hard-headed commissioner had second thoughts about searching Ethan's place. Another encounter with this redoubtable person, his equally formidable wife and his native friends was a thing best avoided. Especially since there was virtually no chance of them finding either a still, or even a bottle of homebrew. He shuddered at the thought of the skull with the bullet hole. If Ethan did have a still on his property, he would have it moved or well-hidden long before they could get back. *Damn it, we should have searched his place when we were there,* he thought. He couldn't wait to tell the RCMP about the skull and hopefully he could accompany them when they came to search the area to interrogate Ethan. Since Ethan appeared to be friends with the Indians, perhaps he was selling moonshine to them. He smugly thought how justice would be served.

As for Ethan, he had a good chuckle at the escapade as he continued on his way riding on the logs. He was glad that Ivan had come for the distilling equipment the previous week, as now there was no shred of evidence by which they could convict Sean. He worried about Jane as word was now out about the location of her school, and soon she would have a confrontation with the school superintendent.

(Footnotes)
[1] Lakota and the First Nations band that he belongs to, were introduced in *Third Time Lucky* along with their special relationship to Ethan.

Chapter Sixteen

It was the last school day of April when the superintendent arrived. It was after last recess and the class was involved in general discussion period. The world map was pulled down as the students wanted a geography quiz. On such occasions, Jane would ask her pupils to find a certain country, large body of water, or a famous river and she would pick from a show of hands for a student to locate it with her pointer on the map. As the session progressed, there was a knock at the door and before Jane could get over to answer it two men stepped in. All activity stopped as the students were also curious as to who these two men might be. One was a tall, anaemic looking middle-aged man with a balding head and spectacles while the other was shorter and younger looking.

"May I help you gentlemen?" Jane asked suspiciously.

"You are Jane Phillips, teacher of this school?" The tall anaemic-looking man said in a tight voice.

"Yes, who might you be?"

"I am Zachery Smith, the superintendent of the school division," he said smugly.

"And your partner?" Jane asked in a flat tone as she swallowed hard. The other man Jane recognised as Arnold from the Goon Squad. He smiled sardonically at her.

"He is my driver. Since he knew how to get out here and I didn't, thanks to the non-cooperation of the people around here."

Jane smiled inwardly then looking at the other man she said with contempt, "You were here before with the Goon Squad."

"You mean the commission for the control and suppression of illegal production of spirits," Zachery

151

corrected her.

"Whatever," Jane replied curtly. "I know why you are here and it is not something to discuss in front of all the students, nor is it the business of your driver."

"You have a point there," Zachery replied. He motioned for Arnold to go out to the car and wait.

Jane said, "If you will excuse me, I will deal with my class." Without waiting for an answer, she went to her desk and called for their attention.

"Class I have a guest from the school board who wants to talk to me about the future of the school." She looked directly at Herman and Thomas. "So, I am going to give you a treat and give you extra recess until your parents come to get you. Thomas and Herman remember your assignments for homework." She winked at them and continued, "Class dismissed."

The two shining stars understood perfectly and would inform their parents of the superintendent's visit.

Helen stuck up her hand and asked, "Do you want me to erase the blackboard and do the brushes, Mrs. Phillips?"

"No, I'll take care of it. I will look after all monitor duties today. Take your jackets and lunch pails with you and leave them on the step until your parents come."

There was a general clamour as the students vacated the building. While Jane was dealing with the class, the superintendent looked over her library and made note of the world map that had been pulled down and other curiosities like the framed map of Europe and the column of Cyrillic letters with their Latin equivalent beside them located on the far side of the front blackboard. Jane stood behind her desk bracing for her confrontation as her students dispersed. Helen, who was last to leave, closed the door behind her.

The superintendent turned to Jane and said abruptly, "Now then, Mrs. Phillips, by what right do you presume to play the role of teacher for these students in this make-believe schoolhouse?"

Jane was immediately put on the defensive by his brusque

approach and replied in a forthright manner. "I presume to be a teacher by the request of the parents of these students because your school board would not provide a school for them. As for this schoolhouse, I assure you it is not make believe but very real. The students in my class are learning to read and write and to do their arithmetic, among other things, and some of them are doing it rather well."

Puffing himself up, Zachery replied, "We didn't provide a school because there are not enough students in this area to warrant one. It costs money to build a schoolhouse and pay a real teacher to teach. Besides, if these people want their children educated, they can send them to Grimstad."

"That's at least fourteen miles for the closest ones," Jane replied sharply. "Surely you don't expect a six-year-old child to travel fourteen miles, especially in winter, to go to school. Use a little common sense, sir."

Zachery's mouth quivered for a moment as he had been warned by Arnold that Jane would be a thorny person to deal with. Then changing his tack he continued, "For the record may I see your teaching certificate."

"You know I don't have one."

"So you admit that you are an unqualified teacher?" he grilled.

"I admit nothing. If I am guilty of anything it is the need to help some very bright children to avoid growing up ignorant of the basic knowledge every child is entitled to have."

"I don't suppose you have a proper curriculum either," he continued relentlessly.

"I have a lesson plan that involves teaching the children how to read and write, to do arithmetic, learn some basic science, history and geography," Jane replied ever defiantly. "Isn't that what any school does?"

"Does your so-called curriculum include instruction in Russian," Zachery sneered as he glanced at the column comparing alphabets.

"Two of my pupils are Russian, and since their father

can read Russian I thought a comparison of alphabets might be interesting for the other students. Surely there is no harm in that."

"Real schools follow a set curriculum teaching various age groups known as grades a certain level of knowledge," Zachery said dismissively. "I suppose you don't have grades either, let alone report cards."

"My students learn according to their ability to absorb knowledge, and I do send progress reports home to their parents four times a year, just like one of your *real* schools."

"But without structure, your students are learning in a mishmash way. What if some of them want to go on to high school or university, how will they know what grade they passed?"

"Surely there are tests for them to write, should any of my students and I can think of at least two, who will likely go on for higher education," Jane shot back.

"My dear lady, the Department of Education explicitly declares that any student educated in Alberta must have a report card filled out by a competent teacher declaring the student's proficiency level."

"All I know is that nine children would be at home illiterate and frustrated if not for this school. I never asked for this job, but accepted when asked by the parents and now I rather enjoy it, and I intend to keep doing it whether you like it or not." Jane's eyes blazed with defiance.

"We'll see about that," he muttered. Zachery was frustrated that this feisty woman could not be cowed down easily, so he tried yet another tack, "Those maps and those books at the back…where did you get them?"

"Most of those books were donated, and people took up a collection to buy the encyclopaedia. The old dilapidated stuff was found in the garbage." Jane replied in a milder tone.

"Do you know that the roll maps and school texts belong to the school board?" he quizzed.

"I was unaware that the school board still claims stuff that is sent to the garbage," Jane replied curtly.

"These items were put in the garbage by accident or possibly design," he continued relentlessly. "I have a mind to confiscate them."

"Why? They are old and worn-out and the maps are out-of-date."

"Because we can use the maps and re-bind some of the books. In real schools in remote areas, we sometimes have to issue them out-of-date maps and second-hand texts until our budget allows for replacements. I think I will definitely take those maps."

"Not so fast," Jane said, stepping between the superintendent and the roll map of the world which was still down. "There is something about finders keepers."

"The maps are school board property and now that you know that, keeping them constitutes theft." Zachery blazed.

"It would be interesting to see how the courtroom scene would play out if you tried to charge me with theft of garbage," Jane sneered.

"You…you…" Zachery sputtered in near apoplectic rage, finding it increasingly difficult to cope with Jane's blatant defiance. "I'll shut this school down, I'll shut you down. This farce of a school cannot be allowed to continue."

"Jane is a good teacher, you leave her alone!" said a shrill voice behind them. They both turned and saw Hella standing near the door. Herman had informed her as to what was going on when she had arrived with Robbie. She left Robbie in his care and slipped into the schoolhouse unnoticed in the heat of the confrontation between Jane and the superintendent.

"What, who the hell are you?" Zachery demanded.

"I am Hella Kepler, ze *mutter* of two of Jane's students. We asked Jane to be ze teacher *und* we want her to continue mit ze chob. You get out *und* leave us alone."

"But Mrs. Kepler, don't you want your children to get a

proper education?"

"Zhey are getting a good education mit Jane, *mein* children love zhere teacher *und* zhey are learning so much. You chust mind your own business *und* leave Jane alone."

"I can see this conversation is going nowhere," said the frustrated superintendent, "but you, Jane Phillips, have definitely not heard the last from me." He turned and walked out the door.

Zachery had barely left when Ethan arrived for Jane. He laughed heartily when they filled him in on the confrontation with the superintendent. "I almost feel sorry for him for tangling with the likes of you two. I wish I could-a been here to hear it."

Then with a sobering thought Jane said, "He threatened to shut the school down, threatened to take the maps and books and forbid me to teach any more."

"He won't get away mit any of zose zings," Hella assured her.

"He can't shut the school down neither," Ethan stated. "It's on my property."

Zachery was still furious by the time he got back to Grimstad. *The impudence of that woman,* he fumed as he thought of Jane. *The audacity... who does she think she is running that so-called school any way she pleases?* He planned to stay the night and confront Mary McKay over the fate of the discarded school supplies so he and his brother-in-law took rooms above the store for the night.

Sean intercepted Mary as she was leaving the school yard, and she agreed to climb into his car. Neither was aware that the superintendent was in town. "So Mary, have ye thought about things? The winter is over and spring has come."

"Are you still in possession of your distilling equipment?" Mary replied giving him a quizzical look as they drove toward the store at a slow speed.

"No, I can honestly say it is out of me hands now. No

doubt ye heard the Goon Squad was back and they searched me place when I wasn't home, and ye don't see me bound in irons for it so that should be tellin' ye somethin','" Sean said with a wink and a grin. "So ye see, the time has passed for them to convict me of makin' homebrew."

"I heard the goons were back and had a run-in with Ethan and Jane," Mary laughed.

"And his Indian friends, they escorted the goons back to town. I don't think you'll see the likes of them around here again." Sean laughed in turn. Then he added, "Would ye like to come out to me humble abode for a taste of Irish stew and praties cooked by a real Irishman. The pot is simmerin' on the stove as we speak."

"You planned all of this ahead of time, Sean O'Malley," Mary said, coyly looking at him with her head down.

"I did make enough for two people," he grinned. "We can talk about things and I promise not to try to take advantage of you."

"Promise," Mary grinned. "They say a woman is not safe alone with an Irishman, you know."

"Now who would be sayin' a thing like that," Sean replied. "But there's only one way to find out."

"I'm a daredevil and a fool, but I'll take a chance this once. Let me go in and tell Kari I won't be there for supper."

Mary burst into the kitchen to inform Kari that she was going out with Sean and wouldn't be there for supper, but her last word trailed off as the superintendent stepped into the room.

"Good evening, Miss McKay," he smiled derisively. "So it seems I won't have the pleasure of your company at supper."

"No, I'm going out," Mary said abruptly as she turned to leave. Her heart was pounding as he was sure to find out that she was seeing Sean again, but it was too late to back out now.

"Oh Sean, what am I gonna do?" Mary fretted as they

headed out of town. "The superintendent will surely know I am out with you."

"Well lass, ye can't be hidin' from him forever. It is none of his business who's courtin' you, especially a law abidn' citizen like Sean O'Malley," Sean said with a wink.

"A reformed law abiding citizen," Mary grinned.

"Take it as ye may. The law can't convict a man who is guiltless."

"You're right Sean," Mary said with renewed confidence. "I am my own person to do what I please, and I am pleased to be with you."

A few hours later when Sean brought Mary back, Zachery, who had a front room above the store, observed their arrival and opened his window a crack with the hope of picking up any conversation should they both get out of the car. Sean got out of the car like a true gentleman and opened the door for Mary. She took his hand as she stepped out and continued to hold it as he led her up the steps to the bottom of the external staircase that led upstairs. At the bottom of the staircase and still visible from the window, Mary turned to face Sean.

"It would be my pleasure if you would let me take you to the spring dance next Saturday, Mary McKay," Sean said.

"It would be my pleasure, Sean O'Malley," Mary replied. "Well, I must get to my bed now thanks for the wonderful evening." She kissed Sean passionately for a long moment and gave his hand a squeeze before turning to go up the steps. He stood and watched her climb the steps with a satisfied smile that the courtship was back on.

Zachery also smiled quietly to himself. Perhaps he could get rid of two teachers with one swoop as he was sure Mary was aiding and abetting Jane since some of the material she threw out was too good to be trashed and it was a little too coincidental that it ended up in Jane's school.

Chapter Seventeen

Mary was joined at breakfast in Kari's kitchen by Zachery and Jesse. Little was said beyond morning greetings. However, when Mary rose to head for the school as she always liked to arrive a half hour ahead of the start of class, Zachery offered to walk with her.

"I should like to have a word with you once we get to the school," he said as they walked along.

Mary swallowed with the suggestion although it was inevitable that he would want to speak to her about Sean. The three-block walk to the school was in silence, but Mary decided this time she would hold her ground come what may. Once at the school, Zachery called Mary into the tiny office and beckoned her to have a seat.

"Now then Miss McKay," he began. "There are a couple of issues we need to discuss."

"Yes," Mary replied with a small voice.

"I paid a little visit to this so-called Opportunity School yesterday and had a little chat with your friend Jane. The woman is quite belligerent."

Mary smiled inwardly as she could imagine how the confrontation unfolded.

"Among other things, I found two roll maps and some tattered texts that belong to the school division. I am curious to how she obtained them."

"Why are you asking me?" Mary said flatly, avoiding eye contact.

"You said last autumn when I was here that you threw away a bunch of what you considered worthless pieces of school property. It seems that these so-called discards found their way to her classroom. How is that possible?"

"She must have retrieved them from the garbage," Mary

shrugged.

"How would she know that these items were kicking around in the school garbage bin?"

"I don't know. Why don't you ask her?" Mary said sharply.

"Listen young lady, I don't like your tone," Zachery retorted. "Furthermore, I suspect you deliberately planted this…this garbage so she could find it and take it to her school," he continued relentlessly.

Mary looked directly at him and replied, "Why do you worry so much about a bunch of old textbooks that were falling to pieces and some out-of-date maps. I was doing the school a favour in getting rid of them, and if Jane Phillips wants to go rooting around in our trash bin for usable garbage far be it for me to stop her."

There was a glaring silence for a long moment, then Zachery said in a more quiet, but firm tone, "I see you are back to seeing the Irish moonshiner. As I said it is not becoming of a teacher to be seeing someone who makes his living outside the law."

Mary rose from her seat, perhaps propelled by the anger rapidly rising within her and replied with a quiet ominous voice, "What I do in my private life and who I see is none of your business, Mr. Superintendent. Yes, I am seeing Sean O'Malley and intend to marry him." Sean had not even formally proposed and until this moment, Mary had not given marriage to him serious thought. "Yes, I helped my good friend Jane and was proud to do so. As much as I love teaching, I will be tendering my resignation at the end of June rather than be intimidated by some tin pot, overbearing superintendent who delights in running roughshod over those in his charge. I am going back to my classroom now where I can do some good, and you sir can go to hell."

She opened the door and stepped out slamming it behind her. Mary stood outside her classroom door for a moment, swallowed hard with resolve, put on a brave face and went in to attend her class.

James, the principal, was called into the office where Zachery bluntly informed him, "I want that woman, Mary McKay, fired! She is insolent and rude. I'll–I'll have her teaching certificate lifted."

"Aren't you overreacting sir," James said mildly.

"The woman is defiant and insubordinate and now admits to helping this woman who has been masquerading as a teacher," Zachery ranted. "She no doubt gave the materials she threw out to that woman…that make-believe teacher."

"If Mary is dismissed immediately, there will be no one to fill her class," James argued.

"I will take care of things when I get back to the office," the superintendent said in a calmer voice, "but before I'm done Mary McKay will be out of a job, and that pretend school up north will be out-of-business. So, unless you have any issues of your own to bring up I'll be heading back. I have a lot of work to do."

"No, I only ask that you find a sub before you fire Mary. Otherwise, we'll be in a real pinch as year end is rapidly approaching."

Zachery said no more as he left the school building, both James and the other teachers breathed a sigh of relief that they were spared a class visit from this overbearing individual. They all felt sorry for Mary and gave their support. James declared at a lunch hour meeting, "I'm going to write a letter to the chairman of the board and risk the wrath of the superintendent by pleading for Mary on behalf of both her past reputation and performance at the Grimstad School, portraying her as an excellent teacher who has done no wrong."

The other two teachers also offered to sign the letter. Mary gave them a teary eyed nod in gratitude but added, "It is best I go at the end of the term as I cannot abide working for that man."

James; nonetheless, sent the letter to the chairman of the school board. He simply felt that Mary was too good of a teacher to let slip away. Mary maintained a brave face for the rest of the day with the certain satisfaction that she told the superintendent off and of knowing the rest of the staff stood behind her.

That evening when Sean called on her; however, Mary broke down sobbing in his arms about losing her job as a teacher.

Sean held her, stroking her hair and speaking with a soothing voice, "But ye stood up to him. He's nothin' but a bloody bully you know that."

"But I love teaching and he's taken that away," Mary sobbed. "I told him I'd resign at the end of the term just to avoid giving him the satisfaction of firing me."

"Well, that's one for you Mary, me dear," Sean laughed, trying to cheer her up. "I guess ye should have said no when I came to ask yer hand in courtin' again."

"It would have made no difference. His main anger is because of Jane," Mary said. "Bringing you into it was just for spite." Then smiling weakly she added, "I can imagine the war of words he had with her."

"I'd a loved to be a fly on the wall for that one too," Sean laughed. "It'll take more than the likes of him to get the best of her. There's a meetin' at Jane's school tonight, would ye be wantin' to go since ye have nothin' to lose."

"I'd love to go," Mary grinned eagerly. "I'm dying to hear how Jane made out with him and what the others have in store."

Later as they drove up the road to the school, Mary remarked, "When the superintendent brought you up I not only told him I was seeing you again, but intended to marry you. Silly, isn't it?" she smiled coyly.

After a moment Sean replied with a grin, "Well Mary McKay, if yer proposin' to me, I accept."

"Sean O'Malley you're incorrigible," Mary scoffed.

"Well then," Sean continued grinning broadly, "Since I accept yer proposal will ye accept mine. Marry me and be me darlin' one and we'll face this thing together."

"Oh Sean," Mary replied. "I do love you, you thick-headed Irishman. Yes I'll marry you, but I ask one condition."

"You women always attach conditions," Sean said with a frown. "I heard that line once before. Well, what is it?"

"I want to be married back in Cape Breton where my family is. If you can't afford the train fare, I'll spring for you."

"Oh, I can afford it lassie," Sean replied. "But I'm thinkin' of our friends out here that would be wantin' to come."

"Well, we could invite them as a token of friendship though few, if any will make the journey, and then we can have a celebration when we get back. Rent the hall or Jane's school for a dance and party."

"That's a condition I could live with," Sean grinned. "Oh, Mary McKay I've been waitin' a good wee while to hear those words. I love ye with all me heart."

Mary leaned over and placed her head on his shoulder. She looked up at him with adoring eyes and kissed him. He kissed back with such passion that the car drifted off the trail and ran into the underbrush stopping against a tree.

"There ye go Mary McKay," Sean laughed. "Yer kisses are enough to make a man drive off the road." She laughed as Sean backed the car out onto the trail and they continued on their way with a piece of poplar sapling stuck in the front bumper. As they drove Sean happily sang, *When Irish Eyes are Smiling* and she soon joined in.

When they arrived at the school Mary and Jane gave each other an emotional hug. "It looks like we're both going to be out of a job," Mary said with a watery-eyed smile.

"You too? The superintendent and I had a rather heated discussion over my right to teach, then Hella came along and tore a strip out of him, but why you?"

"He got on to me this morning about helping you

and giving you the discards and then he started on Sean. It was then that I told him to go to hell and tendered my resignation."

"You didn't!" Jane gasped.

"He would have fired me anyway for standing up to him, so I beat him to the punch," Mary said smugly. "So, I guess this meeting is about the fate of you and your school."

"Apparently so," Jane sighed. "We all knew this showdown would come. We just hoped it would be later."

It was a noisy meeting attended by all the parents and other interested parties such as Audi, Axel, Sean and Mary. While many of the parents, particularly Hella and Sari, were quite vocal. Audi sat quietly taking mental notes. When all was said and done, Ethan assured them they couldn't close the school because it was on private property, and since Jane was a volunteer teacher, it was a private school. This brought cheers all around. Finally, Dave said, "I believe there is a school board meeting next week. I think I should like to attend as it never hurts to see what the other side is planning." There was a murmur of approval. Then Ethan announced, "I think I'll go along with Dave. After all, this school is on my property and Jane is my wife, so I definitely have what ya call a vested interest."

"Zhat's it Ethan, you go down zhere und tell zhem what for," Wolf added amid a clamour of approval.

"What about you, Audi?" Dave said. "You've said very little tonight."

"I'm just taking notes tonight. I'll weigh in on the second round," he said mysteriously. "But you may be sure that they won't shut Jane down without a fight from me." He grinned at Jane and she blushed.

"Well then, I would like to conclude this meeting and break for coffee," Dave said.

"Wait a wee moment," Sean said with a grin. "On the brighter side of things, I have an announcement." There was silence as they waited to hear Sean. He stood up and induced

Mary to join him, holding her hand as he announced, "Mary has agreed to be me wife. We are officially engaged as of this night."

Wild cheers erupted while Mary blushed and bashfully looked down. Sean waved them to silence and continued, "Since I'll be takin' a wife and one-day hopefully be blessed with children, we'll be wantin' Jane to teach them. So ye see, I have a vested interest in this school as well."

Laughter and cheers erupted as the men, Dave included, moved to congratulate Sean while all the women hugged Mary. Nearly everyone, however, was interested in hearing about the two confrontations with the superintendent.

The following morning at the school board office, the secretary was surprised to find an elfin faced man standing in front of her. He held a tweed cap in his hands.

"May I help you, sir?" She said flatly.

"If it is not too much trouble ma'am, I would like to be havin' a word with the boss of the school superintendent."

"The what?" she puzzled.

"You know, that man who runs the school board. I'm not much on titles, but ye know what I mean."

"You must mean Darcy McBride, chairman of the school board." She said pleasantly.

"Darcy McBride ye say, now that's a fine Irish name," he grinned.

"And who might you be, sir?"

"Sean O'Malley at yer service. Now would you be a good lass and tell him that I would like a wee word with him."

"He's a very busy man," she replied. "You just can't come in here on a moment's notice and expect to see him."

"But I drove all the way from Grimstad. It's a long way to come to be disappointed."

"Why is it you wish to see him?" She persisted although she was starting to melt before his Irish charm.

"I am here to talk to him about a certain teacher called

Mary McKay."

"You should take your complaints to the superintendent," the secretary replied.

"Oh no, I'm not here to complain about Mary. It is he who is the problem."

Darcy McBride had stepped from his office in time to hear the last statement. He had been reviewing Zachery's report.

"May I help you?" Darcy asked as he approached Sean.

"This gentleman wishes to see you sir," the secretary said, "but I told him you have a very busy schedule."

"Hello, my name is Darcy McBride," Darcy said extending his hand and ignoring the secretary.

"Sean O'Malley at yer service, sir," Sean replied shaking his hand. "Ye have a good Irish name Mr. McBride."

"Yes, I'm of third generation Irish decent and you sound fresh from the old country. Now how can I help you?"

"I've been here since the end of the war," Sean replied. "Me concern is the teacher named Mary McKay."

"Step into my office," Darcy said. "I've got a half hour before my next meeting."

Darcy beckoned Sean to sit and state his purpose.

"I would like to know why Mary McKay from Grimstad School was pressured to resign her job. It is me understandin' that she is a teacher of good reputation."

"And why is Mary McKay of special interest to you?"

"Well, it is a personal nature sir. She is me fiancée and it seems that your superintendent feels that it is not becomin' of a school teacher to be seen with the likes of me."

"Ah yes, the Irish moonshiner he mentioned."

"It was all a bad rumour sir," Sean said glibly. "The goons, if you'll pardon the expression, raided me place twice and turned it upside down. The fact that I am still standin' here as a free man should tell ye somethin'. And for what it's worth, I work an honest days work for an honest day's pay at Axel Rutland's sawmill."

Darcy thought for a moment then said, "I have here two

things on my desk; a scathing report from our superintendent calling Mary argumentive and insubordinate among other things, demanding her immediate dismissal. I also have a letter from the principal praising her and asking her to be kept on. What do you think, Mr. O'Malley?"

"I think the letter from the principal tells it all, does it not? He is the one workin' with Mary every day. Your mealy-mouthed superintendent comes there accusin' and insultin' her. Does she not have the right to defend herself? What would you do?"

"Well...uh, I'd defend myself," Darcy chuckled. "Perhaps he is overreacting a bit and she does have a sound reputation as a teacher."

"Now you're talkin' sense. I knew one Irishman could get through to another." Sean laughed.

"Then there is the matter of this Opportunity School, which seems to be the eye of the storm and Mary's involvement."

"Well sir, I'm a wee bit involved with that school meself and even helped build it. The teacher there, Jane Phillips, is a good Irish lass with a strong constitution and has a gift as a teacher from what I understand. The parents and students all love her and they are learnin' things as good as in any school."

"But she has no training or knowledge of a proper curriculum."

"I'm not one on all them fancy terms and such, but I know she deserves to be a teacher and I'd be wantin' me children to be taught by her," Sean said resolutely.

Darcy glanced at the clock and said, "You must excuse me. I have to go to a meeting, but thank you for coming Mr. O'Malley; and our conversation has given me much to think about. Oh, and tell your fiancée that her job is safe until at least the end of the term and probably a lot longer."

"Thank you sir," Sean smiled. "She'll be pleased to hear that."

"You have me word as one Irishman to another," Darcy

replied, mimicking Sean's brogue. They shook hands.

As Sean passed by the secretary's desk he turned and said with a wink, "I told ye lass that it would take one Irishman to talk sense to another."

Chapter Eighteen

About a week after Ethan's encounter with the Goon Squad, Alan Bates returned again this time with Constable Smith of the RCMP for a second visit to Ethan's place. Ethan had quit the sawmill for the season to tend to his farm. He was out fixing fences when he saw an automobile he didn't recognise come across his field to the yard. He started for the house and as always had his rifle slung across his shoulder. As he approached the house he saw two people get out of the car, Alan Bates and an RCMP constable. He noticed the police logo on the car door.

So that busy-body Bates got an officer and probably a warrant to search my place, Ethan thought. He chuckled at the thought of how it would be a total waste of time for the constable since he was completely innocent of anything to do with moonshine production.

The two men, unaware of his approach despite the barking dog, knocked on the house door.

"I'm over here," Ethan called as he approached.

They turned to see him lumbering toward them with his Winchester slung over his shoulder.

"Careful, he's armed and possibly dangerous," Alan said apprehensively.

The constable had one hand near his holster but made no effort to draw his revolver since Ethan made no effort to unsling his rifle.

Ethan walked directly up to them with his usual expressionless mode then spoke, "Good day officer." He ignored Alan and continued, "What can I do for you?"

"Good day. Are you Ethan Phillips?"

"Yes, I am so," Ethan replied with a half-grin.

"My name is Constable Smith and I have a warrant with

me to search your place with reasonable suspicion that you may be involved in the production and, or distribution of illegal spirits." Alan waved a document at Ethan.

"Did he drag you all the way out here thinkin' I'm a moonshiner?" Ethan scoffed, looking at Smith but ignoring Alan.

"There's a little more to it than that," Constable Smith said gravely. "However, under the circumstances the judge allowed us a warrant."

"Well, he can search all he wants but he won't find a drop of the stuff here or anythun to make it with," Ethan sneered.

"Should we start with the house?" Alan said.

"You go ahead and search. I have a few questions for Mr. Phillips on another matter," Smith said evenly.

As Alan started for the house, Ethan stepped in his way, "You ain't goin' in there. That's my home where my family lives. I'll not have it turned upside down."

Alan gave Smith a pleading look.

"He does have the right," Smith said to Ethan.

"All the same, sir," Ethan replied. "If my house is to be searched, you be the one doin' it with me watchin'. Let this goon search the barn and sheds if he wants."

"With Mr. Phillips cooperation, I'll look inside. You go check the outbuildings." Then looking at Ethan, Smith continued, "If that's all right with you, sir."

"Yeah," Ethan sighed. "Get this nonsense over with and then maybe you guys will leave me alone."

"Could I ask you to set your gun aside?" Smith asked politely.

"Oh sure," Ethan grunted. Smith watched Ethan carefully as he unslung his rifle and leaned it against the wall. Ethan added with a wry grin, "I carry it with me when I'm out and about. Never know when I can pick off a coyote, or even a bear. I don't use it on people."

"I understand sir," Smith smiled.

"Now then, I suppose yuh wanna look inside," Ethan

sighed.

"Just for the record," Smith replied.

They stepped into the house while Alan headed for the outbuildings with the smokehouse as his first stop. Meanwhile, once inside, Smith glanced around and looked at the bedroom door while asking, "What's in there?"

"The bedroom," Ethan smiled. "If you think I got a still or a stash of 'shine under the bed be my guest, but try not mess it up too much when yer lookin' because Jane is a fussy housekeeper."

"That won't be necessary," Smith smiled, doubting that he'd find any evidence of moonshine in there.

"That's good," Ethan laughed. "My good wife is a temperance woman and God forbid that even if I dared make 'shine, I'd never be allowed to keep it in the house."

Smith chuckled and looking at the steps added, "Another bedroom upstairs?"

"Yeah, my young son is gonna start sleeping up there soon. We also store stuff in the loft." Then with a twisted grin he added, "The missus wouldn't let me have a still up there either, but yer welcome to look."

Smith climbed the ladder far enough that he could see into the loft then came back down saying, "Somehow I think our over zealous commissioner is wrong. I don't believe you're a moonshiner."

"Glad to hear it," Ethan replied. "I try to live within the law."

"Well, we might as well go outside," Smith said. "It's a nice day and I can ask you a few other questions."

"Fire away." Ethan chuckled as they stepped outside. "I'll try to answer."

"Do you know Sean O'Malley?"

"Yeah, he's my neighbour down through the bush there," Ethan gestured, maintaining his poker face.

"You probably know from all the commission activity around here that he is under suspicion for making moonshine."

"Yeah, I heard the goons were harassing him but couldn't get anythun on him."

Smith cleared his throat at the reference to the commission as goons and continued, "I don't suppose you know anything about his activities?"

"Not a thing. As I said my good wife won't let me touch the stuff. I'd be lyin' if I said I didn't know Sean, or that he don't come over, but if he's bin makin' 'shine he hasn't told me."

"I see," Smith replied. While he didn't expect that Ethan would snitch on his neighbour, he had to ask the question anyway and watch for a reaction. Ethan's stone face revealed none.

"So where are your wife and children today?" Smith said, "If I may ask."

"The wife teaches school and a neighbour looks after my son during the day so I can get on with other things."

"She's an unqualified teacher of an illegal school," Alan said smugly as he came upon the scene. They turned to face him and Ethan glared menacingly.

"Leave her outta this," he snarled at Alan. Then turning to Smith he said in a milder tone, "My wife teaches at the school you passed on the way here. We built that school and she volunteered to teach since the school board said there weren't enough kids in the area to build a school." Then he added in a harder tone, "Tell this no account commissioner to keep his mouth shut about my wife, or I'll shut it for him even if you have ta arrest me for assault."

Turning to the commissioner, Smith said in a firm tone, "I don't think Mr. Phillips' wife has anything to do with why we are here so she is best left out of it."

"Thank you," Ethan replied. "It's good to see a real policeman has some common decency."

Alan scowled at him while Smith asked, "Did you find any moonshine or evidence of a still in your search?"

"Afraid not, if he had any evidence he must have moved it."

"Look, I've had just about enough of this, this so-called commissioner," Ethan rumbled in an ominous tone.

"I personally do not believe Mr. Phillips was in any way involved in the production or distribution of moonshine," Smith declared. "And I also do not condone the harassment of innocent citizens. As far as I am concerned the matter is dropped. So, unless you can prove otherwise, I don't want to hear anymore about Mr. Phillips' possible involvement with moonshine."

"What about the trail between here and Sean O'Malley's place?" Alan continued, "The one that goes by the muskeg where I found the skull and other remains."

"Didn't know it was a crime to cut a trail through the bush to a neighbour's place," Ethan replied. Ethan laughed and continued, "So yuh went out into Dead Man's Muskeg lookin' for a still and found a body instead."

"Yes, that's primarily why I am here and supported Mr. Bates request for a formal search warrant," Smith said evenly. "He said he found human remains out there and I am required to investigate any unreported deaths. I'd be obliged if you would take me out there."

"Can do," Ethan said. "It's just over there." He pointed to an area just south of the garden where the tops of tall spruce could be seen above the surrounding aspen forest. "I was only ever inside that muskeg once, kind of a spooky place."

"Anywhere associated with a dead body generally has a spooky aura," Smith laughed.

"Mind if I take the rifle," Ethan said, "unless you think you can kill a bear with your revolver. That muskeg's a good place for bears to hide out."

Alan looked apprehensive but Smith said, "I would prefer if you sling it over your shoulder though."

"I always carry it that way," Ethan grinned. "Mr. Bates here thinks I'm gonna add yer bodies to that of Black Pete."

"Black Pete, is that the name of the person whose

remains are out there?" Smith asked as Ethan slung his rifle over his shoulder.

"That's the rumour. It was before my time out here." Ethan replied as they started out.

"You knew about the body?"

"The rumour is that one was found out there in the muskeg," he replied as they walked across the barnyard. "I never saw a body the time I was out there, but then I didn't fancy lookin' for one neither. I seen enough dead bodies in the war to last a lifetime."

"So you were in the war," Smith said as they headed across the barnyard angling for the muskeg and bypassing the garden hill. "How long have you been out here?"

"Since 1922, this place was Black Pete's place you know," Ethan said with a grin.

"Is that so? So you knew him then?" Smith probed as they walked along.

"No, he was gone before my time. The place was abandoned and unclaimed so I just moved in," Ethan continued. "If a place is abandoned and if taxes ain't kept up a new person can claim it."

They walked in silence for a few moments as they approached the rail fence at the south end of his pasture.

"I see. So this was all rumour when you got here?" Smith continued as they all climbed over the rail fence. As they continued on a gentle downward slope through the forest, the muskeg became increasingly more visible. "Tell me the story about this Black Pete according to what you've heard."

"Well, as near as I can tell Black Pete built this place sometime before the war, and I gotta say he was a good log builder," Ethan began. "He lived by himself, but was said to be a womanizer. He took liberties with any woman willing, even if they were married. So you can guess he wasn't very popular with the men. To make a long story short, he had an affair with a neighbour's wife when that neighbour was out working in the bush and got her pregnant. When that neighbour got back, and I never did get his name, he found out his wife was in a family way by Black Pete. She claimed she was raped. He paid Black Pete a visit one day and Black Pete was never heard from again. The neighbour moved away as did his wife, going in separate directions."

"It was sometime later when one of the Grimstads was out huntin' and he cut through the muskeg and found part of a skeleton with a bullet hole in the skull. Everybody said it was Black Pete so they buried it right in the muskeg where it stayed until Mr. Bates dug it up. That's how it got the name Dead Man's Muskeg."

"That's quite a story, Mr. Phillips," Smith remarked. "So nobody knows where the aggrieved husband or his wife went."

"Not a clue," Ethan replied as they reached the willow tangles at the edge of the muskeg. "Just call me Ethan, by the way. If you're looking fer more information on this try askin' one of the Grimstads or Dave Higgins since they've been around here the longest."

"I'll likely do that," Smith said. "It is my job to investigate an unsolved mystery that appears to have been a murder." He noticed the skeletal remains of an animal nearby and studied it for a moment.

"That's the remains of my old mare that died last fall," Ethan said sadly. "She dropped dead right in the barnyard, so I drug her out here far enough so I didn't have to smell her rot." Changing the subject Ethan continued, "We'll have to fight our way through the willows and Mr. Bates can show us where," Ethan said as he looked for a potential path through the willow tangle in front of them.

"I-I'd like to stay out here if I could," Alan stammered. "Phillips here probably knows all about where the remains are."

Ethan glowered at him but said glibly, "I've only bin in this muskeg once and I wasn't lookin' fer no bodies."

"Probably helping O'Malley hiding his still," Alan said in a low voice.

"Look, I've had just about enough," Ethan growled as he turned to physically attack Alan, but Smith stepped in the way saying, "As Mr...uh Ethan says, kindly keep your mouth shut and show us where the remains are."

Alan's mouth quivered. Though he still believed that Ethan had a hand in helping Sean, by covering his tracks, nothing could be proven and now Ethan had the constable on his side. He led them into the muskeg without further comment. Constable Smith observed that the trees, tall and spindly and in places extremely dense, had a dark forbidding character about them. The standing remains of long dead spruce were weathered in sometimes grotesque shapes that appeared like strange monsters. When a breeze came through the trees made creaking noises in unsettling ways.

"Something was dug out of here recently," Alan observed as he came to the spot where Sean's still and stash had been removed in the prior weeks.

"Probably some animal, maybe a bear," Ethan shrugged. Although Ivan and Sean accessed the muskeg through his place, Ethan was not personally involved in removing the distilling equipment or any of Sean's remaining moonshine.

"I don't see any tracks though," Smith replied.

"True," Ethan said evenly.

"Is this muskeg on your property, Ethan?" Smith asked.

"No, my property ended at the fence. As far as I know this is crown land," Ethan replied with his expressionless face.

Alan wanted to mention the trail leading from the muskeg to the garden hill, but in view of Ethan's extreme hostility he held his tongue. Ethan would probably have an explanation for that as well.

Alan stepped over, just beyond a clump of swamp spruce and said, "It's over here."

The others quickly came over and there on top of the moss was a human skull with part of a backbone attached. Smith knelt down to closely look at the skull and saw a small round hole in its forehead. "Looks like a bullet hole all right," was his comment.

He poked in the moss and found a few more bones, then straightening up he said to Alan, "How did you come by these remains?"

"Well, we followed what appeared to be a trace of a trail into muskeg and saw where something had been dug up, and then we found this spot with an old rotting cross of spruce branches sticking out of the moss. Thinking that is was a marker for moonshine or distilling equipment we dug into the moss and about two feet down we found the skeleton."

"They didn't find what they were lookin' for, but they found this," Ethan said dryly.

"These forests hold a lot of secrets," Smith said. "When people are few and far between and the law spread out, strange things happen." Then turning to face both of them he added, "I'll need to come back with a bag and some tools to dig around. Would you be interested in helping me, Ethan?"

"No problem there. I got some sacks and a shovel," Ethan replied.

"I have a proper body bag in the car," Smith replied, "you can help too," he said to Alan.

"Me," Alan faltered.

"Yes, and who knows, you might even find a stray bottle of moonshine," Smith chuckled.

When they emerged from the muskeg by the skeletal remains of Bessie, Smith noticed a trace of a trail that led up the hill. Aware of the constable's observation Ethan stated, "I drug old Bessie down here from the garden hill as the bush was more open. Her body sort a made a trail."

Just as I thought, Alan frowned to himself. *Ethan has an answer for everything.* Nonetheless, he added as he looked down, "Some one's been by here recently."

Both Ethan and the constable looked at the boot tracks on a soft place near the willow tangles.

"Some of those tracks could be mine," Ethan said

quickly. "I go by here all the time checkin' my traps. I have both a weasel trap and a coyote snare further along in these tangles."

"Makes sense," Smith shrugged. "Well let's get some tools so I can lift those remains out of the muskeg."

In one last act of desperation Alan said, "What about his Indian friends? Maybe him or the Irishman have been peddling the stuff to the Indians."

The constable glanced at Ethan for an answer and Ethan replied directly, "He's talking about my blood brother Lakota. When Mr. Bates here confronted me on the trail the last time he was here, Lakota and some of the band members of the reserve east of here came by and they escorted Mr. Bates back to Grimstad."

"This Lakota, you call him your blood brother?" The constable quizzed.

"I lived for a time with the people of his band and they made me an honourary member," Ethan replied.

"Do you believe that Indians should be allowed access to spirits?" Smith asked carefully.

"Not particularly," Ethan replied. "Their culture is unfamiliar with alcohol and some Indians have been poisoned by shady whiskey traders. Even if I was makin' the stuff, I wouldn't sell it to my good friends and see them get ruined by it."

"Thank you. That will be all," Smith said with a smile.

As they walked back to Ethan's place, he glanced at Alan and smirked as Alan glowered back at him. Every effort he made to try to link Ethan to moon shining, or whiskey trading had been thwarted. They both knew that further investigation would focus on the mystery of Black Pete.

Chapter Nineteen

On the same morning that Ethan and Dave boarded the train to take them to the school board headquarters, Mary received a letter. When it was presented to her by James she was almost afraid to open it, as she feared it would be a formal declaration of her dismissal as a teacher at Grimstad School. James anxiously watched Mary read the letter and saw a broad grin sweep across her face. She handed it to him and he read the letter:

> *Dear Miss Mary McKay*
>
> *I have considered all sides of the situation surrounding the issue of the request for the termination of your teaching contract with our school board and a couple of interesting appeals on your behalf. This, coupled with your past excellent reputation as a competent teacher, has given me cause for reconsideration.*
>
> *I hereby inform you that your contract with us will not be terminated now or in the foreseeable future. I would like you to reconsider your request for voluntary resignation at the end of this term and report for class at Grimstad School September next.*
>
> *Respectfully Yours,*
> *Darcy McBride*
> *Chairman of the School Board*

"Thank you James," Mary beamed. "Your letter must have done it."

"I am surprised," James replied. "Usually a

superintendent's word stands very strong when it comes to dealing with teachers. Now our dear superintendent, who is no doubt fit to be tied, will save his venom for me and leave you alone."

"I feel sorry for you though."

"I can handle it," James assured her, "I gained the upper hand by giving him the end run as according to that letter the chairman overruled the superintendent."

Mary looked at the letter again and commented, "I notice he said a couple of appeals. I wonder who else stuck up for me."

"Jane maybe," one of the other teachers ventured.

"No, I doubt they'd listen to Jane since they are out to get her," Mary replied. "Anything she might say on my behalf would be used against me."

"I guess time will tell," James shrugged.

Dave and Ethan arrived at the school board headquarters just ahead of the weekly meeting. The secretary looked curiously at the two men who stood in front of her desk with hats in hand. Dave was reasonably well-dressed, but Ethan merely wore a clean pair of bib overalls. Jane suggested that he should dress up more for the occasion but he dismissed her saying, "They can take me as I am. I ain't there to impress anybody but to state my piece."

"You're Mr. Higgins," the secretary said upon recognising Dave from his previous visits. "What can I do for you?" She looked at Ethan as if to say, *who is the hick you brought with you?*

"We would like to sit in on the weekly meeting if we may," Dave replied.

"Does Mr. McBride know you are coming?"

"Actually no, we're here about the fate of Opportunity School and its teacher." Dave replied as Ethan shuffled uneasily while maintaining his stone face.

Presently Darcy came by to see if some documents he required for the meeting were ready. As he approached, the secretary said, "I have two gentlemen here who wish to attend your meeting."

"Mr. Higgins I believe," Darcy said, shaking his hand. "You are here about the school no doubt."

"Yes, and I brought along Mr. Ethan Phillips, owner of the land the school is on and husband of the teacher."

"My pleasure sir," Darcy said extending his hand.

Ethan grunted a response and shook his hand.

"The school is a topic of our discussion, so you are welcome to join. I'll put your concerns first on the agenda. That way, you won't have to sit through the whole meeting if don't wish to."

"Thank you, that is considerate of you," Dave replied.

"Follow me then. In view of recent developments I'm glad you came."

After calling the meeting to order, Darcy introduced Dave Higgins, president of the Opportunity School Association, and Ethan Phillips, husband of Jane Phillips, the teacher and centre of the controversy concerning the illicit school.

"Now gentlemen," he said to them, "how may we help you?"

"As you know I was here last year requesting a school for our area," Dave said. "The request was denied due to a lack of sufficient numbers of students."

"That is correct," Darcy replied.

"So they took matters into their own hands," Zachery interjected.

"The esteemed superintendent is quite correct," Dave continued with just a trace of sarcasm. "We did take matters into our own hands because it was impractical to send our children to school in Grimstad. As you know we built our own school and got our own teacher with no cost to the school division."

"An unqualified teacher with no clue about a proper curriculum," Zachery again interjected.

Ethan glared at him.

"I guess we wish to find out what is in store for our school since we heard talk of that the board is trying to shut us down," Dave said ever mildly.

"You will be shut down," Zachery again spoke up.

"Does your superintendent control this meeting?" Dave said with a sneer.

"You are out of order," Darcy reminded Zachery. "Mr. Higgins has the floor."

Darcy continued to address Dave and Ethan. "We are fortunate that you two have chosen to come because there are some new developments regarding the education of the children in that area. Now, Mr. Phillips, you are the owner of the property on which the present schoolhouse exists, are you not?"

"I am," Ethan replied in his rumbling voice.

"Our recent census of the area suggests that from the families with students presently attending, there will be more school age children next term bringing the level up to twelve, the minimum needed for a school to be established," Darcy stated. "With two more families moving in, the number could go up to fourteen or fifteen. In view of that, we would like to take over your school and staff it with a trained teacher."

"That school's on private property," Ethan rumbled, "you ain't doin' anythun with it without my say so."

"But this is outrageous," Zachery again cut in. "The school is already built. He can't stop us."

"That school is on private property, my property. It was built for my good wife Jane to teach in and nobody else. If she can't teach in it, I'm repossessing it and makin' it over into my house."

"But surely Mr. Phillips you won't impede the education of the children by denying them a schoolhouse," Darcy said.

"I ain't impedin' or denyin' anythun, I'm just tellin' yuh you can't use that building or build another school on my property without Jane." Ethan declared. "I'm just tellin' yuh the facts, and if that superintendent thinks he's gonna bulldoze his way in and take over that school he's got another thing comin'."

There was a strong murmur among all those present until Darcy restored order with his gavel.

"We will not take anything from you Mr. Phillips, but we had hoped for your co-operation," Darcy continued. "Since we're not likely to get it, we'll pick another school site from the crown land in the area and build a new one from scratch."

"What if we want Jane to continue to teach our children?" Dave argued.

"Yeah, it was Dave and the others out there who asked Jane to be their teacher and they won't settle for anybody else," Ethan added.

Again there was a general outburst and Darcy had to restore order. Zachery asked for the floor and it was granted.

"As you gentlemen may know," Zachery began in his smug tone, "basic education is compulsory in this province. Furthermore, if a proper school with a qualified teacher is provided for your area you will be compelled to send your children there whether you like it or not."

Ethan and Dave both glowered at him. "What if we declared it a private school?" Dave retorted.

"Declare what you want, but anyone coming from that school will not be recognised as having a proper education, and in the end we will win," Zachery scoffed.

As Ethan sat scowling, clenching and unclenching his fists in a smouldering rage, Dave quietly urged him to calm down.

"Gentlemen, this present course is going nowhere," Darcy stated, seeing the rising hostility between his confrontational superintendent and the formidable Ethan. "Your school can continue to function until the new one is built, hopefully by September. I applaud your wife, Mr. Phillips, for her efforts and it sounds like she's doing a good

Eric J. Brown

job, but our education must maintain certain standards that we adhere to. If we allow people to set up schools anywhere they please and choose anyone they please to preside over them, we will have educational chaos. Surely you gentlemen and Mrs. Jane Phillips understand this."

"So there is no long-term hope for Jane's school then?" Dave said sadly.

"I'm afraid not. Once a new school is built, we hope she will bow out quietly," he smiled.

"So that's it then," Ethan rumbled. "For all Jane has done and for all those kids who love bein' taught by her yer just gonna throw her out like so much garbage."

"I'm afraid we are bound by the Department of Education. While no doubt your wife may be an excellent teacher Mr. Phillips, and we especially appreciate that she volunteered her time so those children could get a basic grasp of literacy, she is not qualified and cannot be allowed to continue."

"I think we should go, Dave," Ethan said as he rose from his seat. "It seems they ain't interested in reason."

"It would seem their minds are made up," Dave added as they headed for the door.

At the doorway Ethan turned and said, "You ain't heard the last from us."

"Yes we have," Darcy replied. "The case is closed. There will be no more talk of Opportunity School. Don't send any more delegations as they will not be admitted to our meetings."

That evening there was another noisy meeting at Opportunity School with all interested parties, including Sean and Mary, in attendance. When Sean arrived to pick up Mary, she was overjoyed to say her teaching career had been saved and showed him the letter.

"So that chairman listened to sound advice after all," Sean said nonchalantly. He did not actually look at the letter since he was driving the car.

"How do you know him?" Mary asked. Sean grinned

184

without comment.

"Wait a minute; did you go down to the school board on my behalf, Sean O'Malley?"

"Well, I didn't want the love of me life pinin' about her lost job as a teacher all for the likes of me, so I went down there to set things right. Bein' Mr. McBride is an Irishman of sorts it took another Irishman to reason him down."

"Thank you darling Sean," Mary leaned over and kissed him.

"Careful there Mary me love. We don't want to be runnin' in the bush again." They both laughed at the comment.

When they arrived at the schoolhouse, Jane and Mary greeted each other with warm hugs. "Guess what, the school board reinstated me. They want me to stay on." Mary was ecstatic.

"That's wonderful. I'm so happy for you," Jane smiled. "What changed their minds?"

"Well, Sean went down to the school board and gave them a piece of his mind," Mary continued in an excited tone, "and he reasoned them down."

"Oh, I'm so glad for you," Jane smiled radiantly, but beneath the veneer of her smile Mary could sense a troubled mind.

Dave called the meeting to order and Jane was unusually quiet as it progressed. Ethan had broken the bad news to her when he arrived home. Although she was mortified she was not entirely surprised. Throughout the meeting everyone voiced their options, insisting they continue to operate the school even if another one is built as they could declare it a private school on private property while Jane sat quietly, lost in thought. Finally, she asked permission to speak. Silence fell over the gathering as she rose and came to the front to address them as she would a class.

"I want to thank you all for the wonderful support and confidence you have shown me this past year. You have been wonderful and your children wonderful, but the school board is right. I was only deluding myself in imagining that I could run a school without guidelines or proper qualifications. If another school is built and staffed with a trained teacher I will step aside."

There was a loud murmur from the gathering, but Jane waved them silent.

"You know it is the right thing to do. All these bright young students, especially my shining stars, deserve to be taught in an organised way and be properly graded so they can easily get admitted to high school and ultimately university. Whatever happens in the future I will have the great satisfaction of knowing I helped nine bright young minds get a start in life by opening the door of basic literacy to them. God bless them and may they all find their way to college. If a new school is built and a new teacher is hired, I will give that person my blessing as I hope you will. Again, thank you all for your confidence. This last year has been a wonderful experience for us all."

With the last sentence, Jane's voice broke as there were tears in her eyes and it looked like she might faint. Ethan rushed forward and caught her in his arms and she sobbed on his shoulder for a long moment. The others rose to give her a standing ovation. Ethan then guided Jane to her seat.

When everyone was seated again, Sari and Hella were still muttering to each other about how this was a great crime and they should still carry through. Audi was again very quiet and was heard muttering to himself, "This should not be allowed. We must not let this happen." He left the gathering when the meeting was adjourned saying little to anyone.

All the women hugged Jane in turn. Sari and Hella asked what she would do without her classroom. Jane dismissively replied with a watery-eyed smile, "I'll stay home and raise Robbie instead of dragging him out of his house every day, especially in the winter. Maybe we'll have another child or two. I'll be able to get Ethan his supper on time and above all give my garden the attention it deserves. I do love gardening almost as much as teaching."

"It chust isn't fair," Hella reiterated. "Zhey had no right."

"Well, life is seldom fair and no one knows that better than me," Jane smiled weakly. "It was a nice dream, but the sad thing about dreams are, sooner or later you wake up to reality."

Mary came over and hugged her, "Oh Jane, I feel so sorry for you." Then she added, "We had them on the run and you gave up."

"I accepted defeat because it was a grand illusion," Jane said. "If they put up another school in this vicinity, it would be unfair for the students if I went on pretending to be their teacher."

"But you weren't pretending," Sari interjected. "It is astonishing what Thomas and Helen have learned since coming to your school. I still say it's a bloody shame what they are doing to you."

"Well, it's done and I'm done." Jane sighed heavily with resignation. "I will give them my best until the end of June."

"And in September if there still is no school?" Sari asked.

"We'll see when September comes," Jane replied, "but please accept my decision."

Chapter Twenty

At the school board's next scheduled meeting, the secretary looked up from her desk to find a handsome, well-dressed man standing in front of her. He gave her a disarming smile and said, "Has the weekly school board meeting started yet?"

"They are about to start. Are you expected, sir?"

"Well, yes and no," he replied.

"And who might you be?"

"My name is Audi Dykstra," Audi said ever smoothly.

"Do you represent one of the schools then, Mr. Dykstra?"

"Yes I do. It is important that I attend this meeting."

"Come this way then," the secretary said as she got up and started down the hall with Audi following. When they reached the meeting room door, she turned and said, "I will need to know which school you represent when I announce you to the chairman."

"Tell him Audi Dykstra, Director of the Opportunity School Association, wishes to address this meeting."

"Opportunity School!" Her tone suddenly turned cold. "I have strict instructions not to allow anyone representing that school to attend any meetings or seek appointments with the members of the school board authority."

"Tell him it is urgent that I address this meeting, or I will walk right past you through that door," Audi said firmly with a smile.

"All right," she sighed with resignation. "But they won't let you in."

The secretary knocked and stepped into the room closing the door. Audi; however, opened it a crack and pressed his ear to it.

"Sorry to interrupt sir," she said to Darcy, "but a Mr. Audi Dykstra, Director of the Opportunity School wishes to address this meeting."

"I thought I told you that no one representing that school is allowed past your desk," Darcy replied bluntly.

"But he is most persistent sir and he is standing just outside the door."

"Very persistent," Audi said as he opened the door and stepped inside.

"This is most improper," Darcy said. "You can't just walk into this meeting."

"I am here and I insist on being heard. By your own word sir, if I used proper channels I'd be sitting in the waiting room in perpetuity."

"We made it clear to the last delegation, Mr. Higgins and Mr. Phillips that all discussions with this school are over since Mr. Phillips denied us use of the facility. When are you people going to understand that school and its teacher are finished," Darcy stated.

"I think your board is too dismissive and not seeing the whole picture," Audi continued. "You people and your *astute* superintendent, in particular, are throwing Jane to the wolves without a second thought. It is not right and it is not fair," Audi said. "How does that old saying go, 'Forgive them Father; they know not what they do'."

"I fail to see what a biblical quotation has to do with this situation," Darcy said curtly.

"Throw him out. He is wasting our time," Zachery demanded. "We need to get on with planning that proper school."

"On the contrary, Mr. Chairman, my quote has everything to do with it," Audi said ignoring the superintendent. "All I ask is a few moments of your time, after which neither I nor anyone will bother you again in regards to Jane and her school."

"Is that your solemn word?" Darcy said.

"I swear to it," Audi said smoothly.

"Well, we might as well hear what you have to say," Darcy sighed. "We won't get rid of you any other way."

"I must protest," Zachery insisted. "We agreed that this joke of a school and its farcical teacher are beyond further discussion."

"Your protest is noted," Darcy said, "but I will grant Mr. Dykstra his piece. I am starting to get curious as to what there is about this particular school that has caused such a kerfuffle and why the people involved are so fiercely protective of this Jane Phillips, even in the face of being offered a proper school with a qualified teacher. Mr. Dykstra, you have the floor."

The superintendent made a few grimaces and gasping noises but made no coherent protest.

Audi came to the front of the room to stand beside the chairman and spoke to the gathering in his clear, resonant voice.

"Gentlemen of the board, my name is Audi Dykstra, I live only three miles from this school which is the eye of the storm as it were. I came from Holland, a country that prides itself in providing a first rate education for its citizens. I hold a Bachelor of Arts with an English major from the University of Amsterdam, so I think I know something of the value of a good education. I am also well acquainted with both Jane Phillips and the parents who send their children to this school. Although I am a bachelor with no children of my own, I became intrigued with the idea of this independent school and its *very* capable, if untrained, teacher so thus became involved."

"Am I correct in assuming that a delegation of parents came to this office about a year ago requesting a school for our area?"

"Yes, but there were not enough students to justify the expense of setting up a school in that area at that time," Darcy replied.

"I can appreciate the economics of the situation," Audi said. "Schools cost money to build, equip and staff and because of this, children in remote areas sometimes slip through the cracks and grow up to be illiterate." Audi continued, "But now, suddenly, you have determined that there are enough children in the area to justify a school."

"Well...uh, we did a head count and discovered as of this autumn there will be at least twelve school age children in that area," Darcy faltered.

"Did you not realise that last year?" Audi persisted.

"Mr. Dykstra, this meeting is not a board of inquiry. Please get to your point or I will have to ask you to leave," Darcy demanded.

"Very well, forgive me for getting off topic," Audi continued with a condescending smile. "What happened last year is water under the bridge, but as a result the people of the area took it upon themselves to build a school and asked Jane Phillips to be their teacher since she was already tutoring two of them anyway. It was a job she accepted with initial reluctance but grew to love, as teaching children is her true calling. I have overheard her teach and have sat in on parent days when she had the children recite what they knew to their parents. I stood in awe as I listened to a ten-year-old boy recite the very profound poem, *Abu Ben Adhem*. He not only recited flawlessly but could actually comprehend its meaning. I saw others perform mathematical calculations and recite matters of history and geography beyond their years. I had to agree that not only do we have some gifted children, but a gifted teacher in back of them, a teacher of rare quality indeed and you would cast her aside like yesterday's garbage."

"Yes but..." Darcy interjected.

"You are going to say she is not qualified," Audi cut him off. "This brings me to the point; what constitutes a qualified teacher? Is it someone who can conduct an orderly classroom and convey to their students the information these students need to know, or is it someone who has a piece of paper declaring them a qualified teacher? Is it someone who is given the gift to teach, or is it someone who merely passed a course?"

Darcy was about to say that one still needs standards, but Audi continued relentlessly, "You will say she does not follow a proper curriculum. Without help or guidance of any sort, Jane was forced to create her own curriculum — one I may add is working rather well. Her pupils can read and write, they can do mathematical calculations, and they know something of the history of our land and something of science. And you sit here and tell me that woman is not qualified because of some piece of paper? You would cast her to the wolves rather than help her. You have a rare and gifted teacher in your midst and you are throwing her away. Did anyone sit in on one of her classes? Did you, Mr. Superintendent?" He looked directly at Zachery. "Did you ask her about her curriculum or lesson plan?"

"I didn't need to," Zachery shot back. "That woman has no right trying to teach when she has no idea how. Her school is a charade."

"Indeed, sir," Audi said pointedly. "I ask all of you," he continued, looking around the room, "after what I have told you today can you honestly say her school is a sham? I implore you to reach out to this woman of unsurpassed talent. Go out there and see what she is doing before you condemn her and close her school. That is all I ask. Good day and thank you for your time."

Audi turned and walked toward the door. Darcy, who had been digesting Audi's oration, called out, "One moment of you time, please." He rose to follow Audi out the door. Audi stopped just outside of the door and Darcy closed it behind him.

"I grow more intrigued by this whole situation by the day, and your speech in there was most impressive," Darcy said.

"Thank you, though it probably won't save Jane," Audi replied.

"This meeting will be over by noon. Could you come to my office at one o'clock sharp? I would like to talk more about this school and its teacher as there is obviously more here than meets the eye."

"Obviously," Audi replied with a half grin. "I will be at your office. Be sure to tell your secretary so she won't throw me out."

When Darcy returned from lunch, Audi was waiting for him. "Come to my office, Mr. Dykstra." He beckoned. Once they were seated he continued, "Now then, how do you propose a way out of this situation?"

"Well, a good place to start is, I would like to invite you to spend a day in Jane's classroom as an observer. See for yourself what I am talking about and why this very gifted woman deserves a second chance."

"Interesting," Darcy replied. "After all I've heard of late I'd like to meet this Jane Phillips even though Zachery says she's quite belligerent."

"Belligerent is not a word I'd use," Audi chuckled, "feisty perhaps, but not belligerent. Jane will not be cowed down by anyone. Trust me sir, you will be impressed when you meet her, impressed with her the person and especially with her the teacher."

Darcy looked at his calendar and replied, "Let's do it first thing Monday morning. I will come out to Grimstad on Sunday evening and stay over if there is anywhere to stay over," Darcy said enthusiastically.

"You can stay in one of the rooms above the store. As it will be closed on Sunday you'll have to go around back," Audi replied. "I'll meet you there bright and early Monday morning and take you out to the school and sit with you for the day."

"I may want to bring someone with me," Darcy said.

"As long as it isn't the superintendent," Audi replied. "His presence would be counterproductive."

"Agreed, his mind is already made up," Darcy confided. "I was thinking of my assistant who specialises in one-room schools."

"Excellent, until Monday then," Audi said, standing up.

"You know that area out there has some rather interesting people," Darcy said also rising from his seat. "Not long ago I had another fellow, an Irishman, come here to defend another teacher our over zealous superintendent had in his sights."

"Oh, Sean O'Malley," Audi chuckled, "quite a character that one. The teacher he was defending is going to be his wife."

"So he told me. Well, at least that issue was resolved in a manner that was satisfactory to all."

"What is the problem with your superintendent? I've never seen such a rigid person in my life," Audi said.

"He's one of those by-the-book people. He has no concept of flexibility. He's a good administrator but lousy around people."

"It sounds like he is in the wrong job then as he certainly bit off more than he could chew when he clashed with those two women," Audi laughed.

"Yes. Well, that's an issue we're looking into; having said that I would appreciate your confidence."

"You have it. The politics within your administration is of no consequence to me," Audi assured him.

"Thank you, Mr. Dykstra. It was a pleasure talking to you."

"Yes, I better get going," Audi replied. "I drove here in the Model-T. It'll take a couple of hours at least to get back and you have a busy day." Audi and Darcy shook hands. "Oh, I won't tell her what's coming so there will be no chance that she can put on a show for us, not that she would, but it's for your sake."

"I appreciate that, Mr. Dykstra. She won't be angry about that, will she?"

"I'll explain it to her when we get to her school."

Later, Darcy would announce to an astonished board that he was going out to Jane's school to spend a day observing her classes. He invited Nathan, his assistant, who specialises in one-roomed schools to come with him.

"You can't be serious," Zachery said. "It is my understanding that you closed any dealings with that so-called school."

"Mr. Dykstra's impromptu address to our meeting tweaked my curiosity concerning this teacher, Jane Phillips. Perhaps we are not looking at the total picture here."

"I don't understand," Zachery said with a puzzled look.

"It is doubtful that you ever will," Darcy said. "You tend to judge things way too harshly and treat people too unsympathetically. If you would have taken time with Jane Phillips and observed what sort of instruction she was really offering, perhaps I wouldn't need to go out there myself."

"But..." Zachery groped for words.

"Furthermore, I rejected your request to dismiss Mary McKay from the Grimstad School and asked her to reconsider her voluntary resignation."

"But that woman was insubordinate and rude," Zachery insisted. "She has been helping this Jane Phillips. I am sure she was deliberately generous in discarding materials from her school, such as the maps, so they could be taken to this Opportunity School. Besides that, she is being courted by a known moonshiner."

"That moonshiner came to my office to plea for Mary McKay and assures me that it was a bad rumour. Furthermore, the private lives of our teachers are not really our concern unless it compromises their ability to be effective in the classroom. Perhaps Miss McKay was over zealous with her discards we have no proof that she directly gave them to the other school. Also, she was only rude to you because you were accusing and insulting her."

Zachery was taken aback by Darcy's bluntness, but had no comment.

"This brings me to my next point," Darcy continued persistently. "Taking all of this into consideration, along with other complaints, I'm going to ask you to step down as superintendent and take another job in administration."

"But I was only doing my job," he protested.

"Effective immediately," Darcy said firmly. "When this meeting is over, I will start considering a replacement for you. Meanwhile, I want the committee to continue with plans for the new school, but we will not initiate any steps toward construction until I return from my planned trip."

Chapter Twenty-One

It was midway through Thursday when they spotted the bear. The students were out playing at noon break when Thomas noticed a bear watching them from the edge of the muskeg. It reared up on its hind legs for a better look.

"Hey Herman, look a bear!" He cried.

"Holy smokes we better get everyone into the school," Herman replied.

The two older students quickly gathered up the other seven and told them to go inside because of the bear. Helen went running to Jane who was sitting at her desk having lunch.

"Mrs. Phillips, there's a bear outside!" She cried, her eyes filled with terror.

"There is!" Jane exclaimed as she came to her feet. The other eight students came running into the school with Thomas and Herman coming in last and closing the door behind them.

"There's a big, black bear outside, Mrs. Phillips," Thomas said with a relative calm.

"We thought it best to get all the kids inside," Herman added.

"You did the right thing," Jane smiled. "That was good thinking on both your parts."

Jane went to the window and looked out apprehensively but could not see the bear from there. "Where did you see the bear?" Jane asked.

"By the edge of the muskeg," Thomas replied.

"Yeah, and it was up on its hind legs looking at us," Herman added in an anxious tone.

"Oh, there he is," Jane said as the bear came lumbering past the school and headed for the shady spot where everyone had left their lunch pails. "Or maybe I should say she. Look it has two cubs with it!"

The students all carefully came to the big windows to watch the bear and Jane told them to be quiet.

"Is it gonna eat our lunch, Mrs. Phillips?" Lydia asked with wide-eyed apprehension as the bear and cubs all began pawing over the lunch pails devouring any morsels that they found including the wax paper. Several lunch pails were tossed aside by the bear's snout after it had devoured the contents. It was almost comical to watch one of the cubs having difficulty getting a lunch pail off its snout.

"Better the lunch than us," Lech remarked.

"Don't say that Lech, bears won't eat people." Jane said. "But it would be dangerous to go out there especially when she has cubs."

"I bet you wish you had your shotgun handy Mrs. Phillips," Thomas remarked.

Jane frowned at him, *Will I ever live down that bear incident?*

They watched the bear family in relative silence as the mother bear sniffed around. At one point it reared up again, and then dropped back on all four legs to lead its cubs across the trail into the bush on the other side of the road.

"Do you think the bear will come back?" Helen worried.

"No, it will move on to look for more food elsewhere," Jane replied.

"Can we go outside and play?" Herman asked.

"Let's give it a half hour to get far away, and then we can go outside and look at the tracks," Jane assured them with a smile. "Meanwhile, let's all take a seat to talk about the bear. I'll give you an extra long recess to make up for lunch break."

The students eagerly talked about the bear. When Jane asked what kind of animal a bear was, Willy said, "A mammal."

What kind of a mammal?" she added.

"A carn..." he faltered then said, "the kind that eat meat."

"A carnivore," she corrected him. "What else do they eat?"

"They like honey and berries," Helen added.

"And garbage and our lunches," Mark added. The others laughed.

Willy added, "Bears will also kill pigs and calves. Dad lost a calf to a bear last year."

Thomas mentioned that grizzly bears were a lot meaner than black bears, but lived near the mountains, and Lech added that polar bears were white and lived in the arctic.

Helen asked what a momma bear was called and Jane replied, "A sow, I think."

"What about a daddy bear?" She continued.

"I'm not sure," Jane replied looking at Herman for a possible answer.

"I don't know Mrs. Phillips," Herman replied, "maybe a boar?"

"No, I don't think so," Jane replied. "Boars are daddy pigs."

"Unless they are castrated," Lech said in a quiet voice.

Jane looked sharply at him and thought, *Oh no, not again. Someday I'm going to have a talk with that boy about what is acceptable to talk about in the classroom.*

There were snickers among Thomas, Herman and Willy while Lech realised he again had possibly spoken a forbidden word.

Jane barely had time to compose herself when Sonya innocently asked, "What does castrate mean?"

Jane grasped the edge of her desk while her face flushed. Finally, she said, "That is a word only older people use and it is not to be used in this classroom."

"I'm sorry Mrs. Phillips, I didn't mean to swear," Lech said sincerely.

"You didn't really swear," Jane said with a tight voice, and then continued, "the private areas of animals — like those of people — should not be discussed, in public. Please do not make any further reference to such things on class time."

"I'm sorry Mrs. Phillips," Lech said, "I'll be careful from now on."

"Thank you Lech," she smiled. Then turning to the class, she said, "Okay class, lets go outside now and see if we can see bear tracks."

They all hurried outside, giving Jane a much needed change of subject. They soon found and marvelled at the bear footprints.

"They look almost like human footprints," Helen observed.

"Why is that? Can you tell us, Herman?" Jane again quizzed her honour science student.

"That's because bears walk on the soles of their feet just like people do," Herman replied. "Most other animals walk on their tiptoes."

"Thank you, Herman. That was a good answer," Jane replied. "It's too bad we don't have any plaster we could have captured this footprint for the classroom."

"We have plaster at home," Thomas said eagerly. "Dad is plastering the walls. Maybe I could borrow some."

"That would be a good idea," Jane smiled. "Hopefully this deep track will still be here tomorrow. Meanwhile, you can now have the rest of your noon break. I'll ring the bell when I want you back in class. Just don't disturb the bear tracks."

As the children dispersed to play, Jane went back to her desk and recorded the bear incident in her school diary though she made no reference to the castration comment. Jane chalked that up to boyhood innocence. She was pleased that she could handle it better than his previous reference in the fall where he compared his mother's nursing to a cow and calf. The following day during art class she asked them all to draw and colour a picture of the bear and cubs. The artwork was later hung up on the chalk ledge of the side blackboard.

Darcy and Nathan arrived at Grimstad on the Sunday afternoon train and secured lodgings above the store. They agreed to Kari's terms for supper at a nominal fee and were taken by her pleasant manner and charming Norwegian accent. At supper they were joined by the only other current occupant of the rooming house, Mary McKay.

"Hello," Darcy smiled. "My name is Darcy McBride and this is my associate Nathan Hale."

"I'm Mary McKay," Mary smiled in turn. "I'm a teacher at the school here."

So she is the one that was the centre of the controversy, Darcy thought. *I'll keep my purpose a secret and see what I can learn from her.*

"So, Miss McKay, do you enjoy teaching school?" Darcy asked as they tucked into their meal.

"I love it," Mary replied pleasantly. "There is nothing more satisfying than conveying knowledge to eager young minds. It is my hope, like that of any teacher, that at least a few of my students will go on to college or otherwise make their mark on the world."

"Spoken like a true teacher," Nathan added.

"So, are you planning to stay and teach at Grimstad for the long term?" Darcy asked.

"So far that is what I plan to do. Although I plan to marry this summer," Mary replied. "You might as well call me Mary sir, as my name won't be McKay much longer. I'll be Mary O'Malley."

"That's a real Irish name," Darcy laughed.

"Sean, he's about as Irish as they come." Mary laughed in turn. "Your name also sounds Irish." She thought about his name and said, "Your name has a familiar ring, did we meet somewhere?"

"I'm of Irish decent and I guess my father wanted me to keep my heritage so he named me Darcy." Darcy smiled. Then he added smoothly, "I don't think so. I don't recall meeting you." He did not hold his position as chairman when Mary was hired and Zachery processed her transfer from Round Lake to Grimstad School.

"What brings you gentlemen to Grimstad?" Mary continued.

"We're here a day or two on business," Darcy said carefully. "Tell me more about the challenges of teaching in a small town school. I find it interesting how someone can teach in multi-grade environments where, in some cases, some of the students can't even speak English."

"Well it is a little easier here in Grimstad where I only have three grades to teach," Mary replied. "Out at Round Lake I had eight grades. That can be a bit of a juggling act. Out there I had two students that were Ukrainian and couldn't speak English when they started, but kids catch on to a new language quite quickly."

"Do you find much support from school administration way out here?" Darcy asked cautiously.

"Well, yes and no," Mary replied. "We have a school superintendent who is rather intrusive, not to mention offensive, but we seemed to have gotten around him."

"Interesting," Darcy chuckled. "Anyone in supervision is generally like that. I guess it is part of their job."

"I suppose so," Mary sighed. "But I didn't think it was right that he should be telling me how to live my private life. He even threatened to fire me for allowing Sean to court me because of some ugly rumour."

"Yes, that is a little intrusive." Darcy replied. "Your private life is your own business, I always say."

"He was going to fire me, but I resigned first, then the school board reinstated me because my beau went down there and told them off."

"Interesting story," Darcy chuckled, and then continued carefully. "I hear a lot of interesting stories about remote areas including some about unauthorised schools operating without a properly trained teacher. Do you see that as a threat, Mary?"

"No, I see that as a good thing. In those areas where it is not practical for children to go to school, I think it's wonderful if someone is willing to teach them," Mary said directly. "It is much better than to have them grow up illiterate and not be able to add two and two together. Don't you think?"

"Yes, I suppose so," Darcy continued. "There is even a rumour of one such school near here."

"There is one several miles north of here," Mary said. "It is being run by a very capable teacher, albeit one without a certificate, but I understand the school board is going to shut her down."

"And you think that is a bad thing?" Darcy continued.

"Who did you say you worked for?" Mary asked. She was now growing suspicious of his line of questioning.

"I didn't, but I am curious about such things," Darcy said ever evasively.

Just then Sean entered the room and Mary smiled radiantly at him, "Oh Sean, I'd like you to meet Mr. uh…"

Darcy turned around with a grin o his face, and Sean exclaimed, "Mr. McBride, fancy seeing you a way out here!"

"You two know each other?" Mary said in astonishment.

"We've met," Darcy grinned.

"Indeed, we have," Sean replied. Then looking curiously at Darcy he continued, "Did ye come out here to revoke yer decision about keepin' Mary on as a teacher?"

"Nothing like that, I assure you," Darcy replied. "If anything it confirmed that my decision to overrule the superintendent as a result of our previous meeting was the correct one."

"Well, that's a relief then."

"You mean you're…" Mary said groping for words. "Sean went to see you…of course, you were the one who wrote the letter reinstating me and that's where I recognise your name."

"I'm the chairman of the school board," Darcy chuckled. "Your fiancée put up a rather convincing argument about your merits as a teacher. Like he said, one Irishman to another, we were able to come up with an amicable solution to the issue concerning you."

"So why are you here, Mr. McBride? Is it to pick over Jane's carcass now that you've shut her down?" Sean asked suspiciously.

"Actually, we came out here to assess Mrs. Jane Phillips, as another person from out here barged into one of our meetings demanding that we give her a second chance," Darcy stated. "He convinced me to come out here and spend a day observing her classroom."

"And ye took him up on his offer. Well, that's one for you. I think you'll be findin' that it was worth your while."

"I hope so. He is to meet me here tomorrow morning and take me up to her school."

"And who might he be, if ye don't mind me asking?" Sean said.

"A Dutch fellow, he appears to be well-educated."

"Audi the Dutchman, I should have guessed," Mary said. "He would put in a pitch for Jane."

Darcy looked from Mary to Sean and said, "Is there more to this than meets the eye?"

"I wee bit more," Sean said, "but not what yer thinkin'. Audi has been involved with the school from day one. He feels he owes Jane a debt from somethin' personal a few years back."

"I see. Things are complicated even out here in the backwoods."

"Aye, people are people wherever they may be. But if you'll excuse me I've come to ask Mary if she'd join me tonight for fishin' in the river."

"I'd love to," Mary smiled. "I'll go change and get my things."

"Is there good fishing in the river?" Nathan asked

eagerly.

"Aye, there's plenty pickerel and a few trout."

"I'll have to bring my fishing gear next time I come this way," Nathan replied.

"You do that sir," Sean replied, "and I'll take ye to a good spot."

Chapter Twenty-Two

With impeccable timing, Audi delivered Darcy and Nathan to Jane's school just before the start of classes. They had met Hella heading out with Robbie, and all nine students were playing in the school yard in the warm June morning. Darcy noted a dump of sand, a tire swing and a teeter-totter as basic school yard equipment. Aside from the trim log schoolhouse, there was a slab shed that served as school barn, another for wood and coal storage, and two outhouses in the background.

The students looked curiously at the automobile as it pulled up. They all recognised Audi Dykstra as he stepped from the car, but not the other two. Darcy gave the students a friendly smile and greeting.

Audi told Darcy and Nathan to wait in the car while he explained things to Jane. When he had entered the building, Thomas came up to the side of the car where Darcy sat with window rolled down, and said in a concerned tone, "Are you here to make Mrs. Phillips stop teaching us?"

"No, most certainly not young man," Darcy smiled. "We're here to help her."

"That's good," Herman piped in. "We don't want anything to happen to Mrs. Phillips." By now all of the students were around them.

"You like your teacher, don't you?" Darcy asked with a friendly smile.

"Yeth we love her," Tanya lisped revealing a gaping smile showing that her front baby teeth were missing.

"We heard some bad people were going to make her stop being our teacher," Helen added.

"Out of the mouths of babes," Nathan commented from the back seat.

"Did you know that Mrs. Phillips shot a bear with a shotgun," Mark Gogowicz said with wide-eyed innocence.

"You don't say!" Darcy replied, though he exaggerated his astonishment. From what he heard about Jane, he was not totally surprised that she would be capable of such a feat.

"Maybe she is as formidable as they say," Nathan added in a low voice.

"Fascinating," was all Darcy could say.

"She shot it down just outside their doorstep," Thomas added. "But she doesn't like to talk about it much."

"She should be an interesting person to meet," Darcy replied.

Meanwhile, as Audi entered the classroom, Jane gave him a friendly "Good morning," from behind her desk.

"Forgive me for being abrupt Jane, but I have two gentlemen from the school board outside."

Jane's mouth dropped and she added, "I did say I'd step aside once a new school and teacher were established."

"It's not that at all," Audi said. "The chairman has heard so much about you and your school that he actually wants to sit in on one of your classes for the day. He brought along an assistant who specializes in one-roomed schools."

"What for? So they can feed me more rope to hang myself." Jane replied with a tone of bitterness.

"To be honest with you, I convinced him to come and he agreed." Audi said, "I think he is willing to help you rather than throw you to the wolves."

"Help me how?" Jane asked suspiciously.

"I'm not sure, but I strongly urge you to invite them in and carry on with classes pretending that they are not here observing. If they ask questions of you and your methods, cooperate with them. After all, as far as your teaching career is concerned, you have nothing to lose and possibly a great deal to gain."

"Well…uh…"

"Please Jane, you owe it to those nine children out there. It's a chance that won't come again and don't tell me you won't be heartbroken once you walk out that door for the last time."

"All right, invite them in. I will accommodate them," Jane sighed.

Audi came to the door and motioned for Darcy and Nathan to come in, but Jane stood behind her desk in a defensive mode. Upon introduction Darcy said to Jane, "At last I get to meet the legendary Jane Phillips, the centre of quite a controversy."

"I'm just someone trying to help some young people avoid growing up totally illiterate," Jane replied flatly.

"And it seems, according to your students, that you are doing a fine job." Darcy laughed. "So Jane, if I may call you that…"

"You may."

"We are not here to condemn or criticize, but to observe." Darcy continued, "We want you to carry on a normal day's activities and have both you and your students pretend as much as possible that we are not here. Any questions that we may have for you will be asked at recess time. Does that sound fair?"

"Fair enough," Jane replied. Then in a friendly tone she added, "There are chairs at the back where you can sit. I see you've brought satchels, so if you need to take notes use the table that doesn't have anything on it."

Nathan was looking around the room taking note of various things from the heater to the blackboards, to the Union Jack, to finally Jane's library. "Quite impressive," he remarked as he looked over the library. "You have plenty of books and even an encyclopaedia."

"All donated," Jane said proudly, "as was the dictionary, atlas and globe."

"Very remarkable," Darcy said as he fingered the dictionary.

"That's the learning table," Jane said. "Whenever a

student wants to look at those things on it, or one of the encyclopaedias, they must sit there; although I do sometimes make exceptions for my three shining stars."

"Shining stars?" Darcy asked.

"I have three very bright young men in my class who have devoured virtually every scrap of knowledge in this building. You will see who they are as the day progresses."

Darcy commented as he looked over the class layout, "It is quite clever how you arranged all the desks in a semi-circle around your desk."

"Well, we didn't have access to row desks," Jane replied, "and with the few students I have, this way is more efficient as they are all at equal distance from my desk. It also allows me to help any student who might have problems with their school work."

"Very ingenious," Nathan added.

Glancing at the clock on her desk, Jane said, "It's time to call them to class. Please have a seat."

Jane took the cow bell that she used to call in her class from her desk and went to the door and rang it. Soon the nine pupils clamoured into the school making an uncommon amount of noise for their numbers, due mainly because of the excitement about their guests.

"Interesting school bell you have there," Darcy chuckled.

"Well, we didn't have access to a real school bell," Jane replied. "This one is louder anyway."

Jane quickly brought her class to order and announced, "We have guests at the school today who wish to observe, so I will ask all of you to try to be on your best behaviour."

With that, Jane asked everyone to rise and recite the Lord's Prayer. The three adults at the back also stood and recited. Then Jane had them salute the flag with their pledge to serve His Majesty, King George V, the British Empire and the Dominion of Canada. The three at the back also saluted. Nathan noted that her pledge of allegiance was not the standard one used but adequate.

Eric J. Brown

With everyone seated, Jane announced the day would begin with year-end reviews of their knowledge in literacy. Students were randomly selected to read aloud passages that Jane picked according to their perceived skill level.

With the reading complete, Jane reviewed their grammar. Again, the younger ones were expected to know the basics of a sentence, while the older ones demonstrated a more complex understanding of punctuation and compound sentences. Jane made notes as the pupils performed. They finished the session with a brief spelling quiz and were then dismissed for recess.

"So, how did I do?" Jane smiled after the last student left the room.

"Well, I must say you are teaching them to read and write effectively," Darcy said.

"If I may impose," Nathan added. "Have you considered breaking your literacy class up into subcomponents, like reading, writing, spelling and grammar and then teaching each separately?"

"I have thought of that for next year. After all, as an untrained teacher as you people so fondly like to point out, I am groping in the dark." Jane smiled sweetly.

"Yes, well…uh," Darcy faltered. "Do you always teach language first thing in the morning?"

"Actually no, I teach it first thing every second day. On the in-between days I teach arithmetic first. Today I teach arithmetic right after recess."

"Why those subjects first?" Darcy asked.

"Well, they each require a lot of brain power and the mind is more alert and fresh in the morning than in the afternoon," Jane replied. "I alternate because it gives them variety and as the old saying goes, variety is the spice of life."

"Yes, a point well taken," Darcy said.

Class resumed and arithmetic reviews were on the agenda. Again, the younger students were called upon to perform simple addition and subtraction while the older ones

210

performed long division and multiplication with decimals on the blackboard. At one point the younger students were called to the blackboard to add columns of single-digit numbers. Rarely did any student need prompting.

At lunch break, the students were told to eat outside and bring their lunch pails in at the end of noon break as it was a beautiful sunny day out. "I hope you gentlemen brought lunch," Jane laughed as she joined them at a back table. "Because I'm afraid I don't have enough to share."

"We came prepared," Darcy said, "Kari, the woman at the rooming house made us a nice lunch."

"Do you have a lesson plan of any sort, Jane?" Nathan asked in a sincere tone.

"Yes, like many *real* teachers, I spend a lot of time at night thinking about what I'm going to do with the students the next day and sometimes that can be a real challenge. I also keep a diary of daily events for assessment purposes."

"May I have permission to see both your diary and today's lesson plan?" Nathan said. "But you're not obliged to show me if you don't wish to."

"I'll show you, it is not top secret information," Jane said with a friendly smile. She went to her desk and retrieved the diary and notebook with the lesson plan. Nathan would spend much of the remainder of the day pouring over the information and making notes.

Darcy walked around looking at various items such as the artwork featuring the bear and cubs. Jane explained their encounter with a bear the previous Thursday. He then looked at the science table that featured several animal skulls, a piece of backbone, a thin cross-cut slice of tree showing growth rings, a few different kinds of rocks and a casting of a bear footprint.

Upon looking at the bear paw casting he said with a wry grin, "I hear from some of your students that you have a reputation as a bear slayer."

Jane blushed bright and replied, "Yes well...it seems

I'll never live that down. I hope it doesn't reflect badly on me."

"Quite the contrary, it shows you have great courage," Darcy continued. "I'm curious to learn about that incident."

"Well, during the first summer I was out here I was working just outside my door extracting honey when a bear came," Jane said modestly. "Ethan had left me a loaded shotgun while he was out working his fields. He was very determined that I learn how to use the thing just in case of such an emergency. Anyway, I picked up the shotgun and accidently pulled both triggers. The kick from it nearly dislocated my shoulder. As it was, it knocked me down."

"Quite a story," Nathan added.

"As I was telling you," Audi added as he joined them at the science table, "she's quite an amazing lady."

"Well it was purely a self-defence reaction," Jane replied dismissively.

Darcy continued to walk around the room observing everything, and at one point, he pulled down each of the roll maps and remarked, "They *are* out-of-date all right. I can see why Miss McKay threw them out."

Jane swallowed with the comment and avoided eye contact, but Darcy moved on and remarked that the map of Europe was at least up-to-date. As it neared time to call the class in Darcy asked, "So what is next on your agenda?"

"Well, today we have history and geography, which I have every second day and on the in-between days I have science," Jane said directly. "Unfortunately, because you are only here for the day, you won't get to sit in on a science class. That is where my shining stars really excel. Although you'll probably see them perform during general discussion time in the last part of the day."

"General discussion time?"

"On Monday, Tuesday and Thursday we have general discussion time in the last part of the day which is a combination of learning and fun. We do spelling bees, geography bees and students are allowed to ask questions about anything pertaining to schoolwork."

"Sounds interesting," Darcy said. "What do you do during that time on Wednesdays and Fridays?"

"We have music on Wednesdays. I have a whole list of songs that I've taught them to sing, and since I've been involved with music in my former life I am also able to teach them music theory, such as the scale, and help them recognize musical notes. On Fridays we have art. The little ones use crayons and the older ones use water colours. It is a good way to round out the week, don't you think?"

"Yes, a lot of schools have art last thing on Fridays," Darcy replied.

When class resumed, the guests were treated to Jane's geography and history class. Once again according to age and comprehension level, Jane asked various students to find geographical features on the dated map of Canada such as important rivers, lakes and the capitals of randomly selected provinces. At one point she had to help Helen properly pronounce Saskatchewan.

They moved into history class and talked mostly about the explorers, focussing on the ones who explored Western Canada. Thomas presented a brief report on Alexander McKenzie, Herman had one on Anthony Henday and Lech did a presentation on Quebec and how it was different because it was settled by French people. He added that Louis Hebert was Canada's first farmer.

The real treat came during general discussion time as the topic gyrated toward world geography whereby the students made abundant use of the dated world map and the map of Europe. Jane fired questions about various countries like asking Tanya which country had kangaroos; she replied "Australia" and pointed to it with the yardstick. Lydia identified India as a place where tigers live. Little Sonya was asked which country has the same name as a farm animal, and she quickly replied, "Turkey." Italy was identified as the boot-shaped country, Austria the drumstick-shaped country and Czechoslovakia as the carrot-shaped country. Greece was the country that was slippery and Hungary as the one that reminded them of supper time. They also identified countries of origin of familiar people, such as Ireland for Mr. O'Malley, England for the Higgins', Germany for the Keplers, Poland for the Gogowicz, Norway for the Grimstads, Holland, or as Thomas corrected them Netherlands for Mr. Dykstra. When Russia was mentioned, Herman corrected them saying that Russia was now called USSR, for the Malovs.

At the end of the day when class was dismissed, Nathan handed Jane her diary and lesson plan back and said, "Most impressive. For someone who isn't supposed to know anything about teaching, you certainly have a grasp at what needs to be done, even though your freestyle curriculum is not generally acceptable."

"I am most impressed by your method of using comparison to help students identify unusual countries," Darcy added. "I would have never thought of referring to Austria as being drumstick-shaped, very extraordinary."

"Thank you," Jane blushed. "It just seemed like a logical way to teach geography as a fun thing and something they will always remember."

"In all it was a very rewarding day, Mrs. Phillips," Darcy smiled. "All I can say at this point is it isn't over for you until it's over. I will request one thing of you though."

"Yes, go ahead," Jane said with a trace of apprehension in her voice.

"I would like you to make out a year-end report card and to the best of your ability state which grades each student belongs in. If you need assistance you can ask your friend Mary at the Grimstad School to help you."

"Mary," Jane gasped, "but she is forbidden to help me in any way."

"That nonsense is over," Darcy assured her. "On my way back I will stop and see her, and make the request."

"Thank you sir, you will have my every cooperation in having these students ready for my successor."

"Thank you, Jane Phillips. Our school board should have more like you, but we should be going now. Nathan, your board director here and I," he said, referring to Audi, "have much to discuss in regards to the future of this school and the teacher who runs it."

"Thank you for your part, *Mr. Director*," Jane said to Audi with a wry grin.

"Now do you understand?" Audi said as they were driving away. "We have a rare and gifted teacher in our midst. Not the kind you want to throw away."

"There must be a way around this situation," Darcy said. "Nathan and I will review what we've discovered today and make a decision."

Chapter Twenty-Three

Three days later Jane received a letter from the school board. Ethan had gone to Grimstad that morning after dropping her off at the school. He returned during noon break and stopped at the school to deliver her letter.

He wore a peculiar half-grin on his face as he handed her the letter saying, "I got one too, but I didn't open yours."

Jane eagerly tore open her legal sized envelope. As she read, a smile slowly spread across her face.

Dear Mrs. Jane Phillips,

We have assessed your performance as a teacher at Opportunity School and found it exemplary. Based on our observations and conversations with other people familiar with your school we have made an unprecedented decision. We will waive your grade record at high school since it has been lost and will write a letter of recommendation that you be accepted at the Normal School in Edmonton for teachers training during the summer months. Attached is an application form to attend.

Upon successful completion of the course, our school board will hire you as teacher at Opportunity School, which will be integrated into our school system pending agreement from your husband, Mr. Ethan Phillips, to lease the school ground area to us, or in failing that you will be established as teacher at an alternative school to be constructed in the area.

Please fill out the form and send it in as quickly as possible. If you decline our offer, we will go ahead with our original plan to build another school and

staff it with a qualified teacher.
Yours Sincerely,
Darcy McBride

"Oh Ethan!" she exclaimed. "They are giving me another chance. What does your letter say?"

"They want to lease this little piece of land from me for the school until a new one is built."

"Wonderful!" Then with a sobering thought she said, "It will cost us money for me to go to Normal School with tuition and all."

"We'll figure somethun out," Ethan assured her.

"What about Robbie? Who will look after him when I'm gone? You won't be able to do your farm work and look after him. Then there's the garden."

"It'll all be taken care of one way or the other. You're not gonna weasel out of going for that teacher training and don't think you will," Ethan said resolutely.

"Yes sir," Jane replied as she hugged him.

When class resumed for the afternoon, Jane informed her pupils that she would be able to continue teaching if she went to school during the summer to get her certificate. There was wild cheering from the children. In her private thoughts Jane veered from ecstasy about getting a second chance to see her life-long dream come true to worry about how she was going to pull it off financially.

Word spread like wildfire about Jane's reprieve, and the school association quickly organised a fundraiser dance and box social at the school. Kari again set up a donation box at the store. Jane quickly filled out the application and sent it in, informing Darcy by wire so he would send in his letter of recommendation to the Normal School. Ethan also agreed to lease the school grounds.

The day of the fundraising social, the Phillips' family was at the store in Grimstad. Kari's daughter Linda was there making a fuss over Robbie as she always did.

Noticing the donation box, Jane was astonished. "They are taking up a collection for me? I could see taking one up for the encyclopaedias that time, but for *me*? I don't believe it," she gasped.

"Dere are people putting money in dere every day," Kari said. "Da people around here are vit you all da vay."

"That shows how well thought of you are dear," Ethan grinned. He then pulled out the money he had gotten that day from the steer and pig he sold earlier and shoved it in the donation box.

"Wasn't that the money you were going to put toward our new house?" Jane said with alarm.

"Well, I think gettin' you all trained up as a teacher is more important now," Ethan replied with a grin. "There are other pigs and steers we can sell later to build the house."

"Oh, thank you my love," Jane said hugging him. "But I do so much want a new house."

"You'll get one, but first things first," Ethan replied in his usual rumbling voice. "There ain't nothun gonna stand in the way of you gettin' that teachin' certificate."

"Dere you go," Kari laughed. "Dere is no running avay."

"I still don't know what I'm going to do about Robbie while I'm gone," Jane said soberly. "Hella offered to keep him as did Sari, but he'll spend so much time away he won't know where home is."

"Ve have an answer to dat problem too," Kari smiled.

Before she could answer Linda turned and said, "I will stay at your house and look after Robbie while you're gone, Mrs. Phillips. I'll cook supper for Mr. Phillips and even weed your garden."

"So dere you go," Kari grinned.

"That'd be asking too much," Jane said, "for you to spend your summer way out there."

"Why? If I stay here Mom will put me to work anyway and I like babysitting." Linda replied eager for the challenge.

"But your mom probably needs you here."

"I can manage da store vitout her."

"Are you sure you can handle the responsibility?" Ethan asked.

"I am fifteen and have already been babysitting for two years. I babysat for both the Keplers and Higgins'. I can cook too."

"I can always help with that," Ethan said. "I used to be a bachelor."

"If he cooks, you'll get served everything in the frying pan all mixed together," Jane scoffed

"I like a mixed fry," Linda laughed.

"Sounds like yer problem is solved," Ethan grinned as he looked at Jane. "She can sleep in the loft."

"Will you weed my garden?" Jane asked.

"Oh yes, I work for Uncle Rolly in his garden and greenhouse quite a lot."

"Well I guess you're hired," Jane said. "And we will pay you when we can."

"I don't expect payment," Linda said modestly.

"Nonetheless you will get it," Ethan added. "On the day we take Jane to the train, I'll pick you up and bring you back with me."

The box social and dance was a great success as the little schoolhouse was filled to capacity. The heater was taken out while the teacher's desk and back tables had to be stacked outside to make room. Jane made sure the items from the science and learning tables were carefully packed away in boxes and temporarily stored in the woodshed. The student's desks were moved together in a front corner to provide a tiny stage for the band. Many people came all the way from Grimstad as the late warm and bright, June evening made for easy travel by even those with horses and buggies. Axel and Kari did their share of canvassing around town and many of the farmers near Grimstad knew Ethan and Jane. All were intrigued by the story of Jane the teacher who defied the system and apparently won. Confident that the Goon Squad was nowhere around, Ivan brought a couple of bottles of white lightning to spark up the spirits of the men folk.

The music was supplied by volunteer musicians and again Ivan joined them on occasion to give a Russian flavour to the faster tunes. At one point, moonshine-fuelled Ethan took over one of the fiddles and fiddled out a rousing polka with Ivan in accompaniment. Many were amused as he gyrated and fiddled furiously, even coming out on to the dance floor as he fiddled. Jane smiled radiantly and Mary came alongside her saying, "It's good to see that Ethan has gotten over his shyness about playing in public."

"It's too bad he had to be primed on moonshine to do it," Jane scoffed.

Sean, who came alongside Mary as Jane commented, added, "At least ye can't be sayin' that it was my moonshine he was drinking."

"No, but you've had your share of the stuff too," Mary replied shortly, making a face at his alcohol tainted breath.

"Ah, but we're celebratin' tonight," he laughed as he grabbed Mary's hand and pulled her onto the dance floor saying, "With this crowd we're bound to send Jane for teachers training."

When the polka was over Ethan looked at Jane then began playing the strains of *Never-ending Road*.

"No!" Jane exclaimed, indicating strongly that she didn't want to sing. Ethan nonetheless continued to play, causing everyone to stop and listen to the beautiful strains.

As it occurred to several people that this was the song Jane sang at the Christmas concert, they began chanting, "Jane, Jane, Jane..."

As word rippled through the crowd that Jane could sing this song beautifully, the chanting grew more pronounced and Ethan grinned. Finally, Jane capitulated and joined him on the stage amidst wild cheering and scowling at Ethan. When the song was over the cheering was almost deafening, followed by chanting for more. "I'll sing one more, give me *I'll Take You Home Again Kathleen*. One verse, and I want Sean up here," she said to Ethan, he nodded and he began to fiddle. In the privacy of their house she and Ethan sang and fiddled many songs together usually of a Celtic nature. She sang one verse then on cue Ethan stopped and she said in a clear voice, "I'm not the only one here who can sing, we have a singing Irishman in the crowd." Ethan began to fiddle the *Irish Washer Woman* and Mary said to Sean. "She means you," and gave him a shove.

"Now what has got into that daft woman's head, I can't sing in public," Sean protested.

"Do it for Jane," Mary replied and then began chanting, "Sean, Sean, Sean..."

Ethan and Jane joined her and soon everyone was chanting. Ethan began to fiddle the strains of *Cockles and Mussels*, and Jane said, "I'll sing with you." Finally, overcome by the demands of the crowd, Sean caved in and joined Jane on stage with a frown. His mood changed as he joined her in song.

"Are ye satisfied now lass that ye drug me up here," Sean frowned while the crowd roared with applause.

"You owed me that from the time you brought Ethan home dead drunk," Jane grinned. "Remember, you were singing it."

As if Ethan could read Jane's mind he began playing the strains of the powerful Irish ballad, *Raglan Road*. Jane helped him get started then stepped back to allow Sean to finish the moving ballad on his own.

When the applause died down, Sean said to the audience, "Enough of this nonsense now we came here to dance not sing." He and Jane stepped off the stage and Ethan joined them, handing the fiddle over to its rightful owner.

The band struck up the strains of *Over the Waves* while Sean and Ethan induced their partners in a waltz.

"That was quite the performance you and Sean put on," Ethan chuckled as they danced.

"After you went and played that song and got everyone to get me to sing," Jane scoffed.

"Everybody loved it," Ethan grinned, "yer a real entertainer, you and Sean that is."

"He's a good singer and I thought if I was going to be dragged up on stage, he could join me."

"Good thinkin' on yer part," Ethan replied.

When Mary complimented Sean on his performance, Sean replied, "That's a one shot deal, don't be thinkin' you'll get me back up on stage again."

At midnight, when the dance wound down, Audi made a speech thanking everyone for coming, and amid wild cheering he expressed thanks for the surprise vocal entertainment. When the crowd had dissipated he, along with Dave, Jane and Ethan stayed to count the money from the proceedings.

"Still fifty dollars short of what I need for tuition and lodgings," Jane said in a downcast note.

"Don't despair," Dave said. "We don't know how much there is in the collection box at the store."

"Yeah, maybe there's enough there," Ethan said. "We've come too far to quit now."

"That's right," Audi said. "Say Dave, how about I pick you up Monday and we'll both go to Grimstad and add what's in that collection box to what we have here and see where we stand."

"Yes, I have to be on that train this Wednesday to get settled in and get ready for classes. Orientation is the following Monday morning," Jane said in an anxious tone, "and I have no idea how to get around Edmonton."

"Don't worry Jane," Audi said. "You were destined to be a school teacher and so you shall."

"I wish I had your confidence," Jane replied.

Ethan yawned and suggested they all go home. Then it dawned on him, "Where is Robbie?"

"He's asleep under the buggy seat," Jane said. "Linda

settled him in there when he started to get tired."

"She's startin' already is she," Ethan replied.

"Well, I'm heading out too," Audi said to Dave. "I'll pick you up first thing Monday morning."

"Righto," Dave replied. "You might as well hang on to the money."

"Will do, since we all know how much is here," Audi replied.

Monday morning Dave and Audi arrived at the store. They were about to take the collection box to the living quarters to count the money when Sean burst into the store. "Don't think you'll be countin' the money without one last wee donation from me." He pulled out a small wad of bills and stuffed them in the box saying, "That's me last week's wages. If that isn't enough for Jane, I got a wee bit more in the safe."

"Thank you very much Sean," Audi said. "We'll see what we've got after it is counted, and then maybe we'll touch you for more if we have to."

"You're being very generous, I must say," Dave added in one of the rare moments that he spoke to Sean independently.

"Well, as ye know I'll be gettin' married before this summer is out. And in a few years when I have me own children, I'll be wantin' Jane there to teach them." Sean said with a wink.

With all in order, Ethan brought Jane to the train on Wednesday morning right after chores. When the money had been counted they found, to their surprise, that there was at least fifty dollars more than the minimum that Jane required.

"I can't believe the generosity of the people around here," Jane said to Ethan as they drove down the road to Grimstad. "What is left over I will return to the treasury of our little board."

"Like I told you all along, there's a lot of people rootin' for yuh Jane," Ethan replied. "I heard Sean put in a week's wages

"How much is that?" Jane wondered out loud.

"About fifteen or twenty dollars at most," Ethan replied.

"And I needed fifty, now there's more."

"Well, other people put money in the box too," Ethan replied.

"I wonder if...?" Jane said. She was thinking of her mysterious benefactor. "If it is the same person who brought the books, the globe and all those other things to the school."

"Yer mystery man again," Ethan chuckled.

"I'd sure like to know who he is so I can thank him," Jane said with sincerity.

"I have my own ideas on that one," Ethan chuckled. "But I ain't sayin' nothun until I'm sure."

"You do? Tell me," Jane demanded.

"You know who," Ethan said mysteriously.

"Ethan Phillips I demand that you tell me," Jane insisted.

"Not until I'm sure in case I'm wrong," Ethan teased. "It'll give you something to think about all summer."

They crossed the creek just outside of Grimstad and Ethan nudged the horses to a trot. "So you're not going to tell me," Jane continued with a frown.

"Not yet, but it'll come to you if you think about it hard enough. If I find out for sure while you're gone, I'll write you a letter."

"Thanks," Jane said in a disgusted tone. "Now you'll have me wondering all summer."

"Well, if I guessed wrong you'd run off and thank the wrong person," Ethan laughed.

They arrived at the station and stood on the platform to

wait for the train. They didn't have to wait long; however, as the train was on time. Robbie was both frightened and fascinated as the mighty locomotive, with its bell ringing, went chugging past them belching steam and smoke. The train squealed to a halt and the conductor stepped from the coach directly in front of them to usher Jane on board. The station agent took Jane's luggage and a sack of mail to the baggage car near the front of the train.

"Well, it looks like yer gonna get on the train this time," Ethan grinned, referring to an incident three years ago when Jane threatened to leave him.

"But I'll be back and not soon enough."

The conductor cried, "All aboard!"

Jane bent down to Robbie and said, "Be a good boy for Daddy and Linda. Mommy will be back soon."

"Mommy go on train," Robbie said.

"Yes, Mommy is going on the train so she can learn to be a teacher."

Robbie clung tightly to her while she hugged and kissed him. Then she straightened up to face Ethan.

"Take care of my garden for me and don't let the weeds get too big."

"Linda and I will look after it. You just hurry up and get back here with that paper sayin' yer a real teacher."

"Bye," she replied as she hugged and kissed him for a long moment.

"Bye, Mommy," Robbie said morosely as Jane turned to get on board.

Jane stepped on to the train. They waved and she blew them a kiss as the train pulled away.

Chapter Twenty-Four

Jane stepped off the train at the station in downtown Edmonton somewhat lost and bewildered, but she was soon accosted by a familiar voice.

"Nathan is it," she gasped. "You were the person with Darcy McBride."

"Yes, Mrs. Phillips, I was sent to meet you at the train, help you get set up with lodgings and be there at the Normal School tomorrow to present the letter from our school board recommending you."

"Well, this is a surprise and I am grateful. I'm afraid I would be totally lost in Edmonton, though I've lived in bigger cities," Jane gasped.

"Since time is of the essence, Darcy and I thought it best to make sure you find your way to Normal School and get settled in before classes," Nathan grinned.

"Your school board went from one extreme to the other with me," Jane said. "I can't believe this is happening."

"You made quite an impression on us that day. Darcy pulled out all stops to see that you got this chance to go to Normal School and he doesn't want his efforts to fail." Nathan chuckled as he helped stow her bags in the back seat of his car. "Actually, so did your students. Some of them gave us the third degree about firing you."

"I can imagine," Jane laughed. "I have a good rapport with them."

"You are fortunate with the class you have, but it won't always be that easy," Nathan replied as they drove along. "There will be times when you will have difficult students, difficult either in learning ability or behaviour, but they will explain all of that to you in your classes on managing students."

"Yes. I realise I had it pretty easy with those eager bright students, though I did have a few trying times with them asking awkward questions bordering on forbidden subjects."

Nathan smiled quietly and replied, "Did you ever have to discipline any of them?"

"Once I had to punish three of them for using filthy language on school property."

"I see. How did you do it if I may ask?"

"I smacked them on the palm of their hands with the yardstick and made them write lines," Jane replied, "but I think it was the threat to tell their fathers that kept them in line."

"It sounds like you handled it correctly," Nathan replied. "Say, this director Audi Dykstra seems like quite a character."

"In what way?" Jane asked.

"He sure went all out for you. He spoke so well of you and when he barged into our meeting it was hard to refute him," Nathan said. "He said he owed you a great debt."

Jane was silent and thought for a long moment, *could he be the mysterious benefactor. Oh, I wish Ethan were here just now.*

When Jane settled in that night and lay in her bed, she thought again of Audi and how he always seemed to be there at the right moment. He alone would have the wherewithal to get the books and other supplies that mysteriously appeared. He seemed to be around when the necessary donations to both the encyclopaedia and tuition funds were desperately needed. Jane couldn't wait to get back to discuss this matter with Ethan, but that would be six weeks from now.

When Jane attended class at Normal School, she discovered that she was much older than the other students. The others in the class were bright, eager young faces still in their late teens. They were fresh out of high school and determined to begin their careers as teachers. They looked upon Jane as a curiosity who was out of place and belonged with the instructors rather than the students. Some turned up their noses at her still somewhat frumpish appearance. Even though Jane kept her hair down and wore fairly modern dresses that allowed her ankles to be seen, they were out of style. Although she was only twenty-eight years old, they saw her as an old woman. On one occasion she overheard someone call her Miss Frump, but at least to her knowledge, no one called her stork as they did in her younger years.

Whenever Jane felt down about standing out among the crowd, she thought of back home at Grimstad where she was a heroine of sorts by having defied the system and having won over its administration. She thought of her shining stars and how it would be so nice to get back to teaching them without having to look over her shoulders and without the threat of being shut down. Most of all she thought of Ethan and little Robbie. She only had to endure this for six weeks, albeit a long six weeks, but Jane was tough and she could handle it.

As for the courses, they merely helped refine what she already knew intuitively or had been explained to by Mary. There would have to be major adjustments in her class routine in some areas and her free discussion time at the end of the day would likely have to come to an end or be shortened as would music and art time. As she learned about grading she would have to regrettably rein in Thomas and Herman as they would reach Grade Eight, the highest grade she'd be qualified to teach, well before their time.

Finally, the day came for the closing ceremonies and the presentation of the certificates. With the ceremonies over as the students left the auditorium, a familiar smiling face was there to greet her.

"Mr. McBride!" She gasped upon seeing Darcy. "What a pleasant surprise to see you here."

"Well, we'll be signing up three of the graduates for our

school board, and I especially wanted to present you with a contract. Shall we step into the side office I reserved for recruiting?"

Jane followed him and noticed school board officials from other areas were taking some of her classmates aside to offer them jobs. Outside the small office, a young man and woman sat waiting to be interviewed.

"Excuse us a moment," Darcy said to them in a pleasant manner. "Mrs. Phillips here is a special case that I will deal with first."

"I could wait in line," Jane blushed modestly.

"Nonsense," Darcy said. When they entered the office he introduced her to Edwin Jones, the new superintendent of schools.

"Pleased to meet you," he smiled. Though Edwin was a middle-aged man with the look of authority, he seemed less offensive than Zachery. "I've heard a lot about you."

"Hopefully not from your predecessor," Jane replied with a crooked grin.

"Like you said, the lady does have spunk," he commented to Darcy wryly.

"Jane is not a person to trifle with. If you find fault with her teaching methods, you'd better be prepared to defend your criticism," Darcy laughed.

"Oh, I'm not really the ogre they make me out to be," Jane blushed. "I look forward to any helpful suggestions you may have when you come to visit my school."

"I think I'm beginning to like you already," Edwin chuckled.

"Yes. Well, as I have a busy schedule and you no doubt want to get home, I'll come to the point," Darcy said to Jane with a pleasant smile. "Jane, I have here a three-year contract for you to teach at Opportunity School--we will retain that name for obvious reasons. At the end of those three years you will be required to spend another summer at Normal School to get your permanent certificate which will allow you to teach anywhere in Alberta, grades one to eight."

Jane smiled as he laid out three copies of the contract and instructed her where to sign. She positively beamed when he handed her a copy after signing. She was now a fully recognised teacher in every sense of the word.

"Now Jane," he said in a serious tone. "Now that you have learned how to set up a proper curriculum, please try to follow it. We will be sending you a copy of the prescribed curriculum, a school register and a real school bell among other things that a *real* teacher needs."

"What do I do with my three shining stars?" Jane asked. "It will be hard to rein them in."

"I am sure you'll think of something to occupy them. They are too young to go to high school." Then in a dismissive tone he added, "Well, I won't keep you any longer as we both have important things to do."

Jane sighed as she rose from her chair and Edwin, who also rose out of courtesy, said, "I look forward to visiting your class, Mrs. Phillips."

"I hope I will pass your inspection, sir," Jane said flatly.

"Oh, I'm sure you will." Darcy laughed as he opened the door for her. "I might even tag along again."

"Now there's a threat." Jane laughed as she rose from her seat. She then turned and said, "Thank you again Mr. McBride, thank you for everything. You have no idea what this means to me."

"Goodbye Mrs. Phillips and good luck," Darcy replied, and then turning to the young lady waiting by the door he said, "Next."

The train pulled up to Grimstad station and Jane stepped off. At first, there was no one there and then Ethan and Robbie came out of the waiting room and rushed to greet her.

"Are you a real teacher now, Mommy?" Robbie asked as he clung to his mother.

"Yes, I am a real teacher sweetheart," Jane laughed as she scooped her young son into her arms.

Then after greeting Ethan with a hug and kiss she said, "Audi's the benefactor, isn't he?"

"I'll bet that bothered you all summer." Ethan chuckled.

"It did."

"Well, you can ask him." Ethan turned and nodded, and then a crowd of people poured out of the station to meet her. They included all of the families who had children in her class the previous year, Sean and Mary, Axel and family, Kari, Linda and finally Audi who had a woman at his side.

They crowded around Jane to congratulate her as she proudly waved her teaching certificate for all to see. "See, I'm a genuine teacher now and I have a contract in my handbag from the school board to teach at Opportunity for the next three years."

Wild cheering erupted from the others. Then Thomas and Herman came forward to offer their best and Helen presented her with a bouquet of flowers.

"Are you gonna teach me, Mrs. Phillips?" little Krystal Kepler asked.

"Yes, Krystal," Jane smiled. "I will be teaching you the ABCs."

"Congratulations Mrs. Phillips," Linda said as she wormed her way to the front.

"Thank you Linda," Jane beamed. "How did you do a way out there?"

"Really good," Linda smiled. "I enjoyed looking after Robbie and your garden."

"She did a real good job too," Ethan added.

"You didn't get tired of supper being cooked in a frying pan?" Jane laughed.

"Mr. Phillips' pan-frys are really good, but I did cook some of the suppers."

"She's a good cook too," Ethan added, "almost as good as you, *almost*."

Sean and Mary came forward and Jane and Mary hugged for a long moment, "Thank you Mary, for everything. I still think I learned more from you than I did at Normal School."

"So now ye are official," Sean grinned.

"Yes, I have a three year contract and thank you Sean," Jane smiled. "Thanks for your large donation." She leaned over and kissed Sean on the cheek, "And by-the-way you two, congratulations."

"If ye have no objections we'd like to be celebratin' our weddin' at the school come Saturday evening," Sean replied.

"As long as the school is in shape for classes in September."

"We'll have it spotlessly clean to be sure," Sean assured her.

"It looks like the desks are already here," Ethan observed. The agent and porters had just unloaded two sets of row desks from the baggage car along with some large boxes containing textbooks, all addressed for Opportunity School.

"I'll be down to the station first thing after the celebration to fetch them things for yer school," Sean offered.

"We can use my lumber wagon," Ethan said. "You'll need a hand with all that stuff."

"Wonderful," Jane said ecstatically. "I can't wait for classes to start." Then she turned and noticed Audi standing quietly nearby with a woman at his side who was holding his hand. "So Audi really did get a woman like he said he would."

"Yeah, fresh from the old country," Ethan said.

"She was on the train with us when we came back from Sydney," Mary said. "She can barely speak a word of English."

"Well, at least all you other women should be safe now," Ethan chuckled.

"I must speak to him," Jane said as she turned and

walked toward the smiling Audi.

"Congratulations Jane," he beamed. "I knew you could do it. The school board can no longer complain that they don't have a qualified teacher at Opportunity."

"Yes, instead of being threatened with being closed down they are actually going to be paying me to teach."

"And so they should," Audi grinned. "Though probably not as much as you deserve."

"I understand that congratulations are in order for you as well," Jane said, changing the subject. She glanced at the woman beside him smiling uncertainly.

"Oh yes Jane, this is my wife Andrea, fresh from the old country like I said."

"Pleasure to meet you," Andrea said, struggling with her English. "I heard much about you."

"Pleased to meet you, Andrea," Jane smiled. "Welcome to Canada and to Grimstad."

"Ya, you teacher for my children," Andrea faltered.

"I hope so," Jane replied.

"My wife is jumping the gun a little," Audi laughed.

"Audi, could I speak to you a moment?" Jane asked.

Audi spoke to Andrea in Dutch and then he and Jane stepped to the side.

"You were the one who gave the school the books and things weren't you?" Jane asked looking him in the eye, "And probably donated generously to my tuition fund."

"I have to confess," Audi grinned. "Call it investing in the future."

"Why Audi, why was it so important to you that me and my school succeed?"

"You are a woman of many talents. I've always said that," he continued, "and it was obvious from the start that you are a gifted teacher."

"But you were a bachelor with no direct interest in the school."

Audi let out a great sigh and continued, "I owed you an enormous debt from a bit of foolishness three years ago. I

233

knew no spoken apology would ever suffice for that great transgression. When I heard that they were building a school and that you were going to teach, I saw an opportunity to atone my sins, and by being an anonymous donor to your school, you wouldn't think I was trying to buy back your good graces. If you can never forgive me in your heart I can quite understand, but I will have the satisfaction of knowing that I made a partial payment of my debt to you."

"Oh Audi," Jane smiled warmly. "I forgive you. At first, I feared you might have an ulterior motive especially when you went out of your way to be nice to me at school gatherings, but now I realise you were sincere in your motives. So consider your debt paid. While I hope you continue to be involved with the school, don't feel you have to go out of your way for me again."

"Thank you Jane," he breathed. "You have no idea how much this means to me."

"From now on I will call you my friend," Jane added. She extended her arms and they hugged for a long moment.

"Thank you friend," he smiled with watery eyes as they slowly let go of each other. Jane turned and joined her family.

"Well, Mrs. are you ready to go home yet?" Ethan said in his usual gruff voice.

"Yes, I'm anxious to go home and relax," Jane then turned and addressed the gathering of her friends. "Audi and I were just talking about repaying debts. Well, I owe you all an enormous debt that I will bear for the rest of my life. God bless all of you."

Wild cheers erupted from the gathering on the platform.

"I must go home now and tend to my family, and prepare to teach your children in two weeks time. I have to say this year has been one huge learning experience for all of us."

She turned and joined her waiting family as they headed for the buggy to go home.

About the Author

Eric John Brown was born on August 13, 1947 the youngest son of John and Ruby Brown. He was raised on a farm in the community of Magnolia about one hundred kilometres west of Edmonton, Alberta.

Magnolia was, during his childhood, a hamlet consisting of a store, a church and a community hall. The community was a closely-knit one and his family was a warm loving one. During his early grades, he attended a one-roomed school about a mile from home then completed his remaining grades at Seba Beach School from which he graduated. He has always been a keen student of modern history, geography, and science.

Virtually all of his working life has been spent first with Canadian National Railways Signals Department and later with TransAlta at the local Sundance power generating plant.

While on a trip to Scotland to visit relatives in 1971 he met his future wife, Isabella. They were married in Scotland nearly two years later and have since raised two sons, John and Colin.

The author began writing stories when he was thirteen years old but most of his early writings were of the science-fiction genre. Later, as he became more skilled at character development, he turned to standard fiction. He has also developed a keen interest in the ethnic and linguistic background of the vast mosaic of peoples that make up Canada. He, in particular, has focused on peoples seldom mentioned in mainstream literature such as Finns, Latvians, Ukrainians and Scandinavians.

The saga of *Ginny*, his first publication, was conceived when he was only twenty-three years old. At the time however, he lacked the necessary writing skills to tackle a work of this magnitude. It remained, however, in the back of his mind like bedrock, even as he worked on other writings. The details of *Ginny* slowly filled in over the years. Finally after the acquisition of a home computer in 1994, the author tackled this long overdue novel in earnest. As the author set to writing, what was originally to be the story of a community, a strange thing happened. In the author's own words, "the character, Ginny, leaped out of my imagination and took control of the saga making it her story." The result of his literary labours was the publication of *Ginny* on December 11, 1998. Since that time this powerful and warm, loving character has captured the hearts of hundreds of readers of all ages. With the highly successful publication of *Ginny* via the route of self-publishing, the author has continued to write novels which have found broad appeal on the marketplace.

Eric J Brown continues to reside today on the old family farmstead. Here with his good wife Isabella they raised their family and recently they have discovered the rewards of grandchildren. From this rustic setting, he hopes to continue writing stories about the people and times of Canada.

Anna
An Odyssey to Freedom

Anna is a bright eighteen-year-old girl, a member of a happy family and has a bright future ahead of her. Then her world is shattered when the Soviet Union forcibly annexes her tiny homeland of Latvia in the summer of 1940. A year later it is conquered again, by the Nazis. Anna's family is destroyed and she is forced to live by her wits. Her only hope is to somehow find her brother, who is abroad, and the young man in her life who is also lost in these brutal crosscurrents of history. Her only dream is to reach the faraway golden land of Canada. Thus, begins Anna's incredible odyssey to freedom.

Ginny

A Canadian Story of Love & Friendship

Ginny is a rich girl from Toronto who dares, against her family's wishes, to elope with Danish immigrant named Marty Polsen to his homestead in Alberta. Ginny faces many challenges on the homestead such as learning how to cook, coping with homesickness, being chased by a bear, and a difficult childbirth that nearly kills her. With the support of both her loving husband Marty, and her dear friends, Ingrid and Gina, Ginny perseveres.

As you trace Ginny's life, from a time when she was a rich girl adjusting to the rigours of the homestead, to a time when she is offering wise counsel to her grandchildren of the baby boomer era - you will come to appreciate that this work is a triumphant story of love and friendship.

Ingrid
An Immigrant's Tale

Ingrid is only fourteen years old when she is torn away from all that is familiar including her dear friend, Sigrud. This, because her father had chosen to immigrate from Sweden to Canada in 1910 with his family. Ingrid is frightened at the prospect of having to learn a new language, coming to a strange new frontier land and she pines for her friend left behind. When settled in her new home, Ingrid, is pursued by two undesirable suitors, one is a shy clumsy man and the other a raucous ruffian. When Ingrid finally meets and marries the love of her life all seems well, but tragedy and disappointment still stalk her.

Much of this story takes place with World War I looming in the background, and the Great War has its effect on both Ingrid and her neighbours.

The Promise

Full of enthusiasm and patriotism generated by the Great War, young Paul Cunningham enlists in the Canadian Army the day after his nineteenth birthday. His parents of a well-to-do Toronto family, are vehemently opposed to his joining, but cannot stop their determined son's call to duty.

With great passion and fanfare, Paul marches off to war and straight into that man-made hell on Earth known historically as the Battle of the Somme – a battle so horrendous that it consumes a whole generation of young men from both the British and German empires during the summer and autumn of 1916.

As Paul struggles to cope with the horrors of war, he must also deal with a difficult commanding officer culminating in a showdown that threatens to be his ultimate undoing. Away from the madness of the front, two women, his beloved sister Ginny back in Toronto and his sweetheart Chelsea in England, wait anxiously for him. To both he has promised to return.

To the Last Tree Standing

Following up an article in an outdoors magazine, freelance writer Jill Tompkins sets out to find a mysterious mountain man known simply as Brother Nature or more commonly Bro. He is the self-appointed protector a beautiful stretch of forest in Montana. As she begins her trek into the forest, Jill discovers that there is more mystery here than she bargained for. She is followed by a hit man employed by a ruthless logging magnate, whose mission is to kill Bro, and she is watched over by a sympathetic forest ranger. As she plunges deeper into the forest in search of the elusive Bro, the plot thickens, the mystery grows, and the suspense builds.

Last Tree Standing is a fast-moving tale of conservation, ecology, and defence of the innocent. It is a must read for all who fight to save our environment from those who would pillage and destroy our precious natural heritage.

Third Time Lucky

Jane Brody was "as plain as dirt and tough as nails." so her mail-order suitor Ethan Phillips had declared. He also declared that she was "one hell of a cook and could sing like a lark" especially when she sang the haunting ballad *The Never-Ending Road*. Their many, often humorous confrontations, in which her prim frumpish ways clash with his crude sardonic manner, threaten to destroy their precarious relationship at any given moment.

When Jane, the perennial wallflower, becomes entangled in a love triangle with Ethan and the lovable Irish moonshiner, Sean O'Malley, Ethan is at a loss as how to cope, and is left to ponder his belief that either bad luck runs in threes or that the third time can also be lucky.